Gabrielle darted into the nearest alley...

No matter what, she wasn't going to allow the hard-hearted Ranger to recognize her. Unfortunately, Captain Stone crossed the street, eating up the ground with his long swift strides.

"So we meet again," he murmured as he halted in front of her. Bri refused to speak for fear he would recognize her voice.

Suddenly she saw her fiancé ambling down the boardwalk. If Eaton spotted her in her gray gown, he would spoil her charade. Bri latched on to Hudson, clamped her mouth over his, and pulled him deeper into the alley.

To her dismay, the same sensations that had assailed her the previous night spilled over her again. Hudson's tantalizing scent, his taste and the feel of his muscular body pressed against her swept Bri into a dizzying universe that defied logical explanation. Hud clamped his hands on her hips, pressing her against his thighs, making her vividly aware of his masculine response. Then his hand glided up to brush the side of her breast, and another flame of desire scorched her....

* * *

Texas Ranger, Runaway Heiress
Harlequin® Historical #927—January 2009

tell this hard-bitten Ranger captainould recognize his name Like hell

CAROL FINCH

Texas Ranger, Runaway Heiress

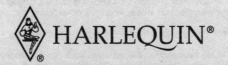

TORONTO • NEW YORK • LONDON
AMSTERDAM • PARIS • SYDNEY • HAMBURG
STOCKHOLM • ATHENS • TOKYO • MILAN • MADRID
PRAGUE • WARSAW • BUDAPEST • AUCKLAND

Recycling programs
for this product may
not exist in your area.

ISBN-13: 978-0-373-29527-2
ISBN-10:   0-373-29527-8

TEXAS RANGER, RUNAWAY HEIRESS

www.eHarlequin.com

Printed in U.S.A.

This book is dedicated to my husband, Ed, and our children
Jill, Jon, Christie, Durk, Shawnna and Kurt. And to our
grandchildren, Livia, Harleigh, Blake, Kennedy, Dillon and
Brooklynn. With much love.

Chapter One

Middle of Nowhere, Texas
Late 1870s

Captain Hudson Stone waited impatiently for Texas Ranger Commander Winston Price to finish his conference with Hud's battalion leader. Winston Price had arrived in camp two days earlier to inspect the troops and assess the situation in West Texas—which had become a breeding ground for trouble the past few months.

When Major John Ketter exited the tent, wearing a carefully blank stare, Hud didn't know what to expect or why the Ranger commander had singled him out. Hud ducked under the tent flap then nodded a greeting to Commander Price, whose alert brown eyes made a quick inspection of Hud's tattered attire and the week's growth of whiskers that he had been too busy to shave.

The commander sank onto the edge of his cot to stretch out his long legs. The former military officer had served, as Hud had, in the Confederate Army. Winston Price was beginning to show his age, although he still was in reasonably good physical condition. He was in his late forties and sported a thick crop of reddish brown hair. A thin mustache and goatee accentuated the commanding features of his face.

"Nice to see you again, Captain Stone."

"What can I do for you, sir?" Hud was in no mood for idle chitchat. He wanted to be done with this impromptu meeting so he could mount up and focus on his quest to track down a ruthless killer known as Mad Joe Jarvis.

"Your battalion seems to be working effectively in this area, all things considered," Winston commented as he braced his arms on the cot.

"We have a dedicated troop of Rangers who are trying to keep the lid on this area. Unfortunately, it is becoming more difficult by the week." *Now get to the point,* Hud mused impatiently.

"Major Ketter recommended you for the duty I require posthaste," Winston said, surprising Hud. He reached for the pipe that sat on the crude nightstand then lit it up. "My daughter notified me unexpectedly that she wants to consult with me as soon as possible. Since the governor sent me out here to expect the battalions and report on the extent of the trouble we've had in this region I need you for immediate escort detail."

"Escort detail?" Hud croaked, stunned. "But sir, I—"

Winston flung up his hand as he surged to his feet. Although Winston was six feet tall and sturdy in stature, he had to stare up at Hud, who towered at six foot three inches in his stocking feet and outweighed the commander by at least twenty pounds.

"I asked Major Ketter to recommend his best Ranger for the task and he says you're it."

"But I'm leading a search to apprehend the outlaw who killed Speck Horton."

Just saying Speck's name aloud sent a wave of grief and frustration pouring over Hud. He and Speck had served in the Confederate Army together and had come to Texas to make a new start. Speck was as close to family as Hud had. The need to avenge Speck's death tormented his waking hours and haunted his sleep. He didn't want to be waylaid by escort detail.

"I have been briefed on your search and I am very sorry for your loss." Winston stared straight at Hud. "I think that might be the other reason Major Ketter recommended you for escort duty. He thinks your vendetta has become too personal and obsessive and that you need a diversion."

Like hell I do! He didn't want to play nursemaid to some prissy tenderfoot female who had no business tramping around in an area that was jumping alive with Indian renegades. Occasionally they sneaked from Indian Territory to express dissatisfaction with conditions on the reservations and their outrage over another of the federal government's broken treaties. Not to mention the problems associated with the influx of white and Mexican outlaw gangs. Plus, ranchers were feuding over water rights, land titles and lease agreements on public lands.

Hud couldn't imagine why Commander Price would allow his daughter to venture out here. Did the dainty female have her father wrapped around her finger? Price had commanded military troops and state Rangers with ease. Apparently he couldn't say no to his daughter. And what, Hud would like to know, was so damn important that the *princess* couldn't wait until her daddy returned to Austin next month to see her?

"Major Ketter has agreed to let you gather your gear and leave for Fort Griffin within the hour." Winston paused to blow two lopsided smoke rings in the air. "I don't want Gabrielle to linger at The Flat longer than necessary. You know what a rowdy place it is."

Teeth clenched, hands fisted at his sides, Hud nodded his dark head. The Flat was the raucous community that had sprung up at the bottom of the hill below the military fort. Buffalo hunters hauled in their hides for transport by wagon to the Dodge City railhead, where they were shipped to tanneries and millineries in the East. Cattle drovers arrived in town and let off steam by drinking, carousing and firing their six-shooters in the streets before trailing their herds to Dodge City. In addition, card sharks, harlots and all sorts of desperadoes, eager to engage in shootings, knifings and brawls, filled saloons and gaming halls. In short, it was the devil's playground. Certainly not the place for a sophisticated lady.

"Sir, I'm not telling you anything you don't know already," Hud remarked, "but not only is this area dangerous but The Flat is as close to hell as most folks prefer to get. Several men have been killed publicly in showdowns. Then there are the ones who have been strung up by vigilantes. Between the cold-eyed killers, crooked dealers at faro, monte and poker tables and the soldiers who trot down Government Hill to carouse when they're off duty, that is no place for a dignified lady."

Plus, Hud had better things to do with his time than pick up a spoiled brat and deliver her to her daddy. Hell! This was the most ridiculous duty anyone had requested of him.

"I am aware of The Flat's reputation," Winston acknowledged before he took another long draw on his pipe. "Which is why I want you to leave immediately. I don't know precisely when Bri's stagecoach is due to arrive at The Flat. Fortunately her new fiancé is accompanying her."

Wonderful, now he had to babysit *and* escort two citified greenhorns across the rugged terrain of the outlaw-infested badlands. Damn it, this unexpected assignment kept getting worse by the minute.

"I will be leaving your battalion this afternoon to inspect another Ranger unit," Winston reported. Frustration must have shown on Hud's face because Winston smiled sympathetically and patted him on the shoulder. "I understand your need for revenge, son. I lost several dear friends in the war. But rest assured that you will be back in a few days to resume command of your manhunt. I will assume responsibility for my daughter while she's here."

That should be fun, Hud thought sourly. The other men would be bowing and scraping over her and she'd probably soak up the male attention like a sponge. Most likely one adoring fiancé and a doting father wouldn't be enough to satisfy Miss La-Di-Da Gabrielle Price.

"Bri is a very unique individual," Winston boasted.

Of course, Winston would say she was unique. He was her father. Either that or sweet little *Bri* was unique because she had an extra finger on each hand or eyes in the back of her head. Whatever the case, Hud considered her an inconvenience of gigantic proportions.

Winston smiled fondly as a halo of smoke drifted around his head. "As a child she tried to be the son I never had. I called her the little general."

It took considerable effort for Hud to keep from rolling his eyes. He had a personal and professional crusade driving him. He had vowed to apprehend Speck Horton's murderer and this ridiculous escort detail was a waste of his valuable time and considerable skills as a Ranger.

"Then Bri blossomed into a woman and men showed up at my doorstep, requesting her company when she came to visit me."

Hud looked at Winston and tried to imagine his broad forehead and angular features plastered on a female. It was not a particularly appealing image.

He didn't know for sure but he presumed by Winston's comment that he and his wife didn't share the same residence. He wondered if Bri played her mother against her father to get what she wanted. It wouldn't surprise him one bit.

"Now Bri's mother has earmarked a young politician for her match and given her stamp of approval. If Bri is coming to ask for my formal blessing then she will have it. *If* this is what *she* wants. Bring my daughter to me, safe and sound, Captain Stone."

The commander's solemn expression and forceful tone implied "or else…"

"I will never forget the favor. Plus, I will alert the other Ranger battalions I visit about your friend's killer so they can provide information to aid in your search."

"Thank you, sir," Hud said begrudgingly.

Then he wheeled around so Commander Price couldn't see his scowl. Hud didn't want to be relieved of his duty of tracking a ruthless killer, just so the commander could have his daughter escorted to him for a formal approval of her politician fiancé.

Swearing a blue streak Hud stalked off to gather his gear, saddle his horse and rush off to Fort Griffin to protect the female who should've had more sense than to venture to the hellhole in the first place.

While Hud was in town, he might take time to single out one of the harlots and scratch an itch that had gone unattended for more months than he cared to count. He ought to get *something* pleasurable from this mandatory trip. For sure and certain, chaperoning a pampered princess, whose father could dishonorably discharge him from Ranger service for disobeying a direct order, could destroy his future plans.

Hud glanced into the distance as he crammed his belongings into his saddlebags. He and Speck Horton had planned to build a prosperous ranch on the land grant they were to receive in compensation for their service to the Rangers. Now Speck wouldn't be around to help Hud make that dream come true.

Still scowling at the unexpected turn of events that interrupted his manhunt, Hud swung into the saddle, turned his back on Angel Mesa—the rugged caprock that dropped into a maze of canyons—and pointed himself toward Fort Griffin. Two hours later, he realized that he hadn't bothered to ask the commander for a description of his daughter.

"How the hell am I supposed to know who she is or where to find her?" he asked Rambler, the sturdy black gelding he was riding. "Right." He gave a caustic smirk. "She'll be the one wearing a diamond-encrusted tiara and who has a wide forehead, straight brown hair and dark eyes like her father."

Hud had yet to meet Gabrielle—or Bri, the pet name her father used. But he disliked her sight unseen.

* * *

Gabrielle Price squirmed restlessly on the hard stage-coach seat and listened to her unwanted fiancé drone his life story to the three male passengers traveling with them to Fort Griffin. She flung Eaton Powell II a disgruntled glance and wished him to be anywhere else but here with her. She hadn't requested his company on this trip. Indeed, she wanted to come alone but Eaton had insisted on traveling with her. He'd spouted something about protecting her from unscrupulous characters and using the trip to campaign for his next venture as a U.S. Senator.

Bri knew Eaton's wealthy family had *bought* him votes to get him elected into Austin's politics. She couldn't imagine how many voters he thought he could contact at The Flat and the fort. The community wasn't known for being public- or civic-minded. But Eaton claimed he wanted to branch out and locate other donors who might fund his campaign.

She wondered if his family had finally objected to his excessive habit of throwing around money and ordered him to find someone else to fund his campaign expenses and his extravagant spending.

Whatever the ulterior reason, Eaton had tagged along, much to her chagrin. She had been stuck on the train and then in a crowded stagecoach with him. So much for this spur-of-the-moment trip that was supposed to take her far away from Eaton.

"My father and brother are bankers in Austin," Eaton was telling the other passengers when Bri got around to listening. "But I am more interested in serving my state and nation and becoming a spokesman for the common man."

Bri knew Eaton had no real interest in serving anyone anywhere. His priority was his own ambition.

She turned her head and smirked while Eaton preened and passed around his manufactured smile. He smoothed his dark brown hair into place with an exaggerated gesture of his hand, and called attention to the gaudy rings that sparkled on his long fingers.

Spokesman for the common man? That was laughable. Not only was Eaton an elitist but he was also an exceptional performer. He could tell a convincing story, make all the right noises and sound sincere when the mood suited him. But mostly he was full of hot air and he bored Bri to tears.

She had observed him at his best, worst and all moods in between and had found nothing endearing or appealing about him. Furthermore, she wasn't naive enough to think he felt any fond affection for her. No, it was her mother's prestigious family name of Roland and their vast wealth that attracted Eaton. Bri's mother and Eaton's aunt hailed from what polite society referred to as two of the "first families" in Texas. They had been lifelong friends and they had machinated this betrothal to promote Eaton's rise to political stardom.

Essentially Bri was the feather in Eaton's cap, the merging of one well-heeled family to another. If Bri's mother had her way—and she did entirely too often— her daughter would become the extension of her own life. A life that hadn't turned out the way she'd wanted.

Mother is not going to get her way in this instance, Bri promised herself resolutely. At twenty-three, Bri was old enough to make her own decisions and accept an engagement proposal, *if* and *when* she wanted to. She had to convince her father to side with her and to stand against his estranged wife. Besides, Bri couldn't possibly plan a wedding while she was accompanying her father on his inspection of Ranger battalions in West Texas, now could she?

The thought of a grand adventure in the great outdoors filled Bri with excitement and anticipation. She thrilled at the prospect of leaving behind polite society and its obsessive preoccupation with her unusual interests and activities.

Bri stared across the countryside, marveling at the broad river valley flanked by rolling hills that were covered with mesquite and oak trees. Pecans and elms lined the creeks that tumbled into the river. Nothing would please her more than to rent a horse and explore this scenic wilderness.

"Tell me, gentleman, what are your opinions of the large ranchers who are objecting to our government's insistence that they *pay rent* on the public lands where their cattle and horse herds are grazing without restriction?" Eaton asked.

Bri wanted to express *her* view about bullying cattle barons. They objected to small ranchers nesting near their domain and using water sources and rangeland that had been designated for public use. Of course, Eaton didn't want her to have an opinion on anything. She was supposed to be window dressing for the upstart politician.

She tuned out Eaton, who had interrupted one of the passengers to express *his* opinion of favoring large ranchers over nesters. Instead, she poked her head out the window to survey The Flat. It was rumored to be one of the four wildest towns in the West. The community was a cultural paradox that not only boasted upstanding storeowners and farmers, but also harbored outlaws, harlots and gamblers.

It looked as if The Flat did indeed have a motley frontier population, she noted as she studied the individuals who were striding down the boardwalks. The place had sprung up at the base of Government Hill and the streets were lined with dozens of businesses. She spotted two freight offices, a large general store, three cafés, a telegraph office and a newspaper office. She also noticed two banks, a theater, gaming halls, saloons, a livery stable and a row of bordellos that seemed to be doing a thriving business an hour before sundown. Bri could only imagine how prosperous the dens of ill repute became after dark, when more of their potential clients were off work and on the prowl.

Bri perked up when she noticed the sign announcing the last performance of a traveling repertory company. Several men and woman milled around the redbrick theater, singing ditties and sporting costumes and props to entice attendance. The actors drew considerable attention, Eaton's included. He came to point like a hunting dog when he spotted four young women flitting around in tight-fitting costumes.

Womanizer, she mused as she watched Eaton's hawkish gaze rove over each woman's physique.

Here was yet another reason Bri refused to spend her life shackled to this blowhard politician whose sexual appetite was whispered about in drawing rooms. Bri knew loyalty and fidelity weren't among Eaton's virtues—if in fact, he had any at all. She couldn't think of one off the top of her head. But then he'd been getting on her nerves all day so it was hard to think past his annoying faults to find his redeeming qualities.

As the stagecoach halted beside the clapboard depot, Bri caught a whiff of a foul odor. She glanced sideways to see the oversized piles of buffalo skins and the unkempt men who wandered around the hide yard that sat on the edge of town.

"Ah, here we are," Eaton said unnecessarily. He leaned close to add, "Honestly, Gabrielle, why must you wear these plain traveling clothes? You look like a sodbuster's wife, not a future senator's fiancée. You can afford to dress like a princess and you should."

"I have no intention of soiling my best clothes in dusty stagecoaches. I don't believe in flaunting family money," she declared.

His gaze narrowed reproachfully. "I must remind you that *your* unfashionable appearance reflects badly on *me*. We are in the public eye because I'm running for office. You need to dress the part and keep up appearances for my sake."

She cocked her head at him then stared pointedly at the three shabbily dressed men who climbed down from the coach. "I thought you wanted to represent the *common* man."

"Represent them, yes. Become one of them? Hardly, my dear." He flicked his wrist, urging her to step out of the coach by herself so he could make his grand entrance into the street. "Please find something flashy to complement my wardrobe before you venture out this evening."

Grateful to escape the narrow confines of the coach—and Eaton—Bri practically launched herself through the door.

Glancing this way and that, Bri sought out a hotel that offered adequate accommodations. She noticed an establishment above a run-down saloon, but it didn't appeal to her. Neither did the foul-smelling stack of hides close by. She intended to stay upwind of hide hunters and their pungent bounty.

The moment the driver handed down her two satchels, she hiked toward Brazos Hotel, which sat at the opposite end of town. The sound of tinkling piano music and boisterous laughter that wafted from the string of saloons was a welcome change from the tiresome sound of Eaton's voice and his haughty criticism. Bri couldn't wait to ensconce herself in a private room and relax.

"Slow down, my dear!" Eaton called out as he snatched up his four suitcases and clatted after her.

Bri glanced over her shoulder in time to see Eaton nod a flirtatious greeting to one of the thespians who all but floated across the street to greet him. It was lust at first sight for Eaton and the red-haired actress, she decided. She shook her head at the ridiculousness of the public flirtation playing out on the boardwalk. The voluptuous actress, with pouty lips and luminous green eyes, was welcome to Eaton. And vice versa. Bri didn't want him. Never had.

One of the main objectives of her journey was to *dis*-engage herself from Eaton. Another was to enjoy the freedom and independence her mother constantly tried to stifle. Despite her mother's browbeating efforts, Bri refused to be no more than a social hostess and devoted politician's wife.

When the redhead twirled gracefully in front of Eaton, who had halted to watch her leap through the air like a ballerina, Bri smiled in amusement. Eaton's arrogance was astonishing. He seemed to have no idea that she could see right through him and tell what he was thinking while he visually undressed the actress. She would be outraged if she had the slightest interest in the boorish dandy.

Her stomach growled as she hiked past one of the cafés. There would time for food later, she promised herself. First, she wanted to wash away the trail dust and relax in the privacy of her room.

Leaving Eaton to ogle the actress—and her friends, who gathered around to promote their farewell performance—Bri scurried into Brazos Hotel to request a room. She dug in to her purse to pay for her accommodations then trudged up the steps.

She expelled a gigantic sigh when she closed the door behind her and appraised her modestly furnished room. She was never so glad to be anywhere in her life! She could tend to the business of hiring a guide to accompany her to the Ranger camp, where her father was inspecting troops. Even better if her father had received her message in time to send someone to fetch her.

Mercy, it had been too long since she had seen her father. Almost six months, in fact, she mused as she shed her dusty calico gown and changed into a drab gray dress, floppy-brimmed bonnet and shawl that downplayed her feminine physique. She was counting on her father to become her champion against her mother's unreasonable demands and expectations. *He* understood her restless spirit, her need for adventure and excitement. She was her father's daughter, not her mother's senseless puppet.

A fond smile pursed Bri's lips as she pulled her bonnet low on her forehead to conceal her facial features. She loved her father dearly and respected him greatly. He didn't lounge in an office at the state capitol. He personally inspected the troops and assessed the situation in the wilderness to ensure the Ranger battalions had enough manpower and supplies to keep the frontier safe. Winston Price was also feeding his adventurous soul. If he didn't remember that Bri was the proverbial chip off the block, she vowed to remind him.

It was dark when Hud arrived in The Flat. His first order of business was to lead Rambler to the livery stable and brush him down thoroughly. In his line of work, a man was only as good as his horse. Hud made certain Rambler received full rations and the best of care.

He glanced down the street and told himself he should be enthusiastic about being back in society—if you could call this collection of misfits in The Flat society. He stared down the dimly lit street, noting the gathering crowds and hearing boisterous laughter wafting from a nearby gaming hall. There were all sorts of entertainment to be had. Ironically, all Hud wanted was a bath and a few minutes to stretch out on a real bed for the first time in months.

Assured that his horse was in capable hands, Hud strode off to find comfortable accommodations for himself. He pulled up short when a woman in a frilly costume pirouetted in front of him then leaped through the air.

"We'll be giving our last performance tonight before continuing our tour to Fort Elliot, Tascosa and Mobeetie," she announced as she circled around him and waved a perfume-scented scarf under his nose. "Come join us, handsome."

Handsome? Hud inwardly scoffed as the woman flitted off to entice another passerby on the boardwalk.

He didn't consider himself anywhere near handsome. Whiskers lined his jaw. The bags under his eyes testified to his lack of sleep and too damn much time in the saddle.

Thanks to Commander Price, Hud had set a swift pace to reach Fort Griffin to look up Gabrielle and play nursemaid and tour guide.

Scowling, Hud veered into Brazos Hotel to rent a room. After requesting heated water for a bath, he slung his saddlebags over his shoulder then scaled the steps. He smiled appreciatively when he entered his room to see the feather bed and the brass tub in the corner.

Tossing aside his saddlebags, he ambled over to the window to look down on the bustling streets filled with hide hunters, gamblers, cowboys and desperadoes. Turning away to heel-and-toe out of his boots, Hud unfastened his holsters and set aside his weapons. His gaze skittered around the room again.

"Hell of a life you lead," he mumbled to himself. "The highlight of your month is bathing in a tub and sleeping on a real bed."

Chapter Two

After a surprisingly appetizing meal at Garland Café, Bri scurried back to her room. She considered searching out a guide and arranging to rent a horse from the livery this evening. But first things first, she decided. She wanted to confront Eaton Powell II immediately. Although Bri could practically hear her mother pitching a fit—all the way from her palatial drawing room in Austin—she was giving Eaton notice that she had cancelled their engagement. Permanently. He could make his way home without her and he could campaign his heart out while he was at it.

All she wanted was to be rid of him for good.

Determined of purpose, Bri hiked down the hall. Two scraggly-looking characters came to attention as she approached. She kept her head down, her face concealed by the floppy-brimmed gray bonnet. She could feel the weight of the derringer she kept tucked in one garter on her thigh and the cool steel blade of the dagger she stashed on the other.

Anna Roland Price would throw a conniption if she

knew what a vast education and unconventional training her daughter had received when she'd been shipped off to that snobbish finishing school in Houston. Bri had befriended a rascally, fun-loving street urchin—who had initially tried to rob her—and then he became her dearest companion.

The thought of Benji Dunlop's life cut short by his senseless death galvanized her determination. She was not going to be the extension of her mother's unreasonable expectations and she could handle herself in adversity, thanks to Benji's thorough training. Bri had become a fair shot with a pistol. She could wield a knife accurately and she had learned to be a scrappy fighter in hand-to-hand combat.

"Don't let nobody get the drop on you," Benji had lectured her countless times. "Gotta guard yer own back 'cause you can't count on nobody else to do it for you."

Regret and sorrow whipped through Bri, remembering the loss of that treasured friendship. Benji had come to a bad end in a dark alley one night before he was to meet Bri for an evening adventure to Galveston. She had waited two hours but he never showed up. It was the next day before she learned that Benji had died at the hands of three knife-wielding bullies because he refused to give up the shiny gold pocket watch she had given him as a gift.

Bri slid her hand into her pocket to clasp the watch she had recovered at a pawnbroker's shop. It was a constant reminder of the loyalty of her best friend and the uncertainty of life. Even after three years she still hadn't recovered from the guilt. If she hadn't given him the expensive gift that he treasured and carried proudly—visibly—he wouldn't have lost his life.

"My, my, ain't you easy on the eye, honey. Care for a little company?"

Bri ignored the tall, greasy-haired hombre whose smile displayed a mouthful of rotten teeth. He looked to be at least a decade older than her twenty-three years and he smelled as if he hadn't bathed in months. When he grabbed her elbow, she jabbed him in the soft underbelly to ensure that he turned her loose so she could continue on her way.

"I bet I could teach you a thing or two about a woman's place," the man growled as he started after her.

"Try it and I'll scream this place down around you. You can spend your evening in jail," she muttered as she glared over her shoulder at him.

His slate-gray eyes narrowed menacingly. When he stepped toward her, his friend clamped hold of him to hold him at bay.

"Leave me alone, Pete," the man said, and scowled.

"Easy, Joe, we got places we gotta be tonight. No need to call unnecessary attention to ourselves," Pete, the heavyset, auburn-haired man insisted. "The boss wouldn't like it."

Bri ignored Joe Whoever-He-Was. She remained on high alert, in case the scoundrel wormed loose from his companion's grasp and came after her.

She was proud to be the daughter of a veteran of the Confederate Army and Rangers' upper echelon, as well as the best friend of a scrappy street fighter. Men didn't expect her to be capable of defending herself. It was that element of surprise that had saved her several times when she chose to venture off alone to escape the restrictions of high society.

Bri silently rehearsed what she intended to say to

Eaton before she wished him a final fare-thee-well. All
the while, she cautiously monitored the whereabouts of
the two men. She breathed a sigh of relief when they
ducked into the room three doors down from her own.
She halted in front of Eaton's room and drew herself up
to full stature, trying to make the most of her five-foot-
three inch height.

She smirked at the thought of Eaton demanding the
two-room dignitary suite. Nothing but the best for
Eaton. He had convinced himself that he was entitled
and he constantly put on airs to assure the public that
he was something special.

Her thoughts flittered off when she heard a burst of
feminine laughter on the other side of the door. Bri
frowned then looked up at the room number. Yes, this
was Eaton's suite. She had come to the right place.

A man's rumbling laugher caught Bri's attention. It
dawned on her that her soon-to-be *ex*-fiancé was enter-
taining a woman. She turned the doorknob and found it
unlocked. When she poked her head around the edge of
the door, she saw a string of garments—male and
female—that formed a path across the small sitting
room to the bedroom. The mirror hanging above the
dresser in the adjoining room provided her with a view
of the bed that sat against the back wall.

Bri gasped in shock when she saw a woman's red
head and bare breasts. She recognized the actress from
the theater troupe. She was tumbling around in bed with
Eaton, who was bare to the—

With a muffled squawk, she squeezed her eyes shut
after she got a clear view of Eaton's buttocks. She cursed
under her breath when she realized belatedly that she
had emitted a sound that interrupted the two lovers.

"What was that?" Eaton said as he yanked the sheet over his bare hips.

The redhead jerked the corner of the bedspread over her breasts. "Did you remember to lock the door?"

"Hell, no, you were pulling clothes off me left and right," he muttered as he rolled off the bed to grab his breeches.

Heart pounding, Bri eased the door shut while Eaton stabbed a leg into his breeches. She really should confront him with his infidelity, here and now, she supposed. However, seeing him naked with the actress rattled her more than she expected. Her face felt as if it had gone up in flames and she couldn't get the image out of her mind.

She became frantic when she heard the wooden floor creak as Eaton hurried to investigate. She glanced down the hall, trying to calculate how long it would take to reach her room and duck out of sight. Too blasted long, she decided.

She had to make a choice. She could face Eaton now while she was struggling to gather her composure or try to slip into the room next door until the coast was clear. She chose the latter.

To her relief the knob turned easily and silently. She darted inside the dark room and eased the door shut with a quiet click.

"What the hell—?"

Bri found herself staring at yet another bare chest. However, the man who owned it put Eaton to shame. Washboarded muscles rippled down his belly. His shoulders were much broader than Eaton's and he stood six foot three inches in his stocking feet. His whiskered face was in deep shadows because his back was to the dim lantern light that was blocked by the dressing screen in the corner.

When Bri heard Eaton whip open his door to check for unwanted visitors in the hall, she glanced wildly at the brawny frontiersman who was staring warily at her. When he opened his mouth—in what she anticipated to be a terse demand to know why she had burst into his room unannounced—she did the only thing she could think to do to silence him quickly.

She pushed up on tiptoe and flung her arms around his neck. She kissed him soundly—sucking the breath from his lungs and the question off his tongue. When he tried to rear back to get a look at her, she held his head to hers and leaned sensuously against his solid chest. She put all she had into the embrace so she could keep him distracted until Eaton returned to his paramour.

A moment later, she heard the stranger's rumbling purr. Then he said, "Well, if you insist, sweetheart…"

His arm glided around her waist to hold her intimately against him. To her surprise, he lifted her off the floor and kissed her back in a way she had never allowed a man to kiss her before. And now she knew why. It was entirely too intimate and personal and demanded more than she preferred to give.

Yet, for a dazed moment, she forgot her objective of keeping the half-dressed stranger quiet until Eaton re-entered his suite. She told herself that she should be thinking about scuttling to her room once the coast was clear. But first she had to recover from the titillating sensation of being swallowed up in the powerful arms of the raven-haired stranger, whose sensuous lips were making a feast of her mouth. Despite the abrasive brush of his whiskers, Bri enjoyed the reckless embrace—in an utterly wicked and devilishly delightful kind of way.

Which was completely out of character for her. She didn't go around grabbing men and kissing them until they gave in and kissed her back enthusiastically. She had become intrigued by kissing this brawny stranger. Then she had been swamped by a flood tide of physical pleasure that surely must be lust in its purest form.

The erotic misadventure left her experiencing the most incredible sensations imaginable. The man tasted good and he felt even better while he pressed her familiarly to his muscled planes and contours. If she was going to behave recklessly and irrationally, who better to experiment with than a perfect stranger who didn't know who she was and had no expectations except sharing a mind-boggling kiss in the dark?

Bri gave herself up completely to the exquisite pleasure that consumed her and promptly forgot Eaton Powell II existed.

Hud's mind went blank and his body hummed with unbridled desire while the mysterious woman, who had darted into his room unexpectedly, kissed him deaf, blind and stupid. His initial reaction upon seeing the woman in gray, whose face was concealed by the droopy brim of her bonnet, had been to lunge for the pistol that he'd tossed on the bed. But she'd caught him off guard when she latched onto him as if he were the missing half of her soul reunited after an eternity.

When she delivered that first lip-sizzling wallop of a kiss, Hud forgot everything he ever knew. It was the most bizarre moment of his life. He couldn't see the color of her hair or the color of her eyes. He couldn't tell much of anything about her appearance because she was no more than a gray shadow within the inky shadows of his dimly lit room. Yet, he kissed her for all he was worth and she clung to him with the same reckless abandonment.

Damn, in all his thirty-three years he'd never been so bewildered or out of control. Even his years of soldiering and rangering hadn't prepared him for a surprise attack that assaulted all his senses at once. The unidentified female left him aching with lust and shaking with need in nothing flat. He responded instinctively to the taste of her kiss and the enticing feel of her shapely body molded to his.

After a long, hungry moment of pressing her hips against his hard arousal and kissing her as if there were no tomorrow—or the day after—he heard the door to the next room snap shut and the lock click into place. Then suddenly the kissing bandit lurched backward. Hud impulsively tried to pull her back into his arms but she bent his wrist at a painful angle and darted from his reach.

"Ouch," he said to the back of her bonnet-covered head. "Mind telling me what the hell's going on here—?"

"Shh-shh-shh!" she said without glancing back at him.

Then poof! She slipped out the door and scampered down the hall.

Hud craned his neck around the partially open door, noting the mysterious female in the dowdy gray gown and shawl was careful to cling to the shadows of the hall. When she reached the staircase, she turned her head away from him to conceal her facial features. Then she flew down the steps and disappeared from sight. He hadn't had a clear view of her from her dramatic arrival to her abrupt departure.

He couldn't describe the elusive night visitor or identify her voice. Yet, he knew the appealing taste of her, knew her alluring scent and he knew how amazingly good her curvaceous body felt in his arms.

Frowning, Hud shook his head to clear the erotic sensations that fogged his senses. He glanced toward the waiting tub of bathwater behind the dressing screen and smiled wryly. If the kissing bandit had arrived two minutes later, Hud would have been stark naked. That would have been an interesting way to make her acquaintance. Of course, her way of introducing herself with a steamy, mind-blowing kiss and "shh-shh-shh" was peculiar enough.

"Ah, well, I guess you have to expect such things in a boisterous town like The Flat," he said to himself as he unfastened the placket of his breeches on his way to the tub.

Hud smirked at the steam drifting from the water. Now he was going to need a *cool* bath instead of a *warm* one, because the kissing bandit had left him hot and bothered.

Bri halted at the bottom of the steps to inhale several bolstering breaths. Lord have mercy! That unexpected encounter, coming so quickly on the heels of viewing Eaton's tryst, left her head spinning like a windmill. At least she'd had the presence of mind to rush downstairs rather than scamper to her room. Otherwise, the raven-haired stranger would have known where to find her. He might have dropped by to ask the kind of embarrassing questions she didn't want to answer, even to herself.

After striding across the boardwalk in front of the hotel, Bri paused to grab hold of the supporting beam to steady herself. She glanced toward the opera house, watching the actors give one last pitch to attend their final performance. Bri was still staring in that direction, lost in thought, when the redhead exited the Brazos Hotel hastily and scuttled down the street to rejoin her troupe. Bri wondered if other thespians spent their spare time giving command performances behind closed doors. One did, apparently.

After five minutes passed, Eaton swaggered from the lobby, dressed fit to kill—as usual. *Unless* he was tripping the light fantastic with a paramour. In which case he stripped naked.

Discarding the unpleasant image of Eaton's soft, pale flesh, Bri drew herself up, squared her shoulders and walked over to plant herself squarely in Eaton's path.

"Ah, there you are, sweetheart. I've missed you," he had the nerve to say.

Missed me? My eye, she thought sourly.

"I'd like a word with you, Eaton," she demanded.

He glanced over the top of her drooping gray bonnet to stare at the opera house. "Can't it wait? I'd like to catch the last theater performance before the troupe packs up and heads west."

"You already did," she said, smirking. "Private showing, I believe you call it."

He tried to look blithely innocent and befuddled, but his demeanor became noticeably cautious. "Pardon? I don't have the faintest notion what you mean."

"Of course you do. Remember that unexplained noise you heard while you and the redhead were naked together in bed?" she prompted. "That was *me* gasping in shock."

Bri took grand satisfaction in watching the arrogant dandy's brown eyes pop from their sockets. His freshly shaved jaw sagged on its hinges. Then he recovered enough to shake his head vigorously in denial.

"I have no idea what you're babbling about." He struck a haughty pose and looked down his nose at her drab garments. "Furthermore, you look hideous in that shapeless gray outfit. Really, Gabrielle, go change into something suitable and we'll attend the theater performance." He flicked his wrist to shoo her on her way. "I'll wait for you here."

"In the first place, you know exactly what I'm referring to," she said in a stern tone. "Secondly, you can stop lying to me. I know who and what I saw. Having said that, you shouldn't be surprised that I am officially canceling our engagement. You can see yourself home on the next stagecoach."

"You are not canceling out on me," he snapped, his polite facade fizzling out. "Your family and mine have made an arrangement and we are sticking with it."

"No, we aren't. Your tryst made it null and void."

"Your mother and my aunt already made the announcement and set the plans in motion," he all but growled at her.

"My mother doesn't speak for me when it pertains to important decisions that affect my future," she replied. "I'm going west to visit my father and I don't want to see you when I return here. You can campaign all the way home if you like, but this is where we part company permanently."

He took a step closer, trying to intimidate her, but Bri didn't scare easily. "You are making a gigantic mistake," he snarled, all his practiced charm gone with the wind.

"My *mistake* was keeping silent so long about this disastrous mismatch." Bri thrust back her shoulders and elevated her chin when he clutched her arm painfully. "Back away, Eaton. There are witnesses here about and don't think I won't land a strategic blow that will drop you to your knees and ruin your next tryst with the redhead."

Eaton's dark eyes glistened with fury. He gnashed his teeth as he released her arm to spin on his well-shod heels. "We will continue this conversation later."

"No, it's over," she said in no uncertain terms.

He paused momentarily to look back at her. His gaze narrowed in a menacing frown. "You are going to regret your decision, Gabrielle. I promise you that."

She silently wished him good riddance and a quick one-way trip to hell as he struck a confident pose, then swaggered down the street. Bri glanced at the pocket watch she held near and dear. She knew it was ill-advised to go gadding about after dark in this rowdy town, but she felt the need to walk off her frustration. Plus, she wanted to make arrangements at the livery to buy a reliable horse and tack for her journey. She decided to save the interviews for a prospective guide and the gathering of necessary supplies until the next morning.

Battling a tired yawn, Bri strode toward the livery stable, following behind a cluster of citizens that were moving down the boardwalk toward the theater. She didn't want to isolate herself and risk being whisked off by the rougher element of society—like the two cretins she had encountered in the hotel hallway—while she was mentally distracted.

Bri glanced around, wondering if there was anyone else *besides* the rougher elements gallivanting at night in a town known as one of the toughest places this side of hell. Probably not. Except for the brawny stranger who kissed like nobody's business and left her burning with forbidden desire.

* * *

After a refreshing bath and a short nap, Hud exited the hotel. He scowled sourly when he found himself glancing up and down the dark streets, trying to locate the mysterious woman in drab gray who had kissed him senseless then pulled her vanishing act without a word of explanation.

Whoever and wherever she was didn't matter, he told himself sensibly. He had ventured out this evening to enjoy a drink and scratch the itch the mysterious kissing bandit provoked. Afterward, he'd swing by the stage-coach depot and inquire about the arrival of Commander Price's spoiled daughter.

Too bad she didn't have the good sense to stay in Austin where she belonged. She could have saved him this frustration. The thought of the prissy socialite and her politician of a fiancé spoiled Hud's mood. He quickened his pace, planning to veer into the nearest saloon. To his dismay, guttural snarls caught his attention. He stopped short when two burly bodies, locked in a bear hug, slammed into the clapboard wall of a saloon. The men— one was a buffalo hunter and the other a cowboy, judging by their style of clothing—crashed across the boardwalk and rolled into the street. Their drunken oaths and vicious growls captured the attention of passersby. Patrons also spilled from the saloon to egg on the brawlers.

Hud glanced toward the marshal's office that sat twenty yards from the fort's guardhouse at the bottom of Government Hill. He sighed in exasperation when Marshal Long didn't rush from the office to break up the fight. Well, hell, he thought. He'd had to separate drunken brawlers in hellholes like The Flat plenty of times. Apparently, tonight was no different.

When the two snarling men threw punches at each other, drew blood and turned the night air blue with foul curses, Hud grabbed the reins to the nearest horse. Then he walked the horse between the two downed men, forcing them to roll away or be stepped on. Their choice.

Disappointed that Hud had spoiled their entertainment, the saloon crowd wandered back to the bar.

"Who the hell do ya think you are?" the scraggly-haired hide hunter muttered as he straightened his buffalo vest and glowered at Hud.

"Yeah, mind yer own b'ness," the cowboy slurred out as he blotted his bloody lip with his shirtsleeve.

"What's going on here?"

Hud glanced over to see the marshal striding toward him. If Hud wasn't mistaken, Calvin Long, the bandy-legged law officer whose birdlike facial features had earned him the nickname of Sparrow, had dressed hurriedly. His shirt was fastened unevenly and the top buttons on the placket of his breeches were gaping. Hud speculated the marshal had stopped in the red-light district while making his evening rounds.

Hud had been on his way to seek out the same diversion, *especially* after the mysterious female had started a fire in him with her scorching kisses.

Calvin Long cocked his head in a birdlike manner and studied Hud for a long moment. "Stone, isn't it?"

Hud nodded.

"Wish you'd stop in more often. Since this town has grown to a population of two thousand, not counting the influx of hide hunters and cowboys who pass through here like blustery winds, I could use an extra hand keeping the lid on this place."

"I'll help you haul your rowdy friends to the cala-boose," Hud volunteered.

He grabbed the cowboy by the nape of the shirt and marched him toward the jail while the marshal ushered the greasy-haired buffalo hunter down the boardwalk.

"Damn cowpuncher," the hide hunter scowled as he wobbled unsteadily on his feet. "I saw her first. He had no cause to interfere with me."

"You were fighting over a woman?" Hud asked as they approached the jail. "I haven't met a woman who's worth a gut punching or a split lip."

"This goon was trying to drag the poor woman into the alley," the cowboy muttered out the uninjured side of his mouth. "I was rescuing her from this ugly brute. I don't belong in jail. He does!"

"Ha! You wanted her for yerself. But she was workin' me over too good without yer interference." The buffalo hunter readjusted his wooly cap then leaned heavily on Marshal Long for support. "She kicked me right square in the crotch when I latched on to her. Then she hit me with *somethin'*. Don't know what but it set me off." He hitched his thumb—which sported a dirty, jagged fin-gernail—toward the cowboy. "Then this cow-faced wrangler showed up to take her away from me."

"I was defending her honor, you smelly bastard," the cowboy sneered insultingly.

"She didn't need no help. She took off down the alley like a gray blur and left me on my knees, tryin' to catch my breath."

Gray blur? Hud shot a quick glance over his shoulder to the alley. *The kissing bandit?* he wondered. *Where was she now? Had she returned safely from wherever she'd come from?*

A shadowy movement in the alley caught Hud's attention. "I'll catch up with you in a minute," he said, striding off.

Hud muttered an oath when the elusive female backed into the deepest reaches of the alley, making it impossible to see her face again. "I want to know who you are," he demanded as he approached. When she pivoted on her heels, he said, "Don't make me chase you down, because I can and I will do it."

She turned to face him and he cursed that droopy bonnet that hid her features as he approached. "Are you all right?"

She nodded and her bonnet flopped over her face.

"You weren't hurt by the hide hunter?" When she shook her head no, he said, "Tell me your name."

She didn't speak, just curled her hand around the back of his neck and kissed him senseless again. Instant pleasure assailed him and he wrapped her up in his arms and kissed her hard and hungrily for a long, breathless moment. Then she traced his lips with her forefinger and backed away.

"Hey! Are you coming to help or not?" the marshal shouted impatiently.

"I'm on my way," Hud called over his shoulder.

To his dismay he glanced back to see that his fantasy woman had vanished like a specter evaporating into nothingness. Grumbling at the kissing bandit's amazing ability to melt down his brain then disappear at will, he strode toward the marshal. He told himself to forget about the mysterious woman and focus on locking the brawlers in jail. *Then* he could quench his thirst, scratch an itch and wait for Commander Price's daughter to arrive in The Flat.

Chapter Three

When the two men were locked behind bars, Hud glanced curiously at the marshal. "Do you know if a female passenger arrived on the stagecoach today?"

Calvin suddenly noticed his improperly buttoned shirt. He smiled guiltily as he corrected the problem.

"Better check your gaping placket while you're at it," Hud suggested with a wry grin.

"Well, hell," Calvin grumbled self-consciously. "It's getting to where a man can't follow pleasurable pursuits when he's on break without being interrupted by gunfights, brawls and such. In the past week there's been a duel on the street, an unidentified body left in the alley and a half-dozen saloon brawls. Not to mention corralling an abusive drunk in the red-light district."

"About the stage passengers?" Hud prompted. "I'm supposed to escort the commander's daughter to the Ranger camp."

Calvin nodded in recognition. "I heard there were a lady and a highfalutin political candidate on board the stagecoach. But I didn't see her in person. The coach rolled in late this afternoon." He lifted a thinning brow. "The commander's daughter, you say?"

Hud nodded.

"I don't know where she is, but I saw that Powell character strutting around like a rooster earlier this evening. He's campaigning for senator and he was shaking a few hands after the theater performance. Then he strutted off with a crowd of cowboys. My guess is that he was planning to buy a few votes by paying for several rounds of whiskey at one of the saloons. The woman is probably holed up in Brazos Hotel since it offers the best accommodations in town."

After Hud fielded the marshal's questions about the reports of Comanche and Kiowa raids against supply wagons and the threat of Mexican and white outlaw gangs stealing everything they could carry off, he stopped in for a long-awaited drink at a saloon.

First thing in the morning he would seek out Miss High-and-Mighty Price and arrange for the return trip to camp. He dreaded the jaunt and the unwanted company, but at least this escort detail would take only a few days. Then he could concentrate on finding Mad Joe Jarvis and his sidekick, Pete Spaulding.

Bri had been lingering in the shadows of the alley, watching the brawny stranger break up the brawl between the lecherous bastard who'd grabbed her and the drunken cowboy who'd tried to come to her defense—and had accidentally gotten in her way. She would've had that stinking hide hunter laid out like a corpse in the dirt, suffering a brain-scrambling blow to his hard head if the cowboy hadn't charged in.

She hadn't lost the knack of self-defense, she mused

proudly. Benji Dunlop had taught her well. She remembered every dirty trick and had used several on the drunken brute before she knocked him to his knees. What she didn't know was why she'd allowed the tall, muscular stranger to approach her when she could have lost herself in the shadows of the alley, despite his claim that he could track her down.

After the stranger and the marshal hauled the two men to jail, Bri wrapped her shawl tightly around her shoulders and scuttled back to the hotel. She could rest easy now. She had contacted the livery owner and purchased a sturdy mount and had gathered a few supplies as well. However, she had yet to hire a dependable guide. She frowned pensively, wondering where she might find a reliable escort in a town jumping alive with scoundrels.

Perhaps she could hire the stranger, she mused as she locked the door to her hotel room. He was obviously competent. She had watched him break up a street fight without sustaining so much as a scratch.

Bri removed her gown to stitch up the shoulder seam the hide hunter had ripped loose when he became pushy and insistent.

On second thought, it wouldn't be wise to approach the ruggedly handsome stranger she'd brazenly kissed twice in the same night. If he recognized her, he might presume that he was entitled to fringe benefits during their cross-country jaunt.

Then again, if he didn't recognize her...

Bri set aside her mended gown to prepare for bed. Maybe she *would* approach the stranger and test the waters. If he didn't recognize her she might offer him a job as her guide. He'd proven himself capable of handling adversity this evening. Whoever and whatever he was, he had remained cool and collected while breaking up the brawl.

Bri admired that about him. Not to mention her appreciation of the arousing way he kissed. The erotic thought sent wicked pleasure rippling through her. Smiling secretively, Bri laid her head on her pillow and fell fast asleep. Two hours later she awakened in the middle of such a vivid fantasy that her body burned with forbidden desire. Chastising herself, she crammed the pillow over her head and tried to sleep without dreaming.

Eaton glanced at his bejeweled pocket watch. He'd bought a round of drinks and encouraged the saloon patrons to cast their votes for him in the upcoming election. Impatiently he finished off his drink and killed another few minutes before the clandestine meeting he'd arranged with his new associate.

He swallowed a grin, remembering that Sylvia would be waiting for him when he concluded his business. Eaton cast aside the lusty thought as he sauntered from the saloon to the gaming hall. When the three men appeared on the boardwalk, he inclined his head toward the alley.

Eaton tapped the butt of the pistol he carried beneath his expensive jacket to make sure he was still armed— just in case. Muggings were commonplace in this hellhole and he didn't intend to become a victim while he arranged for his newfound friend's hirelings to deal effectively with Gabrielle.

"Now, what is this task you require, in exchange for *my* financial support and *your* political loyalty?" Ray Novak asked then puffed on his cigar.

Eaton surveyed his new cohort's bulky physique and

bushy eyebrows. The rancher shared the same fetish of dressing in the finest clothing money could buy. *A man after my own heart,* Eaton thought as he walked deeper into the shadows of the alley so no one could overhear him.

"I'm having a problem with my contrary fiancée," he murmured. "I trust your two men can make the necessary accommodations. I intend to teach her a lesson and to promote my campaign. Of course, this favor will benefit you as well."

"Count on it." Novak smiled around the cigar he had clamped between his teeth.

Then Eaton got down to the dirty business of hammering out the details.

The next morning Bri started when someone rapped abruptly on her hotel room door. She glanced at her watch, surprised Eaton had piled out of bed at this early hour, even if he was driven by the need to convince her to reconsider their engagement.

"Not a chance in hell that I will change my mind," she vowed as she opened the door. She blinked in surprise when the brawny stranger who had tormented her dreams loomed on the threshold, not Eaton.

"Miss Price, I presume."

His deep, resonant voice rolled over her. She was quick to note that he didn't seem surprised to see her. There was no flicker of recognition in his whiskey-colored eyes that were surrounded by thick black lashes. He was as tall as she remembered and his face was tanned. Raven hair protruded from beneath the brim of his hat.

Although he wore buckskin breeches and a dark button-down shirt that looked the worse for wear, he filled out the garments exceptionally well. He did indeed possess broad shoulders and long muscular arms, just as she remembered. Double holsters that sported pearl-handled peacemakers encircled his lean waist. He had horseman's thighs and he wore scuffed high-heeled boots designed to remain in the stirrups when breaking speed records on the back of a horse.

This was definitely the man she had kissed last night. Minus the bristly whiskers, she tacked on. Now he was clean-shaven and she wondered if she'd enjoy kissing him even more without those whiskers.

Bri mentally pinched herself when she realized she was staring at his sensuous lips and studying his striking appearance like a dazzled schoolgirl. It amazed her that she felt such an instant and compelling physical attraction to him. For all she knew he might be a hired killer. Whatever his profession, he was appealing—in a rugged sort of way—and he drew her attention and held it fast.

When his alert gaze roved over her plain blue cotton gown then refocused on her face, she didn't know why she felt insulted by what appeared to be his indifference and his quick dismissal. Nonetheless, she *was* disappointed. She swore that she saw him smirk before he schooled his face in a carefully disciplined stare. Obviously he'd taken one look at her and found her lacking.

True, she wasn't wearing the most expensive gown she owned and she didn't approve of putting on airs the way Eaton did, but she did look presentable…didn't she? She looked better than when she wore the dowdy gray gown, bonnet and shawl that practically made her invisible in the shadows.

"And your name is?" she replied while he studied her with a stare that was no more flattering than the first.

Honestly, she might not be a raving beauty like some

of the debutantes who attended soirées in Austin, but she'd never had a man show such a complete lack of interest. Usually men paid her more attention than she preferred.

"Captain Hudson Stone," he said in a no-nonsense tone. "You can call me Hud. Your father ordered me to contact you. I am to escort you to camp since he is on inspection and is occupied with field reports." He stared pointedly at her. "Perhaps you can schedule your next visit during a time when the commander isn't exceptionally busy. You might save both of us valuable time."

She arched a challenging brow and crossed her arms over her chest. "Are you lecturing me, Captain?"

"Is that what it sounded like?"

Hud stared at her with feigned innocence and watched her hypnotic indigo eyes flicker with irritation. If she was upset by his insult then too damn bad. He was tired, cranky and annoyed that she was so strikingly attractive that it took all his willpower not to react to her. He wanted her to be the female version of Winston Price. She was anything but.

She was positively alluring with those almond-shaped eyes that were rimmed with long sooty lashes. Her oval face was the color of peaches and cream and her pert nose gave her a bit of an impish appearance. Her curly mane of gold hair seemed to catch fire in the early morning light that streamed through the window. He had to clench his fist to prevent himself from burying his hand in those flaming curls.

Hud hated that he found everything about Gabrielle Price appealing. Lusting after an engaged woman was unacceptable. Especially this one. She was also the commander's daughter.

"I don't know what I have done to annoy you, Captain.

Or are you just one of those surly individuals who wakes up in a bad mood and never overcomes it?" she asked with a sticky-sweet smile.

Extremely attractive…except for that sassy mouth, he corrected. Maybe that's what Commander Price meant when he claimed Gabrielle was *unique*.

When she snapped her fingers in his face, disciplining him like an absentminded child, he jerked up his head and glared down at her from his superior height. His steely-eyed stare didn't faze her one whit, he noted.

Feisty and combative, too, he mused, adding to the list of her annoying traits. The more the better, he thought.

"Damn good thing you're pretty," he muttered under his breath.

"Say again?" she demanded.

He shrugged. "Nothing important."

"I figured as much. I'm sure my father kept his best Rangers for patrol duty and left you for me."

He bared his teeth. Not to be outdone, she did the same. They were off to a rocky start. Not that he cared. Escort detail kept him from his crusade to avenge Speck Horton. Because of this delay, a cold trail would be damn hard to follow.

And that snide remark she'd made about other Rangers being more competent? He'd like to shake her until her teeth rattled for saying that.

"You saved me the trouble of seeking out a guide," she commented as she strode over to gather her two satchels. "I still can replace you if you prefer. Apparently you have taken an instant disliking to me, Captain."

She had that right…and wrong. He liked her—in an exasperating sort of way that defied common sense. He had expected a whiny little daisy of a female. Instead, he had clashed with an iron-willed woman who didn't back down easily and gave exactly what she got. He doubted she could follow orders worth a damn, either. Despite the fact that her father had spent two decades in military service and law enforcement, he hadn't managed to teach Gabrielle Price discipline.

When Hud dallied too long in thought, she snapped her fingers at him again, which aggravated the hell out of him.

"Well? Shall I seek out someone else, Stone? Are these questions too difficult for you? I can speak slower if necessary," she taunted unmercifully.

Hud blew out a breath. "No, I'm under direct orders from your father," he replied in a brusque tone. "With any luck, we will dodge bloodthirsty outlaws and Indian war parties to reach bivouac without killing each other. I'm up to the challenge if you are."

"Definitely." She nodded her head and sunlight sparkled in that glorious mass of curly golden hair again. "I'm ready to leave whenever you are."

"At first light *tomorrow*…if you can drag yourself from bed that early," he added caustically.

She smiled snidely at him. "I'm an early riser. As you can see, the early bird is here to greet the worm."

Bri bit back a grin when Hud's amber gaze narrowed on her. If he wanted to continue exchanging insults, she was up to the challenge. In fact, she rather enjoyed matching wits with this particular Ranger, who obviously drew the short straw when it came to unwanted escort detail. He was stuck with her and he wasn't the least bit happy about it. He had no qualms about voicing his displeasure, either.

"I see no reason why we can't leave this morning," she insisted. "I'm packed and ready to ride."

"*I* have other duties to attend while I'm in town."

"Like what? A visit to the nearest brothel and saloons? A diversion to compensate for the unpleasant duty of acting as my guide?"

"Precisely. You're more insightful than I anticipated," he countered. "Might as well have some fun when I can. Clearly, we aren't going to get along well during our journey through a region where danger is the rule, not the exception. I'm warning you now that this is no place for the faint of heart and the tender of foot."

She snickered at his turn of phrase.

"I'll give you a day's rest so you can keep the swift pace I set, Mizz Price." He stepped closer, eclipsing her with his size and stature. "Just so you know, my long-time friend and fellow Ranger was murdered recently. I was trying to track down the bastard who shot Speck Horton in the back, stole his badge and left him to coyotes. Have you ever seen what a pack of hungry coyotes can do to a man, Mizz Price?"

She grimaced at the bleak prospect. "No."

"Consider yourself lucky because it isn't pretty. Speck was my friend and dragging myself here to fetch a greenhorn, who arrived on a foolhardy whim doesn't set well with me."

He stared her down—and he was good at it, damn his brawny hide. "If you and your fiancé had any brains in your heads you'd catch the next stagecoach out of here and wait for your father's return to Austin to visit him. They don't call this place Hell's Fringe for nothing. So pay attention when you sashay down the boardwalk today. And do not go out at night unless you have a death wish."

She would love to tell this hard-bitten Ranger captain

that she could take care of herself, thank you very much. But he was all puffed up like a spitting cobra and it was difficult to get a word in edgewise.

"People in these parts get their throats slit for the coins in their pockets," he said bluntly. "And you don't want to know what can happen to a defenseless woman. Just last night a female came dangerously close to being mauled and raped by a drunken hide hunter."

Not as close as you think, she mused. The foul-smelling brute was seeing double after she clobbered him with the broken wagon yoke she'd found in the garbage bin.

"Are you quite finished trying to scare me, Captain Stone? You can go now." She flicked her wrist dismissively, doing a fair impersonation of Eaton at his snobbish best.

"Quite finished," he grunted out as he stepped across the threshold into the hall. "Tell your fiancé to keep his wits about him while he's escorting you around town."

Bri didn't bother to mention that Eaton was her *ex*-fiancé and that he wasn't accompanying her cross-country. "I might leave him behind," she declared flippantly. "That will give me more opportunity to charm and seduce you, Captain."

"Even if I were interested, *which I'm not,* it would be a waste of your time," he shot back. "I don't dally with an engaged woman, especially when she is my commander's daughter."

The insult provoked her to thrust back her shoulders and tilt her chin indignantly. "Change of plans, Captain," she snapped. "I'll make my own way to camp or find another guide."

"Like hell you will."

"Consider yourself officially dismissed. I've had quite enough of you. Goodbye and good riddance!" she said before she slammed the door in his face.

Hud halted at the top of the staircase and cursed himself up one side and down the other. He had been rude, sarcastic and harsh with the commander's daughter. But she had set him off with that sassy mouth, he thought self-righteously. Moreover, it annoyed him that she was so stunningly attractive and that he had to go to great lengths to pretend *not* to notice. Plus, she was quick-witted and she rose to every challenge. She impressed him—and annoyed the living hell out of him at once. Which made dealing with her a nightmare.

Muttering, he tramped downstairs to have breakfast with Marshal Long, who had requested that Hud add a few more names to his Black Book that he carried to keep track of fugitives. Several Wanted posters had arrived with the mail from the stagecoach. Sparrow wanted Hud to update the other Rangers about the outlaws who had been described and identified as perpetrators of various crimes in the region.

Hud's Black Book—or Bible II, as he and the other Rangers referred to their source of information—was invaluable in the field. He had noted physical descriptions, clothing styles, preferences of weapons and aliases on dozens of outlaws known to be prowling the area.

The damn book was getting so thick that it barely fit into his vest pocket, he mused as he strode to the café.

Hud scanned the street, wondering if Mad Joe Jarvis might be in town. It was a possibility. Before he veered into the café to join Sparrow, he stared up at the second-story window of the hotel. Now that he had settled his ruffled feathers he regretted giving the commander's daughter such a rough time.

Well, he'd apologize bright and early the next morning and find a way to return to her good graces—if she had any. The last thing he needed was for the commander's daughter to run crying to daddy and have him dishonorably discharged. Fiery and contrary as she was, she might do it to spite him.

Hud barked a laugh. He could just imagine what Gabrielle Price thought of him. He made a mental note never to ask her directly. Articulate as she was, she'd have a field day categorically listing everything she disliked about him.

Bri spent the day dodging Eaton, who rapped on her door three separate times. If he thought he could persuade her to change her mind about their betrothal, he was sorely mistaken. After he strutted off to take supper without her, Bri donned one of her drab gray gowns, shawl and bonnet so she could roam the streets and alleys as she had done often in Houston with Benji Dunlop at her side.

She came upon three young lads who were scrounging through trash bins for anything they could sell. She stood in the shadows behind the general store, watching the teenage boys. The scene reminded her so much of Benji that her throat closed up with emotion. She clutched the treasured pocket watch in her fist as she stepped into view.

"What'd you be wantin', lady?" the oldest boy demanded sharply.

She appraised the gangly boy, who looked to be fourteen—or thereabouts. "Find anything in the garbage worth keeping?" she asked conversationally.

The boys eyed her warily, ready to break and run if she made a threatening move toward them.

"Not much. You expect us to share what we got with you?" the second lad, whose long face was surrounded with frizzy hair, demanded gruffly.

Bri shook her head. "No, I'm here to share what I have with you." She retrieved three silver dollars from her pocket and tossed one to each boy. "These are compliments of Benji Dunlop."

"Who's Benji Dunlop?" the youngest, cherub-faced lad asked as he rubbed his grimy fingers over the shiny coin.

"The best friend I ever had. He roamed the back alleys of Houston. His home was a hut made of crates that he fashioned behind a saloon. He shared whatever he had with me." She glanced around curiously. "Where do you call home?"

The tallest boy hitched his thumb over his shoulder. "We got a fortress of sorts under a broken-down wagon behind one of the freight offices."

Bri tossed each boy another silver dollar. "Dinner is on Benji tonight. Enjoy it."

When she turned away, the second ragamuffin called after her. "What's yer name, lady?"

"I'm just a friend who cares about you."

A pleased smile pursed Bri's lips when she heard the boys bounding off, whooping and hollering excitedly. Now that she knew where the boys lived, she hurried off to see their makeshift home. She shook her head in dismay when she located the wagon that served as their sleeping quarters. Broken crates were piled around the dilapidated wagon. Beneath it, tattered blankets served as bedding.

She decided right then and there that she was going

to improve the boys' living conditions and offer them a new start. They would at least have a chance to make a decent life for themselves.

Wheeling around, Bri strode quickly toward the street. She halted near the boardwalk and clung to the shadows as several men, who reeked of sweat and whiskey, sauntered past her. Then her gaze settled on the brawny silhouette of the man who exited the saloon across the street. She shrank back when his gaze settled directly on her. For a moment, she swore those golden cat eyes could pierce the darkness and he could see as well at night as he could in daylight. Would he recognize her?

Bri ducked her head and scuttled down the boardwalk toward the hotel. No matter what, she wasn't going to allow Captain Hudson Stone, the hard-hearted Ranger, to recognize her. Unfortunately, he crossed the street, eating up the ground with his long, swift strides.

"Curse it," she muttered under her breath. She darted into the nearest alley and melted into the shadows. But wouldn't you know that he'd pursue her relentlessly, same as he had last night.

"So we meet again," he murmured as he halted in front of the place where she lurked in a pool of inky shadows.

Bri refused to speak for fear he would recognize her voice. She smiled to herself, thinking that he was nicer to the mystery-woman-in-gray than he had been to the commander's daughter.

"Wandering down these dark streets and alleys is a very bad idea," he warned her. "I was hoping last night's fiasco taught you to—"

Bri latched on to Hud when she saw Eaton and his red-haired actress ambling down the boardwalk. If Eaton spotted her in her gray gown, he would spoil her charade.

"*Awk...*" Hud choked on his breath when she clamped her mouth over his and pulled him deeper into the shadows.

To her dismay, the same bedeviling sensations that assailed her the previous night spilled over her again. His tantalizing scent, his taste and the feel of his muscular body pressed against her swept her into a dizzying universe that defied logical explanation. When she came within two feet of him, her body reacted with reckless abandon. *How was this even possible?* she wondered bewilderedly.

This man didn't like her. He thought she was spoiled and selfish. Maybe she was, but he had no right to sit in judgment. Furthermore, he had no right to arouse her when she didn't want to like him, either. Unfortunately, there was no denying her fierce and lusty reaction to him.

Hud clamped his hands on her hips, pressing her against his thighs, making her vividly aware of his masculine response. Then his hand glided up to brush the side of her breast and another flame of desire scorched her.

Bri told herself to back away now that the potential threat of being recognized by Eaton had passed. But the feel of Hud's palm gliding over the fabric covering her breast made her burn with insatiable need. When he teased her nipple with his thumb, her legs wobbled and her breath sighed out raggedly. The embrace quickly became even more personal and intimate than the ones from the previous night.

Bri moaned in helpless surrender when he lowered his head to kiss her hungrily. He cupped her breast again and insinuated his muscled thigh between her legs, making her weak with need.

"Come back to my room," he whispered between devouring kisses and arousing caresses.

"Hey, mister, get yer hands off of her!" came an irate adolescent voice from the black depths of the alley.

Hud jerked up his head, surprised to see three ragtag boys, each carrying a makeshift club, prepared to defend to the death the Lady In Gray. He glanced down, hoping to get a good look at her features, but she turned her head away from him quickly and looked back at the boys.

"We mean it, mister." The chubby runt from the ragamuffin trio raised his club threateningly. "Let her go…N…O…W."

"Yeah, you better back off right this minute or we'll make you damn sorry," the middle-sized urchin sneered boldly.

Hud was still standing there, his body throbbing with unappeased desire, when the mysterious woman lurched around and darted between the three boys.

Hud shook his head, trying to clear his senses. No doubt about it, the elusive female was spinning some sort of magical web around him. One minute she was kissing him until his brain went up in flames and his body burned into a pile of frustrated ashes. Then poof! Off she went again. This time she had three half-grown guard puppies trailing behind her. Were they her children or her siblings? he wondered.

Scowling at the oddity of his encounters with the Lady In Gray, Hud pivoted on his boot heels. Thanks to that steamy interlude, he needed another drink. He also needed a cold bath to douse the fire the kissing bandit left burning inside him—again.

Chapter Four

Bri half collapsed against the back wall of the freight office to catch her breath and collect her wits. If she believed in voodoo, she would swear that dynamic Ranger had cast a magical spell that boiled her good sense into mush and her inhibitions into a cloud of steam.

Blast and be damned, how could she keep responding so immediately and intensely to Hudson Stone? She melted beneath his scorching kisses and bold caresses in one second flat.

"You okay, miss?" the oldest, whey-faced orphan asked worriedly.

"Did he hurt you?" the second lad wanted to know.

"We'll fix him good if he did," the youngest urchin promised vengefully.

"I'm fine. He caught me off guard, is all." She patted each boy on the shoulder. "Thank you for coming to my rescue. I'm indebted. Will you tell me your names?"

"Tommy," the skinny lad said then gestured to the runt. "This is my brother, Howie. And this is our friend, Georgie."

"I'm very pleased to make your acquaintance." She shook their hands. "My name is…Ellie. I have an idea where we might find jobs that will give you a fresh start away from this rowdy town. If you'll gather your gear, we'll be on our way as soon as possible. Are you interested in an adventure?"

"You mean leave all this behind?" Tommy snickered as he gestured toward their improvised home.

Bri chuckled. "I've always had a thirst for excitement and adventure. I have an idea that will get us out of town and on the road to a promising and rewarding future. We can strike off together after we retrieve our belongings. We'll meet back here in an hour if you're willing."

The boys nodded eagerly then darted away.

Bri started in the opposite direction then paused a few minutes later to glance skyward. "Happy now, Benji? I can see why you pointed me in the direction of those boys. But I'm not particularly pleased that infuriating Ranger got tangled in the middle of this."

At least she'd conjured up a plan to leave town without inconveniencing Hud further. He'd made it glaringly apparent what he thought of her and how annoyed he was with this assignment. She had dismissed him— and she damn well meant it. Now she wouldn't have to make the entire trip alone and she could help the urchins begin a new life while she was at it.

Quickening her step, Bri hurried to the hotel to grab her satchels.

The next morning Hud rolled from bed and cursed the restless night's sleep that made him out of sorts— even before he confronted the feisty Gabrielle Price. His arousing encounters with the elusive Lady In Gray had fueled his fantasies. Unfortunately, the commander's daughter kept appearing out of nowhere to spoil his erotic dreams.

Yawning, Hud raked his fingers through his tousled hair then doused his face in cool water from the basin. Wherever the kissing bandit was hiding out, she had three ragamuffins looking after her. Hud knew he wouldn't see her again so he might as well squelch the lusty anticipation that gnawed at him. He had to suffer through his mandatory duty of babysitting Gabrielle Price and her fiancé. Alluring and intriguing though she was, she symbolized everything he wasn't. Plus, she challenged him and defied him. The chances of her obeying his direct orders during the trip were a fifty-fifty proposition at best.

Hud grabbed his saddlebags, slung them over his shoulder and ambled down the hall to fetch Princess Price. He rapped on the door, but she didn't answer so he knocked harder the second time.

"Mizz Price!" he called out, becoming more annoyed with each passing second. "Rise and shine!"

Damn it, if she was delaying their departure on purpose he'd have more than a few words with her. "Ready or not, I'm coming in."

Hud opened the door then choked on his breath as he gazed incredulously around the room. The pitcher and basin that usually sat on the commode were shattered on the floor. The nightstand was overturned and the bedding lay in a pile at the foot of the bed. Hud walked over to step lightly on the bundle of blankets to make sure Gabrielle wasn't under them. Sure enough she wasn't.

Not only was Gabrielle nowhere to be found but her two satchels were also missing.

"Damn," Hud muttered as he lurched toward the door.

This was his fault. He had shown no enthusiasm whatsoever when he assumed his duty as bodyguard. He had been rude and disrespectful to the commander's daughter and he had voiced his displeasure for this assignment. Then he had left her to fend for herself in this raucous town. She'd had no one but her dandified fiancé as protection and now she was gone!

"What in God's name happened here? And *who* are *you?*"

Hud glanced over his shoulder to see Eaton Powell II— or so he presumed, since he was decked out in the very latest fashion—puffed up like a toad. The snooty politician was glaring disdainfully at him.

"What have you done with my fiancée?" he demanded loudly.

"I haven't done anything with her," Hud replied. "I came to fetch her for the journey and this is how I found her room."

Eaton looked down his patrician nose and struck a superior pose. "I will ask you again. *Who* are *you?*"

"Captain Hudson Stone. I'm the Ranger sent to escort you and your fiancée to Commander Price."

Eaton looked him up and down then snorted insultingly. "If you represent the inadequacy of our state law enforcement on the frontier then I shall be sure to tighten regulations and qualifications when I am elected to the senate."

The cocky dandy shouldered past Hud to survey the ransacked room. "My God! It looks as if there was a struggle. Someone must have realized who Gabrielle was and abducted her for money or for something even more sinister."

He whirled around to stab an accusing finger into Hud's chest. "This is your fault! My fiancée has vanished and I hold you personally accountable. Furthermore, I shall see you dishonorably discharged from your battalion!"

Eaton's voice rose to a roar. Hud glanced sideways to see several tousled heads poke around partially opened doors.

"Hey, keep the noise down." The man with bloodshot eyes, who had rented the room directly across the hall, glared at him. "Some of us are trying to sleep."

Hud approached him immediately. "The woman in this room has been abducted. Did you see anything?"

The man shook his disheveled gray head. "No, I didn't come upstairs until nearly two o'clock. Hell, I don't even remember how I got here from the saloon."

Judging by the man's puffy face and red-streaked eyes, he was indeed sporting a hellish hangover.

"What about you, sir?" Hud asked, glancing at the scrawny little gent who had rented the room next door to Bri's.

The gent bobbed his bald head. "I heard something crash to the floor and I heard a man's voice late last night. But I didn't even know a woman had rented the room. I wasn't about to get involved with a ruffian. I mind my own business and I'm only here to catch the stage to Dodge City this afternoon."

After questioning the six men in nearby rooms, he didn't come up with one useful clue. Hud swore under his breath and cursed the disaster that had greeted him this morning. To make matters worse, Eaton was breathing down his neck, blaming Hud for whatever had happened to his beloved fiancée.

"I'll find her," Hud assured Eaton, who persisted in snapping and growling at his heels like an ill-tempered dog.

"Don't bother," Eaton snarled hatefully. "I'll hire my own posse to pose questions and turn this town upside down."

With an audience of the six men, who were still craning their necks around the hotel room doors, Eaton flung his arms ceilingward and burst out with, "Dear God! I can only begin to imagine the horrors my frightened fiancée must be enduring...*if* she's still alive." He glared at Hud. "No thanks to you, Ranger Stone."

Wheeling around, Eaton pelted down the hall. He ranted about how he had come to Fort Griffin and The Flat to campaign for public office and how calamity had struck. He bewailed the abduction of his fiancée long and loudly.

Hud cursed the unexpected turn of events as he watched the hotel patrons close and lock their doors. To his further frustration, he couldn't find one promising lead as to who might have overpowered Gabrielle Price and abducted her in the middle of the night.

A sense of urgency hounded Hud as he descended the fire escape to survey the horse tracks in the dirt. There were three sets, which didn't coincide with what the man who rented the room next door to Bri had said about hearing one male voice. The kidnapper must have pounced on Bri and she had tried to put up a fight but she hadn't escaped. No doubt, her captor had dragged her down the back stairs while the other man waited with their mounts. They must have tied her to the spare horse then rode off to who knew where.

Hud squatted on his haunches to take a closer look

at the hoofprints. One mount had a chipped front hoof and its back left horseshoe had worn thin. One set of prints indicated a well-tended horse—a stolen one perhaps. The third set of prints was similar to the first—worn shoes that indicated a lack of care.

Following the prints, Hud ended up in a side alley where two horses veered east. He frowned, unsure what had happened to the third horse. Before he could survey the area closely, he heard a commotion in the street. He strode to the boardwalk then scowled at Eaton, who was waving his arms in expansive gestures and calling for the attention of everyone on the street.

"My fiancée has been kidnapped," he bugled loudly. "I'm offering a reward to anyone who has information that will bring Gabrielle safely back to me. I'll also pay any man who will join a posse to search for her." He spun about to shake his fist in the air. "If I am elected to the senate I vow to provide better law enforcement in this town, this state and our nation! There are too many muggings and murderers on these streets. And now this!" His voice broke as he blubbered, "May God help my poor fiancée!"

Hud rolled his eyes when several women rushed forward to console Eaton. The dandy was a mite too melodramatic for Hud's tastes. However, it was possible that Eaton might have been hopelessly besotted with Bri and was overcome with fear and concern. Given her beauty, wealth and social prestige, Hud predicted Eaton was eager to reap all the benefits of marrying the commander's daughter.

While Eaton strode toward the newspaper office to have the story of the incident written up, Hud reversed direction to search for more clues.

"Bad publicity. That's all we need around here. A dignitary's daughter and a politician's fiancée abducted from her room in the middle of the night. Damn, I hope she's okay."

Hud lurched around to see Sparrow scurrying toward him. The expression on the marshal's weathered features testified to his concern for the missing woman.

"Any idea who might have taken her?" Sparrow asked.

Hud shook his head as he stared at the single tracks that led down another back alley. "So far nothing. One set of tracks indicates one rider separated from the other two. Mizz Price might have been slung over the saddle and carried off with one rider while the other rider headed the opposite direction to throw us off track."

Sparrow nodded pensively. "You're right. They're probably trying to confuse us before they join up later."

Hud followed the single set of prints that mingled with several trampled tracks in the street near the stacks of buffalo hides. He blew out his breath in frustration and stared into the distance. Even if he didn't have much use for the spoiled female, he didn't want to see her hurt. Not to mention how Commander Price would react when given the grim news.

The thought galvanized Hud's resolve. He wouldn't rest until he found the two men who had kidnapped Bri. As eager as he was to track down Speck Horton's killer, he had to focus his energy and attention on locating Bri before she suffered untold atrocities.

Hud jogged to the livery stable to fetch Rambler. On his way out of town, he picked up a single trail again. He frowned when he noticed the horse had joined three other horses and three wagons. A half mile down the road, six more horses joined the group.

"What in the hell?" He glanced northwest, survey-ing the trail that led toward two communities and the military fort located in the Texas panhandle. There were also several large ranches along the route. Bri might have been taken to a line shack or to a nester's cabin and held for ransom—or worse.

Leaving her in town—where her inconsolable fiancé was alerting everyone about the abduction and offering a substantial reward—was an invitation for the abductors to be overtaken and strung up by hotheaded vigilantes.

Half-twisting in the saddle, Hud grabbed hardtack from his saddlebag then munched on it. He had planned to eat a hearty breakfast before hitting the road. Now his plans had changed drastically—and so had Bri's. He wondered if she also held him responsible for the terror she faced. Hud was sorry to say that he wouldn't blame her one damn bit if she did.

Eaton returned to his hotel suite to gather his belong-ings. He planned to be sitting on the southbound stage-coach to Austin. Now he was the focus of this god-awful community and soon the entire state would hear the news. Of course, he'd sent word of the abduction in all directions, via the telegraph. By the end of the week, his name would be a household word and he'd give inter-views to every newspaper.

Smiling smugly, Eaton neatly folded his clothing and packed them carefully in his suitcases. This publicity stunt would earn him thousands of sympathetic votes from the bleeding hearts in Texas. In addition, it wouldn't cost him a penny. He'd be featured in dozens of newspaper articles, he predicted. People everywhere would recognize his name and know his sad story. This jaunt to this backward hellhole couldn't have turned out better if he had orchestrated the scheme from beginning to end.

Eaton chuckled at his own cleverness. He had finagled promises from the marshal and upstanding business owners in The Flat to support his campaign. The only one who wouldn't benefit from this clever scheme that had launched his campaign into high gear was Gabrielle Price.

Eaton snorted derisively as he closed his suitcases then exited his suite. He'd told Gabrielle that she'd be sorry for breaking off the engagement. The men hired to abduct her would keep her stashed from sight for at least a week. Then Eaton would decide whether her safe return or her premature death would better serve his campaign.

"Here's your ticket, Mr. Powell." Marshal Long dropped it into Eaton's palm. "All the arrangements have been made for your journey. Rest assured that I will do everything I can to locate your fiancée while you're out of town."

Eaton nodded, looking as forlorn as he knew how. "I cannot thank you enough," he said, pumping the marshal's hand with fake gratitude. "I won't forget how cooperative you've been in this rescue effort. Every time I consider the horrible ordeal Gabrielle faces it breaks my heart."

"All of us hope your fiancée returns safe and sound."

Don't count me in those numbers, thought Eaton.

Eaton ambled off to take his noon meal. The number of individuals who approached him to offer sympathy and political support pleased him. He wondered fleetingly if Gabrielle would be offered a decent meal during her captivity. Then he shrugged off the thought and devoured the meal that the café proprietor announced was "on the house."

Hud topped a rise of ground on the northern trail and paused to stare across the broad valley flanked by twisted ridges of bare rock and deep gullies. His eyes widened in surprise when he looked through his field glasses to see a caravan of three wagons that displayed the logo of the traveling theater troupe from The Flat. Four saddle horses were tied to the trailing wagon and six uniformed soldiers from Fort Griffin accompanied the caravan.

He wondered if Gabrielle Price's kidnappers had bound, gagged and stashed her in an oversize trunk and hauled her away. Who would think to search for her among the crates and trunks that held costumes and stage props? He hadn't considered that the abductors might belong to the troupe. Either that or they were traveling with the group for their own safety. This, after all, was area where renegades occasionally sneaked from the reservation in Indian Territory and crossed the Red River to hunt and plunder.

No sooner had the thought crossed his mind than he noticed a dozen riders trailing single file through a deep ravine so the unsuspecting caravan wouldn't notice them. Military escort or not, the caravan was in danger. The six soldiers were no match for a dozen Comanche and Kiowa braves.

Hud went on high alert when he heard the first war whoop and saw the raiders clambering up the steep ravine to race headlong toward the caravan. He shoved his field glasses into his saddlebag then reined Rambler northeast. He rode hell-for-leather to reach the ravine the raiding party had abandoned. With any luck, he and the soldiers could catch the warriors in crossfire and force them to abort the attack.

If Gabrielle Price had been bound, gagged and tucked inside a trunk, it might be all that saved her from injury. Hud had let her down once by not being there to intervene when she was abducted. If she was with the caravan, he hoped he could save her from being shot full of arrows and bullets.

Hud did not want the unpleasant task of explaining to Commander Price what disasters had befallen his daughter while she was supposedly under his care.

Screams of terror filled the air as Hud raced through the gully to take his position on the raider's blind side. He scowled in frustration when the raiders descended on the small wagon train like demons from hell. The soldiers planted themselves squarely on the battleground like human shields.

Admirable but dangerous, thought Hud. Unfortunately, they had left the wagons exposed, making it possible for the renegades to circle and fire at the opposite side of the wagons where the cast members huddled for protection.

"Head to the creek, you fools," Hud muttered under his breath as he bounded from his horse then grabbed his Winchester rifle.

He blinked in amazement when someone among the troupe apparently read his mind and signaled for the wagons to skirt the rugged cliff, making it difficult for the warriors to attack from both directions at once. "At least one person has some practical sense," he said to the world at large as he grabbed an extra box of cartridges.

The six soldiers held their ground and returned fire against the approaching warriors while the wagons moved alongside the creek bank. Using the protection of the gulch, Hud braced his arm on the ledge and stared down the sight of his rifle. He fired off a shot and one warrior tumbled from his horse. Hud scrambled to another location, took aim and fired again. He hoped to give the illusion that he wasn't a one-man rescue brigade, but rather several men lining the gulley to open fire.

His third shot hit its mark again. The brave grabbed his leg and curled over his horse to prevent toppling off. While the soldiers fired rapidly, along with a few members of the theater troupe, Hud blasted away then changed position again.

The crossfire discouraged the raiders from prolonging the attack, much to Hud's relief. The renegades hoisted their wounded men over their horses then thundered north to disappear into the deep, winding gorges.

Hud was on his horse in a single bound to join the soldiers who raced after the raiders, making certain they didn't regroup and return. Fortunately, the war party rode toward the Red River and the protection of the reservation.

"Thank goodness you showed up when you did." The lieutenant smiled gratefully as he halted beside Hud. He looked around then frowned. "Where are your companions? I saw shots fired from several locations in the gulch."

"There's only me. I was on the move constantly."

The lieutenant gaped at him. "Only one of you to disband the raiders?"

"One of me and only one raiding party," Hud said dryly.

"Er…yes. Your technique fooled the Indians. I'll have to remember that."

Hud studied the young officer whose boyish face, silky chestnut hair and fair skin made him look sixteen. Hell, Hud couldn't remember looking that young. But then, he'd endured a difficult childhood and thus far, his adult life hadn't been much to boast about.

"Also remember that the next time a raiding party attacks, use a canyon wall or creek bed or whatever means available to block your exposed side," Hud insisted as he shoved his pistol into its holster.

The young lieutenant took offense and thrust out his square chin. "You are speaking to an officer in the U.S. Army of the West," he said in a haughty tone.

Hud fished his badge from the pocket of his breeches and flashed it at the soldiers. "I'm Captain Hudson Stone from the Ranger battalion stationed southwest of here. I've been guerilla fighting against lopsided odds half my life, Lieutenant. Remember what I told you and you'll live to receive a promotion."

The soldiers nodded slightly, offering Hud begrudging respect.

"Where are you taking the caravan?" Hud asked.

"To Fort Elliot. Or partway at least," one of the privates spoke up. "Their escort detail should meet up with us tomorrow afternoon so we can return to our fort. After an evening performance, the soldiers will escort the troupe to Tascosa and Mobeetie before we meet them again to bring them back to The Flat."

The lieutenant glanced around the area as they rode back to the caravan. "What are you doing out here alone? Reconnoitering the area for your battalion?"

"No, I—" Hud's voice dried up when he saw the Lady In Gray striding past one of the wagons. To his

incredulous disbelief, he noticed the three boys he'd encountered the previous night following on her heels.

*The kissing bandit was a member of the theater
troupe?* Stunned by the revelation, Hud nudged Rambler
in the flanks and raced downhill. He was going to
confront the mysterious woman—in broad daylight for
a change. Finally, he could see her face and by damned,
she wasn't going to duck out of sight this time, he
promised himself resolutely.

When Hud skidded his horse to a halt, blocking her
path, she glanced up at him. The breeze blew the floppy
brim of her bonnet backward, exposing her facial
features in the sunlight. Hud's eyes popped and his jaw
scraped his chest when he recognized Gabrielle Price's
attractive features.

Bri and the mysterious Lady In Gray, who prowled
the dark alleys and kissed him until his brain melted
down—*thrice*—were one and the same?

Well, there's irony for you, he thought. My secret
fantasy turned out to be my worst nightmare.

Chapter Five

"Hello, Captain Stone, what are you doing out here?" Bri asked politely. "And by the way, thank you for lending a helping hand with the raiding party."

"It was Ellie's idea to move the wagons to the creek embankment for protection," the oldest of the three orphans said proudly. "She knows lots of things like that."

"Ellie?" Hud repeated, growing madder by the minute.

Hud was confused and disillusioned. His passionate mystery woman was Gabrielle Price and that annoyed the hell out of him. Plus, he had wasted emotion and time trying to locate a missing woman whose objective in life surely must have been to drive him crazy and humiliate him to no end.

Glaring holes in *Ellie's* drab gray dress, Hud dismounted. He thrust Rambler's reins at the oldest boy. "Take my horse down to the creek so he can drink. Take the other two boys with you, kid. I want to talk privately with *Ellie*."

"The name is Tommy."

Hud dragged his mutinous gaze off Bri to survey the

pale-skinned, gangly boy who looked to be about fourteen and had yet to grow into his oversized feet. He'd trimmed his hair neatly and dressed far better than he had the previous evening. The same went for the other two boys, he observed.

Tommy's blue-eyed gaze darted from Ellie to Hud, and then to Rambler. "You best not be thinking of hurting Ellie while we're gone or you'll answer to us," he said warningly.

Brave words for three malnourished urchins, Hud mused.

"I'm Howie. I'm Tommy's brother."

Hud appraised the boy, who was somewhere near the age of eleven. He was a stocky, chubby-faced lad with pale green eyes and blond hair. He looked as if he, too, was prepared to defend Ellie to the death—if necessary.

"My name is Georgie," the third kid declared.

Hud nodded a greeting to the thin, frizzy-haired boy who had a long narrow face and big brown eyes. "My name is Captain Hud Stone with the Texas Rangers. Rambler could use a drink since he's been running hard and fast today."

Reluctantly the boys led the horse away and "Ellie" pivoted on her heels.

Hud grabbed her arm to detain her. "Not so fast," he muttered at the back of her head. "You and I are going to have a talk."

"Oh, good. I'm looking forward to it," she said with a smirk as he marched her away from the curious members of the repertory troupe.

"You don't know how lucky you are that you're my commander's daughter."

"What's that supposed to mean?" she asked. "That

you'd dispose of me if I weren't?" Bri jerked her arm from his grasp before he cut off the circulation in her arm.

"I'm thinking about it." He snaked his arm around her waist, forcing her to keep in step with his long impatient strides as he scrambled down the embankment to speak privately at the bend of the creek.

She wasn't looking forward to being upbraided by Hud, who was clearly outraged to discover she had deceived him. She was embarrassed that she'd kissed him into silence *thrice* while she was in disguise. She wasn't sure she could endure the humiliation if she tried to explain her reckless physical attraction to this man who had no use for her whatsoever.

"This is far enough," she decided as she set her feet.

Unfortunately, Hud uprooted her from the spot and towed her farther downstream. He obviously had in mind to yell and bite her head off and he didn't want eyewitnesses.

"I'm ready to get this over with." She wrested her arm free again and squared off for the inevitable confrontation.

When Hud dragged in a deep breath and drew himself up in front of her, she thought he might pop the buttons on his shirt. He looked mad as the devil. Yet, she didn't anticipate physical abuse from him. Hudson Stone was many things, but she didn't perceive him as a man who struck a woman in a fit of temper.

Nevertheless, that wasn't to say that he wouldn't lambaste her with foul oaths for deceiving him. He looked as if dozens of curses had flocked to the tip of his tongue and he was more than ready to spit them at her.

"I know what you're thinking—" she started to say but he interrupted her with a slashing gesture of his arm.

"Do you? I doubt it. I really should kill you outright

for misleading the rest of the citizens in The Flat as well as me. But your adoring father would have my head for that, no doubt. I'm trying to decide if it's worth my own execution." He stalked closer, his hands fisted at his sides, his eyes throwing golden sparks. "I'll have you know that I do not appreciate being made to look like an incompetent fool!"

His voice rose to a roar. The birds nesting in the overhanging branches flew off.

Ah, that she could sprout wings and do the same.

"But we will get to your cunning charade later," he snapped as he bore down on her like an ominous thundercloud.

She wondered how much self-control it cost him to resist the urge to strangle her. It looked as if it was taking its toll on him.

"I have a perfectly logical explanation for the charade," she declared before he exploded with bad temper.

"I'll bet," he said, and scoffed. "As for your staged kidnapping, I should file charges against you for that!"

Bri frowned, bemused. *"Kidnapping?"*

He nodded sharply. "Don't ply me with that innocent look. I swear, given your acting ability you *should* be a member of this theatrical troupe."

"Thank you," she smarted off, annoyed with his attitude and his harsh criticism. He suddenly reminded her of her lecturing mother and she had responded accordingly. "I will admit that pretending to like you has been something of a stretch—"

"Same goes for me, *Princess,*" he interrupted sarcastically. "The point is that, because of your stupid stunt, statewide newspapers are running stories about your supposed abduction. Marshal Long is gathering a posse to search for you. So is the commander at Fort Griffin. Not to mention that your dandified fiancé has been dashing all over town trying to find you and he's blaming *me* for losing track!"

Despite Hud's harsh reprimand, Bri stared curiously at him. "I told you yesterday that I would find my own way cross-country and that I wasn't going to inconvenience you more than I have already," she reminded him sharply. "And what the devil are you ranting about? I didn't stage my abduction. I simply gathered my satchels and hiked off to buy Tommy, Howie and Georgie new clothes so they could make a fresh start.

"Then I contacted Milton and Lelia Korn, the managers of the theater troupe, and asked if they could find jobs for the boys so they could rise above the alleys of The Flat. For God's sake," she added emphatically, "they were living under a broken-down wagon and surviving on crumbs from the garbage!"

Hud ceased glowering furiously at her and relaxed his stance. But his amber-colored gaze still bore attentively into her.

Bri grabbed a quick breath and continued in a calmer voice. "Milton and Lelia consented to hire the boys to set up scenery and props for the shows. Also they plan to give them bit parts if they are interested."

"You go around doing good deeds like this often?" he asked, studying her skeptically.

It was none of his business and she had no idea why she decided to confide in him. "While I was in Houston I befriended Benji Dunlop, who lived in the streets. We became acquainted when he tried to rob me. Then he changed his mind and lectured me for gallivanting alone at night. I asked him to show me what his life was like."

"You are kidding."

Bri shook her head and her bonnet brim flopped over her forehead. She pushed it away. "Despite what you think about me, I detest society's pretentious ways and its meaningless parties. I could never live up to my mother's expectations and I refused to become the prissy debutante she wanted. I decided to make friends with someone who didn't have to like me because I was the commander's daughter or Anna Roland Price's only child."

"Roland?" he hooted and blinked owlishly.

Bri smirked at his stunned reaction. "Recognize the name? Of course you do. Although the Price family acquired their wealth from cotton, *the Rolands* are *made* of money, or at least that's what my mother has always told me. In addition, there are hotel entrepreneurs, land barons and railroad magnates whose aristocratic lineage surpasses all other prominent families in the South. And of course, I have a certain responsibility to my elite family's reputation."

She smiled regretfully. "Because of my birthright, lots of people in Austin and Houston treat me like royalty. They try not to offend me because they might need to drop my name, use me to do them a favor or beg for money. So you see, Captain, you just never know who your true friends are. Money and name recognition confuse the issue to the extreme."

Hud didn't say anything, just kept staring at her with those long-lashed golden eyes and an unreadable expression on his ruggedly handsome face.

"Benji befriended me and taught me how to fight and how to survive in the streets."

A pang of regret stabbed into her chest so she retrieved the pocket watch then brushed her fingertips over the gold-plated case. "My truest, dearest and most devoted friend died in the back alleys, refusing to give up this watch because I gave it to him as a gift." Her eye misted as she stared at Hud. "I loved him because he loved me for who I was on the inside. Because he *enjoyed* teaching me to fend for myself. He made certain I could see beyond the elegant drawing rooms of high society to the underbelly of the city. In addition, I could tell him anything and he never sat in judgment."

Bri stared into the distance, muffled a sniff and tucked the watch into her pocket. "Giving those three boys a chance at a better life is my way of paying homage to Benji. Once Tommy, Howie and Georgie develop pride and confidence in their ability to work and to earn a living I plan to fetch them."

"Very touching, Mizz Price, but staging your abduction—"

"You are not listening," she cut in tersely. "I did *not* stage anything. I simply found an alternate mode of transportation and left town."

"Your room was ransacked. Who did you hire to trash the place?"

"I didn't do it and I didn't hire it done," she insisted.

"I saw the room myself and I suffered nine kinds of hell because I felt guilty for not being there to protect you as your father expected me to do."

"And I told you that I didn't want or need your assistance," she persisted. "I gave you my blessing to continue your manhunt without bothering with escort duty."

"You should have notified your fiancé," he retorted. "He ranted at me until my ears burned."

"Eaton isn't my fiancé."

Hud smirked. "Better tell him that. I don't think he knows it."

"Oh, yes, he does," she countered. "I didn't want to be engaged to him in the first place. That was my mother's doing. She decided to make a match with her best friend's nephew. I tried to leave Austin without the haughty bore tagging along, but he refused to take no for an answer. I have been looking for the right way to call off the betrothal and he provided the reason the first night we arrived in The Flat."

Hud crossed his arms over his broad chest and propped himself against a tree trunk. He arched a thick brow and slanted her a look that said, This better be good. "Please go on. I can't wait to hear this."

Despite his caustic comment she continued, "As it turned out, I caught him with another woman. It was the perfect excuse and reasonable grounds in my book."

"I'm still listening."

Bri shifted self-consciously from one foot to the other. She was not looking forward to discussing Eaton's infidelity because it led to the heated kiss in Hud's dark room. "First of all, you should know that I make a habit of dressing in concealing garments that help me blend into the background when I venture onto the streets alone."

"Because your friend Benji taught you to be cautious and inconspicuous," he guessed.

"Exactly. 'Blending in is always best,' he said." She inhaled a bolstering breath and plunged ahead. "On my way back to my room that first night, I decided to stop by Eaton's room to inform him that I had decided not to marry him. I heard male and female laughter on the other side of the door. Naturally I decided to investigate."

She saw his lips twitch slightly. "Naturally, *you* being *you*."

She ignored the taunt. "I poked by head around the door to see a trail of discarded clothing."

Hud chuckled softly. "That must have been a shock."

Her face went up in flames, remembering that she'd received an eyeful. "Thanks to the placement of the mirror over the dresser in the adjoining bedroom I saw Eaton in bed with the red-haired actress from this theater troupe."

"I'm sorry," he surprised her by saying.

She shrugged nonchalantly. "If I cared a whit for the blustering politician I might have been devastated. But I don't. Never have. Unfortunately, I squawked in embarrassment and unwittingly alerted him to my presence in the sitting room. Eaton got up to investigate the unidentified sound so I had to make a quick getaway before he caught me."

She knew the instant Hud put two and two together and came to the correct conclusion. His gaze settled directly on her. "Eaton's room wouldn't have happened to be right next door to mine, would it?"

Bri looked the other way and nodded. "Yes. Naturally, I ducked into the first door within reach so Eaton wouldn't see me. I was too rattled to confront him after seeing him and his lover naked in bed."

"And there I was in the dark, ready to step into my waiting bath," he commented. "So naturally you kissed me to get even with him."

Bri's face flushed with embarrassment. "I wasn't getting even. I was afraid you were going to call attention to my presence when you demanded to know why I barged into your room. I had to shut you up before Eaton came to investigate."

"A blow to my head would have worked as effectively," he mocked.

She flashed him a disgruntled glare. "I didn't have a club handy. Knowing you as I do now, I realize I should have knocked you silly."

It would have been better than facing him now that he knew who she was. That erotic kiss in the dark was right there between them. She would die of shame if Hud asked her to explain why she hadn't stopped kissing him after the danger of discovery passed. Nor did she want to discuss why she had become carried away with him—again and again—when they met later in the alley.

Her honesty with Hud would only reach so far. She would cut out her tongue before she confided that his smoldering kiss and intimate embrace aroused her. She couldn't even explain her volatile reaction to herself, much less him!

"So…when the coast was clear you darted off." He squinted at her accusingly. "But you failed to mention that we had met previously when I arrived at your room to make a formal introduction the next morning." He frowned momentarily. "You *must* have recognized my voice, even if you didn't have a clear view of my face, just as I didn't have a clear view of yours that night in my room."

Bri refused to meet his probing gaze. She felt awkward enough as it was. She wanted to be done with this conversation so she hurried on as fast as she could. "Your can't-be-bothered attitude toward escort detail annoyed me so I didn't *bother* to mention our previous encounter. You made it abundantly clear that you had no use for your assignment or *me* so I made other arrangements. As for my engagement to Eaton, I *did* confront him later that same evening when he was on his way to the theater to watch Sylvia Ford's performance. I told him I knew about his indiscretion."

"And he said…?" Hud prompted.

"He offered the typical male response, of course," she replied sourly. "He plied me with the nonsense that the affair meant nothing to him and that he was still devoted to me and to our future. Eaton is a pretentious oaf who only sees me as a benefit to his campaign. If he appeared upset by my disappearance it was likely a melodramatic act, coupled with the realization that my family won't promote his campaign."

"So you staged your abduction to *spite* him and me."

Bri rounded on him and stamped her foot in annoyance. "For the last time, you hardheaded, rock-hearted Ranger, I did *not* ransack my own room to worry him or make you look incompetent! I left my room as neat and tidy as it was when I rented it. I have no idea who rummaged around in there or why. *That was not my doing!*" she all but yelled at him.

Hud rubbed his jaw and stared thoughtfully at her. "I interviewed the man who rented the room next door and he claimed he heard a crash of furniture and a male voice. He didn't get involved because he wasn't aware that it was your room, nor that of the man he heard clamoring around in there. You didn't pay someone to make your scheme believable?"

Bri glared at the relentless Ranger. "I have no explanation for what happened after I left. I rejoined the boys in the alley, bought them new clothes, cut their hair and hiked off to make arrangements with the Korns's Theater Troupe. The caravan left before daylight and the soldiers joined us two hours later."

It aggravated Bri that Hud continued to stare at her as if he was trying to decide if he believed her story. Well, she didn't care if he did. She didn't need his acceptance or his assistance to reunite with her father. According to Lieutenant Davis, there was a Ranger camp along the trail that led to Fort Elliot. Bri had decided to visit the site and locate a more willing escort among the ranks.

Indeed, she and Hud already knew each other better than they should. As badly as she hated to admit it, she wasn't sure she could trust herself alone with him. There was obviously some flaw in her character that overrode her usual inhibitions when she came within kissing distance of this man—especially when they were alone in the dark.

"Ellie? Are you all right?"

Bri sagged in relief when Tommy's adolescent voice wafted downhill. She glanced up the embankment to see all three boys staring worriedly at her.

"I'm fine," she assured them with a cheery smile.

"The Korns want to move out now so we can reach a good camping spot for the evening."

"I'll be right there."

She surged forward then stumbled back when Hud grabbed her arm unexpectedly.

"Hold it, *Ellie*. It is my duty to take you to your father and that is exactly what I'm going to do. Whether either of us like it or not."

"I explained that I don't want or need your assistance. Benji trained me well. I didn't need your help when that mangy buffalo hunter tried to molest me, either." She tapped one thigh and then other, calling his attention to her two concealed weapons. "I never leave home without carrying at least two weapons, Captain."

"Nonetheless, I'm doing the job I was sent here to do," he insisted as he helped her negotiate the steep embankment. "We can travel with the troupe today then veer southwest to join my battalion tomorrow."

"Thanks but I'd rather not," she muttered.

"Why not?" He paused momentarily and flashed a scampish grin that she itched to wipe all over his suntanned face. "Because you're afraid you can't resist kissing me again?"

The ornery rascal, she fumed, hating that he was right. "Of course I can resist you, Captain Stone," she said to save face. "I wouldn't have kissed you at all if it hadn't been necessary to shut you up. But I won't resort to such drastic measures again. And I assure you, kissing you was nothing short of *drastic* in the first place."

When he chuckled, she wanted to kick him in the shins. However, he didn't give her the chance. He hoisted her uphill, set her on solid ground and led her along with his swift pace when he strode off to fetch his horse.

Hud's thoughts and emotions were spinning like a Texas tornado. The very last thing he wanted was for the mystery lady he lusted after to be the commander's daughter that he was unwillingly attracted to. She was sharp-witted, intelligent and spirited. She was packing concealed hardware on her slender thighs…

He gnashed his teeth when erotic visions sprang to mind.

Do not go down that road, he told himself. *Gabrielle Price is off-limits for a dozen good reasons.*

Even knowing that, his body hardened, remembering how Bri/Ellie's kisses put him in a sensual tailspin and wiped everything except lust from his mind. Damn it, now he couldn't stare at her petal-soft lips without remembering, with vivid clarity, how good she tasted. Without remembering how he had run his hands over her luscious curves and swells. Without remembering how the tantalizing scent of her perfume infiltrated his senses and fogged his brain.

"Slow down," Bri scolded him. "I can't keep up while I'm wearing this restrictive dress."

"Fine with me if you want to take it off." Hud slammed his mouth shut when he realized he'd put the arousing thought to tongue.

He glanced over his shoulder to see Bri bristling with irritation. "Sorry, that didn't come out right," he mumbled. "I meant that if you want to change into more comfortable traveling clothes then have right at it."

She smiled enigmatically. "I intend to if I have to ride off alone with you. I always place comfort and practicality above fashion and convention."

"Good. A woman after my own heart."

"I am not after your heart," she was quick to assure him. "I'm certain that all you have rattling around in your chest is a chunk of rock. I doubt people call you Captain *Stone* for nothing."

"Is everything all right, Miss Ellie?" Lieutenant Davis asked as they strode past—or more specifically, as Hud *tugged* her along with him.

She tossed the boyish looking officer the kind of smile Hud was certain he would never receive from her, given the conflict and personality clashes between them.

Unless they were alone in the dark and she was kissing him senseless…The thought sidetracked him and he tossed Bri a speculative glance.

"I'm fine, Lieutenant," she declared as she dug her

nails into Hud's arm, silently demanding that he loosen his grasp on her. "Captain Stone and I are former acquaintances."

"I'll be escorting her to my Ranger camp to meet with our mutual friend," Hud added.

The lieutenant's smile faltered. Clearly, the man was hoping to strike up a courtship with Bri during the journey.

"Ten miles north on this road is a fork in the old Comanche trail," Hud reported. "I'll scout ahead while you get this lumbering caravan on the move." On impulse he waved to the three boys Bri had taken under her wing. "You boys need to learn a few tips about surviving in the wilds. Mount up."

He glanced at Bri, surprised to note that she was smiling at him in approval. *"What?"*

She shook her head and the floppy brim on her bonnet bobbed on her face. "Nothing, Captain. We will see you back in camp for supper."

Leaving Bri to the adoring lieutenant, Hud mounted his horse and rode off with the three orphans trailing behind him.

Eaton glanced out the window when the stagecoach rolled to a halt in another nameless little town on the route to Austin. The story of his ordeal, and the loss of his beloved fiancée to an unknown abductor, must've burned up the telegraph lines, because stage agents mentioned it repeatedly. Eaton had cleverly managed to campaign for office without spending an extra dime.

When he emerged from the dusty coach the mayor of the small ranching community was there to greet him.

"I am terribly sorry to hear about your fiancée's abduction," the aging mayor commiserated.

"Thank you, kind sir," Eaton murmured. "Have there been any encouraging words from The Flat?"

The man shook his bald head. "I wish I had good news, but there is no report of her appearance."

There wouldn't be, either, Eaton mused. Not unless *he* ordered Bri's release. And of course that all depended on which ending brought better results for his campaign. He might have more success with a sympathy vote. Then again, most idealistic saps loved happy endings. Eaton wasn't going to worry about that now. He'd let that sassy little snip of an ex-fiancée fret about her fate—one that probably hadn't been too pleasant, considering her abductors.

Swallowing a devilish grin, Eaton strutted off to accept the mayor's offer to buy his supper.

"What are we gonna do about that kidnapping that didn't work out the way it was supposed to?" Peter Spaulding said worriedly as he and Joe Jarvis approached the bunkhouse on Ray Novak's ranch.

"We're gonna keep the money and let that highfalutin politician think we carried out his plan," Joe said, then spit tobacco—just for the hell of it—at one of the cows in the pen.

"What if the boss starts asking questions about where we stashed her?" Peter fretted.

"You worry too much," Joe grumbled. "We won't be workin' at this ranch when the politician makes up his mind what to do about his fiancée."

"Now we have to drift from place to place." He stared accusingly at Joe. "If you hadn't gone crazy and shot that Texas Ranger in the first place we wouldn't be lying low and working for a rancher whose herd has more stolen cattle than legitimate ones."

Joe scowled as he glowered at Pete. "Keep your voice down before someone overhears you. And anyway, how was I supposed to know he was a Texas Ranger? He wasn't wearin' a badge. I didn't find the damn thing until I robbed him."

"Maybe we should clear out before those Rangers catch up with us," Pete said apprehensively. "We can cross the state line into New Mexico."

Joe shot him a derisive glance. "And do what? Herd sheep instead of cattle? No thanks."

"We can't hang around Circle Bar Ranch and have Ray Novak found out that we've been paid a lot of money for a job we didn't complete because Powell's fiancée wasn't where she was supposed to be that night."

While Pete mumbled and grumbled, Joe wondered why he'd allowed the worrywart to ride along with him the past few months. Pete was turning into his walking conscience and Joe refused to be bothered with one.

Lost in thought, Joe strode into the bunkhouse to take his evening meal—his last meal with Pete, he decided suddenly. It was time to put Pete out of his misery. Joe refused to run the risk of his cohort blabbing what he knew about the dead Texas Ranger and the kidnapping scheme gone bad.

Chapter Six

Late that afternoon, Hud gestured northwest, calling the three boys' attention to the flock of birds circling in the near distance. "That's a sure sign of water. But a watering hole presents the possibility of not only birds but also two-legged and four-legged predators."

"Like those Indians that charged at us earlier," Howie mumbled apprehensively as he glanced left then right. "I thought we were goners for sure."

"This land once belonged to the Kiowa and Comanche tribes," Hud informed them. "Our government offered a treaty to preserve their land but white ranchers decided they wanted to graze herds of cattle on it. Not surprising that the tribes felt betrayed and struck out when they were driven off their land and herded onto reservations."

Georgie frowned pensively. "Don't know that I wouldn't put up a fuss myself. I don't have much but I don't like it when some bully tries to take what's mine away from me."

"The less you have the more possessive you are about

your belongings," Hud murmured as he led the boys into a winding gorge to avoid being seen.

"Thanks to Ellie, we don't have to worry 'bout that anymore," Howie remarked. "She bought us these fine clothes and boots and our own horses. She clipped our hair then she arranged for us to take jobs with the theater troupe."

Georgie snickered as he pointed at Howie. "You still think you wanna be in one of those plays? Singing and dancing?"

Howie nodded his blond head. "I can sing better than some of those actors. You've heard me."

After an extended silence Tommy half twisted in the saddle to study Hud closely. "You gonna take Ellie away from us?"

Hud shrugged. "Not by choice. I was sent here to accompany her to a Ranger camp to meet a mutual acquaintance." Her father to be specific, but he honored Bri's wish to keep a low profile.

"Why can't we come with you?" Howie asked. "I really like Ellie. If I had a mamma I'd want her to be as nice and pretty as Ellie."

"Wouldn't we all, kid," Hud mumbled.

"Pardon?" Tommy stared quizzically at him.

"I said she's really something all right."

"We saw you kissing her." Georgie fixed his big brown eyes on him. "Are you sweet on her, Hud?"

"Well, are ya?" Tommy wanted to know that very second.

"Are *you?*" Hud questioned the direct question.

Tommy nodded decisively. "I'd marry her if I was older."

"Then maybe I'd marry her if I were younger," Hud teased.

"How old are you?" Howie asked, and the other boys stared speculatively at him.

"Old enough to know better." Hud grinned playfully. "I'll let you boys in on a secret. There isn't a man alive who understands women. So don't set too high expectations for yourselves."

"I don't have to understand her," Howie proclaimed. "I love Ellie because she cares about us when nobody else does."

"You're right," Hud agreed, biting back a smile. "We all love her because she isn't afraid to stand up for her friends and for what she believes in."

"And you should see her handle a rifle and pistol," Georgie said proudly. "She outshot the men in the troupe. She also promised to teach us to handle weapons after she comes back to fetch us at The Flat."

All three boys stared at Hud with so much hope in their smiles that it hit him where he lived. These three misplaced kids were going to soften him up if he didn't watch out.

When Hud didn't reassure them Howie asked, "Do you think Ellie will come to fetch us like she said?"

"Has she lied to you yet?"

All three boys shook their heads.

"Then there you go." Hud halted when he noticed hoofprints crossing their path. "Comanches," he murmured then glanced in all directions.

"How can you tell?" This from Georgie, who looked uneasy.

"No horseshoes."

"You think they'll take us captive?" Tommy asked gravely.

Hud smiled and tried to sound reassuring. "I won't let them, but they'd be proud to have three young braves like you. Of course, after you learned all the Comanche can teach you about riding, weapons and surviving in places most white men can't, then you could sneak off together."

The comment seemed to appease them.

"Did the Comanche capture you when you were a kid?" Georgie asked. "Is that how you know so much about living out here in the wilderness?"

"I learned by watching Indians while being a Ranger."

"Maybe I'll be a Ranger someday," Tommy decided impulsively.

"Then pay attention." Hud led the way around the mesquite trees that rimmed a small spring at the base of a rocky escarpment. "There are a few more things you boys need to know before you sign up."

Bri glanced anxiously into the blinding sunset as the caravan moved west. Golden rays slanted across the rugged terrain, casting deepening shadows. She hadn't had a single sighting of Hud and the boys since they rode off hours earlier. Although she hadn't heard gunshots, she reminded herself that bows, arrows and knives in the hands of a raiding party were silent and deadly.

This was wild, unforgiving country, with rugged, twisting shelves of wind-swept land that broke off into deep, eroded canyons and V-shaped gorges. Steep slopes often became sheer cliffs on either side of the trail. Although the caravan had halted to refill their canteens and water barrel at a small oasis, surrounded by willows and locust trees, they traveled several more miles without seeing anything but scrub oaks, mesquite, cactus and sagebrush.

"Cursed hide hunters," Bri muttered sourly when she noticed several skinned buffalo carcasses strewn around the bottom of a cliff. "They stripped off the wooly skin and left the carcasses to rot. Now buzzards and wolves compete for the rotting meat."

"No wonder the Indians dislike whites so much," Lelia Korn, who sat beside her on the wagon seat, said.

"Hide hunters have wiped out the Indians' food supply and overtaken their land. Honestly, sometimes I'm ashamed to be white," Bri grumbled.

"Maybe so, girl, but that's no reason to scalp innocent folks who have nothing to do with butchering their buffalo and breaking treaties. You'd think there would be enough room out here for everybody to have his own space," Milton commented.

You'd think.

"Wagons halt!" Milton bellowed then glanced at Lieutenant Davis, who trotted his horse up beside them. "This site okay for spending the night?"

Davis hitched his thumb over his shoulder. "There's a shallow creek below this hill, if memory serves. We can find mesquite wood to make a campfire."

He tossed a charming smile in Bri's direction. He looked to be three or four years older than she was. He also appeared to be eager to strike up a friendship with her. Too bad she was harboring a frustrated attraction for that raven-haired Ranger with the brawny physique and whiskey-colored eyes.

And he had damn well better return to camp in one piece, with the boys tagging along—or else.

Bri didn't realize that she had sagged in relief when the foursome topped the rise of ground, spotlighted by the angled rays of sunset.

Lelia nudged her, silently urging her to climb down. "You okay, hon?"

"Daydreaming is all," she insisted as she hopped to the ground.

While the Korns strode off to unload bedding and cooking utensils, Bri hiked downhill to fetch wood for the campfire. It had been a few years since she had enjoyed a cookout with Benji. Lately she had been trapped in elegant drawing rooms filled with dignitaries and debutantes who postured and preened in attempts to impress each other.

Swooping down, Bri scooped up several fallen branches. She yelped in alarm when she heard a deadly rattle that sounded too close for comfort. She'd been lollygagging rather than paying attention to her surroundings and she had unknowingly disturbed a diamondback. When the six-foot-long viper coiled and raised its head to strike, Bri tossed her armload of logs at it.

When she tried to leap out of striking distance, she tripped over the trailing hem of her dress. She landed with a thud and another yelp.

The snake recoiled when she made the mistake of trying to scramble back to her feet—and unintentionally scattered the dry leaves around her. The extra noise put the viper on highest alert.

Bri wondered how many times a rattler had to strike before depleting its deadly venom. The snake's triangular head rose higher and its forked tongue flicked out. Bri gulped hard when deadly black eyes—the exact color of the devil's soul, she was sure—focused on her.

Hud had been in camp for less than two minutes when he heard two yelps and a gunshot rising up the creek bank. He glanced around, noting that Bri was nowhere in sight.

He raced toward the sound of the gunshot, hoping like hell that Bri wasn't on the wrong end of it. He didn't like the idea of anyone shooting at her. He reserved that luxury for himself because she had made a fool of him when she disappeared from The Flat without so much as a fare-thee-well.

Shoving saplings and underbrush out of his way, Hud bounded down the steep embankment like a mountain goat. He could hear the three boys thrashing behind him, calling out Ellie's name, but he didn't look back.

Hud's thoughts scattered like buckshot when he spotted Bri. She was sprawled on the ground. Her skirt and petticoats rode high on her legs. Two bright red garters encircled her creamy thighs.

The sight of her shapely legs distracted him to such extremes that he tripped over his own two feet. Scowling, Hud jerked himself upright before he dived the rest of the way downhill. It took another moment for him to plug his eyes back into their sockets and assess the situation that had provoked her to yelp loudly and fire off a shot.

She was holding a piddling little single-shot derringer in her right hand. She had a thin-bladed stiletto clamped in her left fist. Her breasts heaved beneath the bodice of her gown as she stared at the granddaddy of all rattlesnakes that lay four feet in front of her.

Hud wasn't sure if she was damn lucky or deadly accurate with her pistol. Nevertheless, the viper's head was no longer attached to the long body that continued to coil around a pile of logs. Assured that Bri was safe— more or less—Hud's gaze drifted instinctively back to her legs. When she heard the boys clambering toward her, she swooped down to jerk her skirt modestly to her ankles.

"Nice shot," Hud praised as he hooked his forearms under her armpits and hoisted her to her feet. When she swayed slightly he held onto her until she could stand on her own. "Where'd you learn to shoot like that, Princess?"

Bri drew in a deep breath, squared her shoulders and gathered her composure. Hud unwillingly admired the way she pulled herself together rather than blubbering tears.

"I'm a soldier's daughter," she reminded him. "During Papa's visits I insisted that he teach me to handle weapons. He always accommodated me because my mother objected strenuously, and we both delighted in ruffling her aristocratic feathers."

"Are you okay, Ellie?" the boys asked in unison as they stumbled to a halt in front of her.

She smiled reassuringly as she tucked her derringer into her pocket. Then she reached out to smooth each boy's mussed hair into place. "I'm fine. The rattler and I startled each other. I should have been paying more attention."

Howie bobbed his head in agreement. "That's what Hud said. 'Always pay attention and never approach a watering hole without looking for predators.'"

She arched a brow and glanced at Hud before fixing her gaze on the boys. "Wise advice. What else did this fount of frontier knowledge teach you while you were scouting?"

"He showed us how to read hoofprints," Georgie replied.

"And how to locate watering holes from a distance," Tommy added.

Bri smiled approvingly. "Thank you, Captain Stone."

"Hud," he insisted then turned his attention to the boys. "Gather up the wood and haul it to the campsite, will you? Ellie and I will be along in a minute."

Nodding agreeably, the boys collected the logs Bri had dropped then added more to the stack.

When they were out of earshot, Hud looked her over carefully. "Now that you don't have to put up pretenses to reassure your devoted puppies, I want to know if you're really all right."

"I'm fine, Cap—"

"Hud," he corrected emphatically.

When Bri turned her back and hiked up her skirt to replace her pistol and knife in her garters, Hud had to bite his tongue to prevent offering to help. Damn it, the sight of her creamy thighs would be forever burned into his eyeballs.

"I can't imagine why you're fussing over me," she said with a smirk. "I thought you were perturbed with me."

"I am. Nevertheless, you're still my responsibility and my assignment. Direct orders from your father, in fact."

"I don't want to be your responsibility," she said as she pivoted to face him. "I can take care of myself."

It was Hud's turn to smirk. "You think your father won't have my head on a platter if something—a nasty snake-bite, for instance—causes you injury on my watch? I get the impression that your father is especially fond of you."

She grinned impishly. "Of course he is. It's my sparkling personality and charm that endears him to me."

Hud snorted then gestured toward her left leg, where she kept her stiletto stashed from sight. "He's probably afraid to cross you, for fear you'll come at him with weapons drawn if he doesn't cater immediately to your every whim."

He didn't know why he was baiting her. Maybe because he liked to see that flash of fire in those luminous blue-violet eyes. Maybe because he liked to tease her and watch her rise to the challenge.

She didn't disappoint. She took a bold step toward him then surprised him by running her hand down his rawhide vest. Her light touch distracted him and he peered helplessly into those hypnotic eyes as her hands descended over his hips.

"Are *you* afraid of me, Hud?" she murmured softly.

Honest to God he was. He was afraid this woman was getting to him when he didn't want her to. For sure, he had received a jolt of fear when he'd heard a yelp that was followed by a gunshot. He had pictured her bleeding all over herself, the victim of an attack. He'd been worried—and not just because she was his responsibility. He was afraid this turmoil of complicated feelings she aroused in him were beginning to rival his need to avenge Speck Horton. And that, Hud told himself, had disaster written all over it.

Hud wanted nothing to stand between him and his crusade. Yet, deep down he liked this extraordinary woman. She looked like a dainty fairy princess, but she was capable of fending for herself. Tough and tender, that was Gabrielle Price.

"*Are you?*" she prompted when Hud lingered too long in thought.

"Afraid of a five-foot-nothing female?" he teased, but his voice evaporated when he felt the barrels of his own peacemakers gouging his ribs. Stunned, he glanced down to see that she had picked his pockets—his holsters to be more accurate—and he hadn't realized it until it was too late.

"Another street trick?" he presumed as he retrieved his weapons from her.

"Yes, compliments of my mentor from Houston."

Hud slid his arms around her waist, drawing her closer, feeling forbidden need spurt through him. He angled his head, as if he were about to kiss her. Then he glided his hands over her hips in a light caress.

"Very impressive skills…" He surrendered to the erotic temptation by brushing his lips over her responsive mouth.

Suddenly hungry need gnawed at him—as it always did when he came within two feet of this attractive female. He inhaled her scent, tasted her and felt her shapely body mesh against his. She took his breath away when she kissed him back and it required every ounce of willpower he could muster to withdraw when his male body was shouting obscenities at him for refusing to take as much as she was willing to offer.

Steeling himself against the onslaught of unappeased need, Hud raised his head and nudged her elbow with the edge of her gold pocket watch. He saw her eyes widened in surprise when she realized that he had deftly picked *her* pocket.

"I grew up in the same stinking back alleys as your friend Benji," he told her, his voice not as steady as he would have preferred after sharing a scalding kiss.

Her eyes widened in surprise. She studied him intently.

"The only difference is that my alleys were in New Orleans. Speck Horton was the brother I never had and we watched each other's backs. Thanks to the kindness and compassion of a café owner who set out leftover food for us then hired us to sweep up, we survived."

He handed the pocket watch to her. "Look out for

more rattlers, Bri. And scorpions, too. They're thick in this region."

She didn't utter a word when he turned and walked away, but he could feel her attentive gaze on him. Hud wasn't sure why he had divulged that tidbit about his past. He never had before. Indeed, Mizz Bri was getting to him more than he cared to acknowledge.

Bri inhaled a fortifying breath as she watched Hud ascend the steep embankment. Sweet mercy, she thought as she hiked up her cumbersome skirt and tried to squelch the warm glow of pleasure as she sidestepped uphill. What sort of mystifying spell did that tawny-eyed Ranger hold over her? This time *he* had initiated their kiss and *she* had prolonged it. Then he had snatched her pocket watch as expertly as she had slid his pistols from his holsters.

Learning that Hud was a child of the backstreets made her entirely too sympathetic toward him. She could picture him with Benji, scouring for food to survive, struggling like the three orphans she had brought along with her.

"Well, damn," she mumbled to herself. Not only was she suffering from this infuriating sexual attraction to the tough-as-nails Ranger, but now she was also impressed by how far he'd come from his hand-to-mouth existence in the streets of New Orleans.

Impressed or not, Bri reminded herself that this was a dead-end fascination that could only last a week at the most. After visiting her father, she planned to rejoin the theater troupe in The Flat then take the orphans to see the sights in Colorado—and then venture all the way to California. The boys would make fine traveling companions and they would discourage men from pestering her.

It was Bri's dream to see the world, to escape the rigid confines of society that her mother had imposed on her the past few years.

When Bri returned to camp, the boys were working industriously. They had the campfire roaring and they were helping the Korns set up the Dutch oven. The cast members were unloading trunks from the wagons to roll out their sleeping gear. Several women headed down the creek to bathe.

She wondered if Hud would volunteer to stand guard over them. When Bri walked over to tease him about the possibility, he glanced curiously at her.

"Which actress was dallying with your fiancé?"

"Why do you want to know? So you can question her about the authenticity of my story of finding them together?"

He shrugged noncommittally as he watched the four women amble away.

"Or did you want to try your luck to see if Sylvia is as partial to Rangers as she is to politicians?" A ridiculous surge of possessiveness rolled over her and she wished she could retract the question—especially when Hud grinned rakishly.

"Jealous?" he teased.

To salvage her pride she gave an unladylike snort and said, "Don't be absurd. The redhead is more than welcome to you. I could care less."

She watched him focus on the buxom redhead, who paused to toss Hud a flirtatious glance. Apparently, Sylvia's interest in Eaton had been a passing fancy because she looked Hud up and down—and found not a single thing she didn't like about him.

Bri discovered that she had the same problem herself.

"There's all the invitation you need, Romeo," she

declared. "If you want my blessing or permission then you have it." Or so she tried to convince herself.

"One question," he asked, staring thoughtfully at her.

"Ask away."

"Why did you kiss me both times in the alley?"

Bri was reluctant to answer the complicated question. Her *excuse* was that she wanted to distract him and she didn't want Eaton and the redhead to notice her when they ambled down the boardwalk. The *reason* was that she'd wanted to test her befuddling reaction to Hud. Plus, there was something deliciously thrilling about a secret rendezvous without consequences…until he realized who she was.

"Too personal to answer?" he prodded, refusing to release her from his probing gaze.

His comment tweaked her feminine pride again so she said, "Hardly. It was always about distraction and diversion. Plus, Eaton and the redhead were behind you on the boardwalk. I used you as a shield so he wouldn't recognize me. I wanted to keep you quiet so they wouldn't notice us."

When he continued to scrutinize her for another long moment, she felt compelled to turn the tables on him to divert his attention. "Why did you kiss me down by the creek earlier? Or is that *too* personal for *you* to answer, Captain Ranger?"

He took a step closer, eclipsing the last rays of sunset and leaving her standing in his shadow. Bri was forced to tilt her head back to meet his amber gaze. She found herself staring at his sensuous mouth and she chastised herself severely for becoming hopelessly distracted. Curse it, she could feel the heat radiating from his muscular body and she remembered—with alarming clarity—his enticing scent, his tantalizing taste, his intimate touch.

"It was all about picking pockets," he said in a husky voice that swept over her like a caress. "Why else?"

"Ellie?" Tommy called out, shattering the trance like broken glass. "Where shall we bed down for the night?"

"Yes, where shall we?" Hud murmured and grinned. The ornery scamp.

"*You* won't be sleeping with us," she was quick to assure him then called back to Tommy. "Close to the horses. They are always the first to know if trouble is lurking."

When the boys trooped off to place their new bedrolls by the picket line of horses, Bri glanced back at Hud. "Anything else before I help prepare the meal? If not, you are dismissed, Captain."

She took impish delight in watching him frown in annoyance. When he pivoted on his heels and strode off Bri breathed a sigh of relief. She made a mental note to antagonize Hud every chance she got. It seemed the only deterrent that prevented her from thinking about him as a virile, appealing man. And when that happened, she lost the good sense she'd been cultivating for twenty-three years.

"Are you okay?" Lelia Korn asked when Bri strode up beside her.

"The incident with the rattlesnake was a bit unnerving," she admitted. *So was my latest encounter with Hud,* she added silently. "But I'm fine now."

At least she would be if Hudson Stone kept his distance. Two miles should be about right, she decided. Any closer and she couldn't trust herself alone with him.

Chapter Seven

"So…they tell me you're a Texas Ranger."

Hud glanced over his shoulder to see the redhead sauntering toward him, wearing the come-hither glance Bri had noted before supper. Now, with the meal over and the utensils stashed away, the flirtatious actress had followed *him* down to the stream, where he had hoped to bathe in privacy.

"My name is Sylvia Ford," she purred as she sashayed up to him, rolling one well-curved hip at a time. "I'm thinking it might get lonely out here tonight. What are you thinking?"

She trailed her fingernails over his bare chest and smiled invitingly. Unfortunately, Hud couldn't work up much interest. A damn shame, too, because he hadn't been with a woman for months.

"Maybe I could help you wash your back, Hud."

When he arched a brow she smiled provocatively and said, "I asked the boys who you were. They are very fond of you, by the way. I could be, too…with a little friendly persuasion."

Hud found himself being kissed soundly. Sylvia upped the ante of her seduction routine by rubbing her full breasts deliberately against his chest. Then she entwined her hands around his neck and gyrated her hips against his crotch.

Since Hud wasn't inclined to close his eyes and give himself over to her kiss, he noticed the movement within the shadows of the trees. Shadows of gray in black, to be specific. He knew instantly who was watching. Having found out what she wanted to know, no doubt, the Lady In Gray vanished like a specter.

Hud pressed the heels of his hands against Sylvia's shoulders to pry her loose. He held her at bay when she tried to clamp herself around him again.

"One question, Sylvia."

"You can ask me anything, Hud," she whispered, all puckered up and ready to kiss him again.

"Did you use the same lines of seduction on Eaton Powell or did *he* proposition *you* first?"

The question caught Sylvia completely off guard and inflamed her temper. She snapped up her head and stepped back quickly. "How do you know about Eaton?"

He grinned wryly. "I'm a Texas Ranger. I know everything. For instance, I know that Eaton's fiancée disappeared and her room was ransacked. You wouldn't know anything about that, would you?"

"Fiancée? I didn't know he had a fiancée," she insisted with feigned indignation.

"No?" Hud eyed her skeptically. But professional actress that she was, she tried out her wide-eyed innocent stare on him—for all the good it did. "I fail to see how that's possible. Everyone else in town knew the politician was with his fiancée. Surely Eaton mentioned her after she walked into his room and found the two of you in bed together."

He watched her carefully while she emphatically disavowed any knowledge of a fiancée, the ransacking or an attempted abduction.

"Do you derive fiendish satisfaction in stealing another woman's beau? Is that why you singled me out tonight? Because you saw me with Ellie?"

"Don't be absurd. Just because you're trailing after that mousey little woman in drab gray means nothing to me. I can't fathom why you enjoy staring at her when she isn't looking."

Hud made a mental note to be more cautious about that.

"Damn if I can figure out her lure to you and Lieutenant Davis," Sylvia said with a marveling shake of her head. "I don't know if she even has a face. Most of the time the floppy brim of her bonnet conceals everything but her chin. And the way she hunches over I'd swear she has a crick in her spine. Besides, she has those young whelps dogging her steps. They could be her brats for all I know."

"Forget about the boys and tell me what you know about the fiancée's room being tossed," Hud demanded with growing impatience.

"I don't know anything about anything," she said stubbornly. "I came down here to while away the hours with you in pleasurable pursuits. If you aren't interested, I'll look elsewhere. But believe me, you'll be sorry you missed out."

Hud wasn't the least bit sorry when Sylvia stamped off. Furthermore, he wasn't the least bit pleased that the thought of another woman had popped instantly to mind when Sylvia nearly sucked off his lips and plastered her considerable attributes against him. It was Gabrielle's forbidden memory that leaped to center stage of his mind and refused to leave.

"Hell and damnation." Hud scowled as he doffed his boots then stepped from his breeches.

Sighing audibly, he sank into the waist-deep water to give himself a good scrubbing.

"That didn't take long. You must work fast."

He glanced over his shoulder when Bri emerged from the shadows to stand beside his discarded clothing. He shrugged nonchalantly as he lathered his arms and chest. "Want to get naked and join me? I have extra soap."

"Tempting but no. I have my own fragranced bar of soap in my satchel. I've selected a more secluded location downstream for my bath this evening."

"*I* didn't kiss her," he blurted out—and for the life of him he couldn't fathom why he wanted her to know that.

"Really? It looked like you were involved from where I was standing," she countered.

"Then you were standing in the wrong spot."

"Of course. My mistake. What was I thinking?"

Bri had cursed herself mightily for following Sylvia, who had followed Hud from camp after supper. Yet, she hadn't been able to stop herself. She wanted to test Hud to see if he was as weak and unfaithful as Eaton. She wanted to watch him embrace Sylvia so she could convince herself that Hudson Stone was no better than any other man she'd ever encountered.

She couldn't think of one logical reason why she'd felt a jolt of betrayal when she'd seen Hud and Sylvia kissing. She had felt absolutely nothing except embarrassment and shock when she'd discovered Eaton and Sylvia in bed together.

"She was trying to seduce me but I wasn't a willing participant," Hud declared as he rubbed soap bubbles over his muscular chest. "I was questioning her possible involvement in ransacking your hotel room."

Bri sniffed caustically. "That's how you interrogate suspects? By nearly kissing them to death?"

"Did I have my arms around her?" he asked.

She frowned, trying to recall how involved he actually had been in the embrace. Being annoyed at the time, she hadn't paid particular attention. But come to think of it, he hadn't clamped Sylvia to him the way he'd clamped hold of Bri and kissed her until her senses exploded with indescribable pleasure.

"If you can't say for sure what was what then you aren't a trained observer." He clucked his tongue. "I thought your dear daddy would've drilled something like that into your head. Either he or your beloved Benji should've taught you to pay strict attention to important details."

Bri detected a hint of disdain in his voice. She didn't know what Hud had against Benji but she took immediate offense. "Do not take that tone with Benji's name attached to it," she ordered sharply.

"Right. Sorry. The love of your life, I presume. *Excuse me,*" he said as if he didn't mean it. "Now back to my question."

"No, now that I think on it, you didn't have hold of Sylvia," she replied pensively.

"Then there you go."

When he reached around to wash his back she watched the dappled moonlight spray over his swarthy physique. The enticing sight mesmerized her temporarily and she had to give herself a mental shake to restart her stalled brain.

"Why didn't you kiss her back?" she heard herself ask.

He turned his head to stare directly at her with those entrancing golden eyes. For a moment, she didn't think he was going to answer.

"The boys have convinced themselves that I'm sweet on you because they saw us kissing in the alley. I can't teach them loyalty if I can't set a good example, now can I?"

Bri wasn't sure what she wanted to hear him say but his remark endeared him to her in a heartbeat. She was trying exceptionally hard not to become sentimentally attached to a man who had no place in her future. That road led to heartache and folly. Yet, she was touched that Hud had taken the boys under his wing to teach them about surviving in the wilds and to stress the importance of honor and fidelity. They desperately needed a man they could respect and pattern their lives after.

Although she hated to admit it to herself, she wanted to hear Hud confess that he hadn't been interested in kissing Sylvia because he was attracted to *her*…

Heavens! What was she thinking? She wanted to *terminate* her attraction to Hud, not pursue it. If she knew what was good for her she would remain emotionally detached from Hud—the way she had been to other men after she'd lost Benji, even though theirs had been no more than a devoted but platonic friendship.

His death had tormented her as nothing else in life had. She wasn't going to put herself through that emotional meat grinder again. She had made that promise to herself three years ago and, by damn, she was sticking to it.

"You can turn your back while I wade ashore. *Or not,*" he said, breaking into her thoughts. "Your choice,

Bri. I want to dress so I can reconnoiter the area before I call it a night."

He didn't give her time to whirl around, just came ashore, exposing his broad chest then his washboarded belly, his trim waist... Bri swallowed a gasp and lurched around before she received an eyeful of naked masculine flesh.

She heard his soft laughter close behind her. "Chicken."

Careful not to allow her gaze to drop below his neck, for fear her face would explode with embarrassment, she spun around. She noted the look of surprise on his craggy features. She also noticed how quickly he clamped his breeches in front of his bare hips. "I am many things, of which you don't approve, but I am neither a chicken nor a coward." She reached out to wipe away the soap bubbles beneath his left ear. "If you need assistance reconnoitering the area I'm your woman."

"Thanks but I'll take along the boys. They have a lot to learn about the frontier. You, on the other hand, have considerably more skills than I expected."

Presenting her back so he could dress, Bri smiled to herself. "I'll tell the boys to look you up," she said before she hiked downstream to find a secluded spot for her bath.

She was immensely pleased that Hud acknowledged her abilities and exceptionally proud of herself for meeting his teasing challenge. She had faced down Hudson Stone—while he was naked—even though her face pulsated and her heart hammered in her chest so hard it nearly cracked a rib.

Yet, for one moment—clearly the most wickedly reckless moment in her life to date—she had wanted to make a thorough and deliberate study of Hud to appease her feminine curiosity. It was sinfully outrageous, she knew. But there you had it. Seeing Hud in his splendor and glory was her secret fantasy.

"You should have looked," she murmured to herself then grinned impishly. "Now you'll lie awake half the night speculating on what you missed."

Sure enough she did.

The next afternoon Hud watched Bri say her farewells to the boys, who were reluctant to part company with their new guardian angel. He swallowed a chuckle when Howie clamped his thick arms around Bri's waist, laid his blond head against her abdomen and practically hugged the stuffing out of her.

"You promise you'll come for us?" Howie said tearfully.

"I promise," she told him very seriously. "In the meantime you obey Milton and Lelia Korn and help them prepare for the theater performances. Will you do that for me?"

Muffling a sniffle, the eleven-year-old nodded.

Bri gave Howie a smacking kiss on his rounded cheek then moved on to Georgie, who was doing a damn fine job trying not to cry. "I shall miss you, Georgie. Take care of yourself." She gave him an affectionate hug then raked back his frizzy hair to kiss his forehead. "It is important for other people to know you are reliable and that you will do what you say. Make sure the Korns can count on you."

"The way we can count on you and Hud," he murmured.

She glanced sideways at Hud. "Exactly."

Bri halted in front of Tommy, who stood with his thin-bladed shoulders thrust back, his chin up. He was trying to be the man of the group. "I'll take care of 'em," he volunteered.

"I know you will. You will take care of each other because that's what brothers do. Now you are all brothers in every way that counts." She hooked her arm around his shoulder and playfully tugged him to her. "You might think you're too old for hugs, but humor me. I'm giving you one nonetheless."

It was the opening the proud young orphan needed to display his affection. Bri gave him a quick squeeze then she brushed a kiss over his pale cheek.

When stilted silence prevailed, Hud strode over to shake hands with the boys. "I'll take good care of Ellie, not to worry on that count. Now you boys take good care of *you*."

"We'll see you again when Ellie comes to fetch us," Georgie insisted as he pumped Hud's hand.

Hud didn't lie to the orphans. "That depends on my next assignment. If I'm on the trail of outlaws or raiders someone else might accompany Ellie." Hud herded the boys toward Milton Korn's wagon. "Off you go. Remember to pay attention to your surroundings so—"

"—Trouble can't sneak up on you," Howie quoted Hud's previous warning word for word.

Hud walked over to hand Lieutenant Davis a note. The soldier stared curiously at him, but Hud didn't divulge who Bri was or that she was supposedly missing. "Just hand this note to Marshal Long when you return," he requested.

Hud watched the caravan and its military escort ride away then glanced down to see how Bri was holding up. She was smiling, much to his surprise.

"Benji used to say that tomorrow is a grand adventure

that you should never miss. At least the boys can look forward to a future instead of wasting away in The Flat."

"Benji sure had a lot to say," Hud muttered as he strode to his horse. "Benji the orphan philosopher."

"I don't know what you have against him, but he was wise beyond his twenty years," Bri defended as she grabbed the reins to her sorrel gelding.

"Not wise enough to give up a costly trinket that you could have replaced easily for him," Hud said with censorship in his voice.

Bri's head snapped up. The brim of her bonnet flapped in the breeze. Although she filleted him with a glare, Hud refused to back down because they both knew he was right.

"There is a lot to be said for a fond memory, Bri. Benji's youthful face will never wrinkle with time and he will never age. The moments you spent with him have become more meaningful now that he's gone. He can never upset you or anger you because memories don't make mistakes or cause trouble. A flesh-and-blood man sure as hell can't compete with him."

"Why would you possibly want to try?" she asked.

He didn't reply, just watched Bri fashion her full skirt into breeches so she could ride astride. Hud wrapped his hand around her arm to assist her onto her horse.

"I don't, but you placed Benji on a pedestal where he remains to this day," he said belatedly. "I gave up my grandmother's heirloom necklace that my mother overlooked in her haste to abandon me. I didn't fight to keep it, even if it was the only link to my heritage. It paid for food and supplies that tided Speck and me over for more than six months."

Bri settled herself on the saddle then stared somberly

at him. "So you're saying that Benji was a fool, not the wise sage I've made him out to be."

Hud mounted up then reined Rambler southwest. "All I'm saying is that if you don't know when to give up something, valuable or not, to spare your life, then you made the wrong decision. *You have to know when to let go.*"

On that parting comment, Hud led the way through a deep gorge. He silently asked himself if maybe Bri was right on the mark when she suggested he was a tad bit jealous of her loyal affection for her lost friend. At least Hud was smart enough to know that his forbidden fascination for this unconventional, intriguing female would be over and done when he delivered her safely to her father.

Until then Hud vowed to hold himself to a higher standard and to keep a respectable distance. If his secret fantasy ever collided with reality, he knew he'd be in serious trouble.

Bri had always loved horseback riding, but she was sorry to say that it was rapidly losing its appeal after a full day of keeping Hud's relentless pace. She had no complaints about the spectacular scenery of wind-swept gulches, steep escarpments, jagged cliffs and fascinating rock formations in striated colors of red, white, green and gray, but the riding was getting old quick.

Her thoughts trailed off when she spotted three lobos feasting on carcasses the buffalo hunters had left behind after one of their ruthless shooting sprees.

"Damn them," she muttered angrily.

Hud nodded in agreement. "The buffalo hunters have turned lobos, coyotes and panthers into dangerous beasts."

She frowned curiously. "How so?"

"The hide hunter's policy of leaving so many carcasses to rot has turned predators into gluttons. Not only have the hunters wiped out nearly two hundred thousand head of buffalo with their high-powered rifles, but now predators are turning to cattle, sheep and humans to continue feeding their voracious appetites."

She glanced apprehensively at the rugged gorges and towering cliffs. "Have you encountered killer wolves?"

"Once," he confirmed. "I was on scouting patrol with Speck. When we bedded down for the night, the wolves went after our horses. They bit the hamstring on Speck's horse before we could drop them in their tracks. Then we had to trade off riding and walking beside Rambler to return to our base camp."

Bri noticed that the wolves feasting on the carcass glanced up but didn't dash off when they caught human scent. "I'm going to need a bigger pistol," she mused aloud.

Hud dug into his saddlebag to retrieve a spare revolver then he leaned away from his horse to hand it to her. "Have you used a Colt forty-five before?"

She tested the balance of the weapon then spun it around her middle finger. Smiling she said, "I cut my teeth on a pistol like this, thanks to my father's instructions."

"Good. If you have to bring down a mountain lion or wolf make sure you aim for—"

"—Its neck so it can't keep coming at you," she finished, paraphrasing her father's comment.

Hud appraised her for a pensive moment then asked, "Is there anything your father didn't teach you to do?"

She pretended to think about it for a few seconds then said, "Except how to change the opinion of a man who has his heart set on disliking me, you mean?"

"Yeah, except for that," he replied, lips twitching.

"Then no. He was very thorough with my training, much to my mother's dismay. But Benji—"

She slammed her mouth shut. Although Hud was the first person Bri felt she could speak openly to about Benji, he was tired of hearing about her dear friend already.

"Tell me about Speck Horton," she said, quickly changing the subject. "I presume Speck was his nickname."

Hud smiled faintly as he shifted to a more comfortable position in the saddle. "His given name was Charlie. He had thick red hair and a generous smattering of freckles."

"Hence the name Speck. How long did you know him?"

"Twenty-two years. I found him in an alley one summer day, bawling his head off. He said his mamma sent him into the alley to fetch a wooden crate from a trash bin. When he returned to the street, she was gone. To the day he died, Speck preferred to think that someone abducted his mother and that she hadn't abandoned him on purpose."

Bri inwardly winced, knowing what a traumatic ordeal that must have been for a young child, knowing Speck had held the hope that he hadn't been discarded, unwanted and betrayed by the one person in the world he should have been able to count on to love and protect him.

"My mother wasn't that creative," Hud remarked while he kept a watchful eye on their surroundings to check for possible trouble. "She sent me off to school, same as she did every day when I was ten. She packed up and darted away before I came home. All that was left was the necklace she overlooked and some pocket change."

Bri silently cursed the heartless woman who had left her child to fend for himself while she flitted off to begin her new life. Although Bri and her mother were polar opposites, and anticipated visits from her father were far between, she'd had a warm bed, nutritious meals and a roof over her head.

"I never knew my father, only the string of men who came and went through our back door," Hud continued. "I suppose my mother found someone who offered her more than a night's pleasure and money to pay the bills. But obviously he didn't want a bastard child in the bargain so I was left behind."

The thought of Hud's difficult childhood tugged at her heart. Before she could stop herself, she eased her horse close to Rambler then leaned over to give Hud a one-arm hug.

"No one deserves to be treated like that, Hud."

"No one promised life would be fair." He removed her arm and placed it on the pommel of her saddle. "The point is that you have to make the most of the cards you're dealt. I made it out of the alleys and into the Confederate Army. Speck and I still had to scratch and claw and defend ourselves against flying bullets. But we did have food and clothing."

That was a step up from survival in the streets? she mused. The next time she felt sorry for herself, she would remember Hud's challenging existence and recall how easy she had it, despite dealing with her domineering mother.

"After the war Speck and I came to Texas to join the Rangers. The governor wanted to hire several men who weren't born and raised in the state. He was having problems with local law officers who went easy on outlaws because they were family or acquaintances. We didn't have any family ties, only military experience, so we fit the bill."

"What happened to your friend?" Bri asked gently.

For a moment she wasn't sure he was going to reply. He gestured for her to follow him into what looked to be a box canyon with sheer, hundred-foot walls looming overhead. Bri became sidetracked when she noticed the secluded oasis, surrounded by lush trees and spring grass. A small waterfall trickled from the fissures in the rock wall into a hollowed-out limestone basin.

"We'll stop here for the night," he announced.

Bri glanced up, startled. "Aren't we wasting daylight?"

Hud shrugged. "Yes, but it's a long way to the next spring. A day's ride, in fact. You can bathe, if you like. I'll see what I can scare up for supper."

In other words, they weren't going to discuss Speck's death in detail right now, she presumed. Clearly, Hud held his friend in the same high regard that she held Benji. The pain was still fresh for Hud.

Bri remembered what that was like. Vowing to give him time to discuss Speck's death, Bri dug into her satchels for a bar of soap and clean clothing.

"Ah…" She sighed in delight as she sank into the re-freshing pool to soak her aching muscles. She hoped there were dozens more springs like this between here and the mountains of Colorado that she wanted to explore. Even if she anticipated a grand adventure of traveling the frontier, she wouldn't mind the daily luxury of a relaxing bath.

Bri closed her eyes and lounged against the edge of the pool, convinced this was the closest thing to paradise this side of heaven.

* * *

Joe Jarvis looked downhill at dusk to see a caravan of three wagons advertising the Korn Theater Troupe. A military escort rode beside them. Surely no one in the group knew who he was. How could they? He didn't make a habit of hanging around The Flat for more than a few days and he rarely walked the streets in broad daylight. He slept most of his days away, recovering from hellish hangovers.

The thought reminded him that he could use a drink. He twisted in the saddle to fish out the bottle he had confiscated from Pete Spaulding's belongings, along with the other half of the money the cocky politician had paid them.

Pete sure as hell wasn't going to need it now that Joe had tossed Pete's lifeless body into a deep ravine and kicked dirt over him. Pete had died with a surprised look on his face, Joe recalled.

After guzzling whiskey, Joe stashed the bottle from sight then wiped his mouth on his shirtsleeve. He used water from the canteen to slick back his unkempt hair and make himself more presentable. Then he stuffed Pete's hat on his head. He nudged his horse into a faster clip. If he played his cards right he might wrangle an invitation for a decent meal. He might even have a chance to swipe extra money or jewelry from the unsuspecting theater troupe while he was at it.

"Ho there!" Joe waved his arm expansively to announce himself before some trigger-happy soldier tried to blast him out of the saddle.

The young, boyish-faced lieutenant gestured for him to approach. "Are you traveling alone?"

Joe nodded his shaggy head. "Am now." He put on his sad face to draw sympathy from the soldier. "My partner was killed recently. Damn Indians, always swooping down when you least expect it."

"We warded off a raiding party yesterday," the fresh-faced soldier replied. "It might have been the same ones you encountered. A dozen Comanche and Kiowa braves?"

"Yeah," Joe said, taking the opening the unsuspecting soldier offered. "They were on us before we knew what hit us."

"I'm sorry about your friend. Why don't you join us for supper? You can travel under our protection if you like. An escort detail from Fort Elliot will be here soon to relieve us from duty, but you can join them."

"Thanks for your hospitality," Joe said, making the most of what little manners he had.

"I don't believe I caught your name, sir," the soldier commented as he escorted Joe to the wagons.

"Pete Spaulding." Joe smiled devilishly at his own cleverness.

Pete hadn't turned out to be as dead as he thought he was.

Chapter Eight

Hud skidded to a halt on the embankment overlooking the isolated oasis. Twilight glowed in the western sky and the spring-fed pool glistened invitingly. A small campfire built according to military specifications flickered in the gathering darkness.

"Well, hell," he muttered in frustration. The scene was entirely too cozy and welcoming for a man who was having a devil of a time battling his attraction to a woman who was completely off-limits to him for a dozen good reasons.

To make matters worse, "walking temptation" had bathed and dressed in trim-fitting breeches, a shirt and boots that displayed every curve and swell she possessed. And she had plenty of them in all the right places, he noted as his all-consuming gaze flooded over her.

How was he supposed to remain indifferent to an alluring female like Bri? His shoulders sagged defeatedly, but he did his best to shore up his willpower as he followed the narrow footpath downhill. When Bri glanced up and smiled, another chunk of the armor surrounding his heart broke loose.

"Rabbit for supper?" she said, nodding her curly red-blond head toward the game he carried in his hand. "Sounds good. I'll clean it and put it on to cook while you bathe. I found some wild plums and a few berries to go with it."

Hud surrendered the rabbit that dangled from his fist. He was so busy watching the provocative sway of her hips and the enticing jiggle of her breasts beneath the cream-colored shirt that he was hopelessly distracted and didn't even notice her grabbing it.

Immediately his traitorous thoughts circled back to the previous day when he had bounded downhill to the creek to see Bri's exposed thighs after she retrieved her derringer to shoot the striking rattlesnake. He closed his eyes, clenched his jaw and told himself to think about *anything* except how appealing Bri looked. But when he took a deep, steadying breath, her fragranced soap instantly became his favorite scent.

"Are you okay? You look like you're in pain."

Hud jerked to attention to see Bri staring worriedly at him. He was in pain all right. She was the cause of it…and the cure, if she were so inclined. But Commander Price would kill them both, so appeasing his desire for her was out of the question.

"I'm fine," he said shortly. "Why wouldn't I be?"

She cocked her head to the side and squinted at him. "You're also cranky all of a sudden. Mind telling me why?"

"I've missed out on a lot of sleep lately." He peeled off his vest and hooked it over the pommel of Rambler's saddle.

Thankfully, she let it go at that and he hurried off to soak in the bubbly pool. Ten minutes later Bri ambled from the shadows of the trees while he was lounging in the water.

He elevated a brow and gave her a go-away stare. "Yes?"

Nonchalant as you please, she sank down cross-legged on his discarded clothing. "You were going to tell me about Speck," she prompted.

"No, I wasn't."

"What happened?" she persisted.

He glared at her, not that it fazed the strong-willed female. He was beginning to realize that she wasn't scared of much of anything. "Are you going to interrupt my bath *every* blessed day?"

She pretended to think about it then grinned, undaunted by his scowl. "No. If you recall, I didn't interrupt your bath the second day I met you."

Another corner of his heart eroded when she flashed him an impudent smile and batted her eyes playfully at him.

"Supper is cooking so we have plenty of time for you to tell me what happened. I was going to wait you out, but I decided now is as good a time as any."

Maybe it *was* time to get it off his chest. He'd kept it bottled up inside him for almost two weeks. "Speck and I were on patrol, checking a report of two bandits who robbed a stage station south of Tascosa. Rambler picked up a rock in his shoe and was favoring his back left leg so I had to take time to let him heal properly. Speck decided to scout the area and question the station attendant while I remained in camp with Rambler for a couple of days."

"He didn't return when he should have," she concluded.

"No, he didn't…You might as well make yourself useful. Toss me the razor," he requested.

Bri scooped up the razor he had placed on the edge of the pool then she lobbed it to him. Hud became sidetracked watching her walk away in those trim-fitting black breeches. Scowling at himself, he lathered his face and hair with soap then soaked his head, hoping to drown the titillating vision in his mind. Not that it helped one whit.

"I found Speck a day later. He'd been shot in the back. I killed the three coyotes standing over him. His money and his badge were gone. I buried my friend and vowed to hunt down the bastard who murdered him."

The memory caused his heart to twist in his chest and the resentment of being removed from the search for the killer to take escort detail gnawed at him again. He didn't want to be here with Bri. He didn't want to like this woman who challenged him, aroused him and kept him from his manhunt. She set off such a riptide of emotions inside him that he battled himself constantly.

"I'm so sorry, Hud," she whispered. "I was serious when I volunteered to travel without you so you can track the killer. You admitted that I'm not the greenhorn you thought I was."

"No, you aren't," he agreed, "but this is wild country where two sets of eyes are better than one. With luck, the other Rangers will have gathered information. They might have taken Mad Joe Jarvis and Pete Spaulding captive during my absence."

She stared curiously at him. "How did you find out about the killers?"

"I questioned the stage agent and he gave me a description of the two men. He reported that Joe seemed more bloodthirsty than Pete. Joe pistol-whipped the agent and Pete tried to get his drunken cohort to back off."

"Joe and Pete?" She snapped up her head and stared intently at him. "What do these men look like…?"

Her voice trailed off when an eerie scream echoed around the canyon walls. She bounded to her feet to jerk Hud's Winchester from the sling on Rambler's saddle. In the meantime, Hud waded ashore. He snatched up his breeches and hurriedly stepped into them while Bri charged off to protect the horses. He hobbled barefoot across the pebbles and spotted the oversized panther perched on the ledge above Bri's horse, which nickered fearfully and strained against the tether.

Hud forgot to breathe when the tawny-colored, one-hundred-fifty-pound cat turned its deadly attention on Bri. When the cat screeched again then gathered itself to pounce, Hud reached for his pistol—and cursed foully because he didn't have his holsters draped around his hips.

A second later he realized he didn't need to be armed because Bri had assumed a shooting stance and snapped the rifle into position against her shoulder. When the muscular cat leaped through the air, she aimed and fired.

To Hud's amazement, the giant cat dropped like dead weight. It hit the ground with a thud and lay unmoving ten feet in front of her. Bri, however, yelped and stumbled back because the rifle kicked hard against her shoulder.

"Ouch," she grumbled, rubbing her upper arm. "Your cartridges must pack as much firepower as cannonballs."

Hud was unwillingly impressed with Bri's marksmanship and her ability to remain cool and steady under pressure.

First the rattlesnake, then the mountain lion. Hell, what does she need me for?

"I'm going to finish my bath," he mumbled as he pivoted in the direction he'd come. "I'll dispose of the carcass later."

On the way back to the pool, Hud kept picturing the gun-toting heiress on the arm of the dandified politician of a fiancé. Bri was right, he realized. Powell would have been a disastrous mismatch for her. Despite Hud's original misconceptions, Bri didn't need a man to protect her. She'd proved that she was pretty damn good at it herself.

In fact, she didn't need Hud any more than he needed her. And he didn't *need* her, he assured himself as he walked gingerly over the sharp pebbles to reach the pool.

It was *wanting* her that was giving him so much trouble.

"Pete? We were wondering if you might've crossed paths with our friends Ellie and Hud."

Joe glanced up belatedly and reminded himself that he was answering to Pete Spaulding's name these days. He squinted at the three boys, who stood like stair steps in front of him.

"Ellie and Hud?" he repeated before he gobbled another bite of the tasty meal.

The stocky little brat nodded his blond head. "They headed southwest this morning."

"Ellie was wearing a gray dress and bonnet and riding a sorrel gelding," the frizzy-haired kid added helpfully.

"Hud is a Ranger and he rides a black horse. He was wearing a dark shirt, vest and breeches," the gangly adolescent spoke up.

Joe snapped to attention when he remembered the

woman in gray, who'd turned him down flat in the hall at Brazos Hotel a few days earlier. The same woman, it turned out, that he and Pete had been paid to kidnap. But she had vanished into thin air before he could get his hands on her. And that had sent him into a drunken rage.

Although Joe had been drinking heavily at the time, he remembered that dandified Powell character boasting that the woman was the daughter of some uppity government official connected to the Rangers. Despite her drab gray dress, she was supposedly wealthy and well-connected.

"Sorry, boys, I didn't see anything of 'em."

The boys' shoulders slumped in disappointment. Not that Joe cared. He had no use for brats. When the kids wandered off to bed down for the night Joe grabbed his bedroll and strode off by himself. After a few drinks and some pensive deliberation, Joe smiled wickedly.

If he could catch up with the woman and take her captive, he could make a pile of money from two sources at once. The woman's father would pay to have her back and her fiancé would pay to keep it quiet that he'd *hired* Joe and Pete to abduct her. Once Joe collected both ransoms, he'd be set for life. He could make a new start and settle down where nobody knew him.

"Hell of an idea," Joe mumbled then guzzled some whiskey. First thing in the morning he'd ride off to overtake the lady and dispose of the Ranger.

The wind picked up and whistled around the canyon walls sometime after midnight. Bri watched the glowing embers from the campfire dance over her sleeping pallet. The cold north wind sent chills down her spine and the drifting smoke clogged her nostrils. She needed to gather her bedroll and move upwind from the fire.

Unfortunately, Hud had bedded down on the north side and she wasn't sure she trusted herself to be too close to him.

"How long are you going to lie there eating smoke and dodging flying sparks?"

At the sound of his deep, resonant voice, Bri stared across the glowing coals. The reflection of light in Hud's golden eyes was downright eerie. So was the rumbling noise that swept along the caprock overhead. It reminded her of a thundering herd stampeding in the night.

"What is that sound?" she asked as she propped her head in her hand.

"According to the Comanche it's the combined spirit of more than a thousand horses that Colonel MacKenzie's soldiers slaughtered and left to rot when they attacked the camp," Hud explained. "When the moon is full, like tonight, and the wind howls to foretell of a coming storm, the ghost herd thunders across the escarpments and plunges down the gullies in this place that was once known as the Comancheria."

Normally Bri wasn't a superstitious sort, but the haunting sounds that gushed down the canyon walls, not to mention the effervescent shadows floating over the caprock, were getting to her. She rolled to her knees and gathered her bedding. She would rather be tempted by her maddening attraction to Hud than to be trampled by ghost horses.

"Scared?" he teased when she tossed her bedroll down beside him.

"Of course not," she said with bravado. "I simply can't tolerate being separated from you. Besides, the wind is cold and I figure you'll generate valuable heat."

The moment Bri stretched out beside him she felt

reassured and comforted. That was not a good thing to know. She was battling a lusty attraction already. Taking comfort in Hud's presence contributed to her mounting frustration.

"Better?" he murmured from so close behind her that his warm breath skimmed over her neck.

Desire rippled over her and hot tingles chased each other through her all-too responsive body. "I haven't decided whether this is better or not," she muttered.

When he draped his arm over her waist and pulled her against his muscular torso, the tantalizing sensations assailing her became even more pronounced. All she had to do was roll to her back and she could kiss him for as long as she wanted. No one would know of her lack of self-control.

But he will know that you're exceptionally vulnerable to him, came that sensible voice in her head.

Bri tensed when Hud's hand curled around her hips and he gently rolled her onto her back. Her heart thudded against her ribs while she stared into those mystifying amber eyes. Forbidden need delivered another devastating blow to her faltering willpower, leaving her stumbling along the crumbling edge of self-restraint.

"I'm wondering if it would be bad luck to break our pattern," he whispered as his hand glided up and down her thigh in a light caress.

"Pattern?" she repeated stupidly, completely distracted by his evocative caresses. "What pattern…? Mmm…"

Her thoughts scattered and her voice trailed off as his hand skimmed between her legs then drifted over her lower abdomen. Sensual lightning streaked through her, sensitizing every inch of her skin.

"You've kissed me every day since we met," he prompted huskily. "Except for today." He angled his head and brushed his lips tenderly over her eyelids, her cheek and her chin.

"And you're saying that you feel like you've missed out?" she asked breathlessly.

His mouth curved into a wry grin. "Definitely. When you become accustomed to tasty daily rations you start looking forward to them and you don't want to do without."

When he dropped a tempting kiss to her lips, the tension melted from her body instantly, replaced by a burning need that Bri was tired of fighting.

"Then by all means," she purred. "We should finish the day off right. Here's to fulfilling necessary daily rations...."

As if her arms possessed a will of their own, they glided over his broad shoulders then measured the muscled wall of his chest. She raked her fingers through his thick raven hair, held his head to hers and kissed him ravenously.

The eerie sound of ghost horses thundering across the canyon rim couldn't override the erotic sensations streaming through her body. *Just for tonight,* came the voice of reckless need. She could appease her lusty desire for Hud and then the curious lure he held over her would cease to exist. She would discover what she had been avoiding these past few years when it came to intimacy between a man and woman.

Pleasure cascaded through her as Hud nudged her legs apart and settled over her. He pressed his hips against hers, assuring her that she aroused him and that he was as involved in their embrace as she was. She could feel his hard length against her abdomen and she arched instinctively against him. She couldn't get close enough to satisfy the empty ache burning in the core of her being and hungry need blazed through her, hot and unrelenting.

The pressure of his lips became more intense and his hand moved familiarly over her breasts and belly. Her breath caught in her throat when his hand dipped beneath the waistband of her breeches and skimmed over the sensitive flesh of her inner thighs. Flames scorched her from inside out as his tongue darted into her mouth at the same moment that his finger glided into the molten heat between her legs. Bri cursed the layers of fabric between them, cursed the insane need that made her want to be naked with him, made her want to touch him as intimately as he was touching her...

Her thoughts scattered when a pack of wolves howled in the distance. The horses nickered and stamped uneasily. Hud stilled above her, his keen senses on alert. When he came to his knees then rocked back on his haunches, Bri sat up. She silently thanked the prowling lobos for jerking her back to reality before she cast common sense to the wind and answered the call of wild desire.

"I'll stand guard—" she tried to volunteer.

"No," he interrupted her quickly. "You've already shot a snake and a panther. Can't let you have all the fun. I'll stay by the horses until the pack moves on to easier prey."

After he pulled on his boots, grabbed his rifle and walked away Bri collapsed on her pallet. She listened to the eerie sounds swirling around her and watched phosphoric ribbons of light drift along the escarpment.

For a fleeting moment, she had been wrapped in a warm cocoon, savoring wicked pleasures of the flesh.

The thought of danger had been a million miles away. *This is the dark side of desire at work,* she mused as she snuggled up in her bedroll. *It tosses all sorts of temptation at you while you're weak and vulnerable.* She wondered how long she'd be able to resist the tantalizing lure when each breathless moment she spent with Hud left her teetering on the brink of no return.

Bri contemplated her adolescent infatuation with Benji Dunlop. It was disconcerting to realize her crush on Benji was nothing like the feverish craving that fed upon itself when she was in Hud's sinewy arms, reeling from the sizzling sensations provoked by his heated kisses and bold caresses.

"Go to sleep before you drive yourself crazy," she chastised herself harshly.

Taking that sound advice she clamped her eyes shut and tried to discard the tempting picture of thick raven hair, whiskey-colored eyes and a ruggedly handsome face hovering above her. She could resist the wicked lure of lust for a couple of days, if she really tried. Soon she'd be surrounded by a camp full of Rangers. The welcomed companionship of her father would chase away these forbidden fantasies.

"Two more days," she chanted as she drifted off to sleep.

Hud sat with his back against the rock wall. He cradled his rifle in his lap while he watched over the horses and kept an eye on Bri, who slept on the far side of the campfire.

Damn it, he'd let temptation take a fierce and mighty hold on him when he invited Bri to bed down beside him. He'd let down his guard tonight—again—and look what had happened. He'd savored the taste of Bri's honeyed lips, caressed her lush body and touched her familiarly.

"You made another stupid mistake," he castigated himself sharply. "When are you going to learn you can't trust yourself with her?"

The imprint of her curvaceous body might as well have been branded on him because his flesh burned each place they'd touched. He remembered, *vividly,* how it felt to lie intimately upon her. He remembered her taste, her scent and the delicious heat of her desire burning his fingertip. He knew what it was like to want her almost beyond bearing. It was pure hell not giving in to his fierce need to bury himself inside her and feel her silky heat burning around him.

Hud blew out his breath, stretched out his legs and laid his head against the stone wall. What was that stupid comment he'd made about not breaking the habit of kissing her? He'd kissed her all right—and he'd practically gone up in flames, right on the spot. Damnation, he had to stop torturing himself like that or he'd drive himself loco! He *could* resist sweet, tormenting temptation, if he set his mind to it. He *had* to.

"Two more days," he murmured.

He could control himself a little while longer and he'd deliver Bri to her father. Then he'd ride off to search for Joe Jarvis and Pete Spaulding. His crusade would take his mind off that indigo-eyed siren who kept blasting his noble intentions and willpower all to hell and left him aching with a need that intensified with each passing day.

"Eaton!"

Eaton Powell groaned miserably when he heard the shrill voice echoing down the hall of his lavish mansion in Austin. He'd arrived in town late the previous night, after riding on that dusty, uncomfortable stagecoach for hours on end. Then he'd boarded a train for the final leg of his journey. He'd celebrated his return to civilization with a warm and willing bit of fluff. Afterward he'd drunk himself to sleep and he hadn't planned to rise and shine until afternoon. If then.

"Eaton! Get up this instant!"

The familiar voice played havoc with the rhythmic throbbing in his head. Grimacing, Eaton levered himself against the headboard and blinked owlishly.

Anna Roland Price flew into his suite like a furious witch—minus her broom. Attractive though she was with her blue-violet eyes and blond hair, she could cut you to the quick with her condescending stares. The derisive twist of her lips assured you that you could try but you could never be as important and powerful and well bred as an almighty Roland.

"How dare you!" Anna railed in a grating voice that raked over Eaton's frazzled nerves like fingernails on a chalkboard.

He grabbed his head before it imploded then groaned sickly when his stomach pitched and rolled.

"You incompetent dolt! You allowed *my* daughter, *your* fiancée, to be abducted right out from under your nose."

"It happened in the middle of the night," he mumbled. "I wasn't on hand. We had separate rooms, of course."

She stormed over to the bed, jerked the pillow from beneath his aching head and pummeled him with it repeatedly.

"Then you had the gall to leave her in that godforsaken hellhole and *you* came home?" Her voice rose to an eardrum-splitting squawk that made Eaton want to howl in agony.

"There is no one of any consequence to oversee the search!"

"The Ranger on escort detail was there." He grabbed the pillow from her fist and clamped it under his arm so she couldn't hit him with it again.

Anna scoffed disdainfully. "Obviously the irresponsible hooligan whom Winston sent to accompany Gabrielle is as big an idiot as you are." She fisted her hands on her hips and glowered hot pokers at him. "If you think for one minute that you are going to lounge in the lap of luxury while my daughter faces untold terror at the hands of some ruthless heathen in the wilderness, you are very much mistaken, Eaton."

"Perhaps you should travel to Fort Griffin to oversee the search. I'm sure you'd be much better at it than everyone else," he said snidely.

"Be that as it may, *you* are going back immediately." Her arm shot toward the wardrobe closet. "Get dressed and get on board the afternoon train that heads north. You are going back to Fort Griffin. Do you hear me, Eaton?"

Who couldn't? The walls of Jericho couldn't hold up against the crazed woman.

"I've been in contact with the city marshal—" he began.

His voice became a yelp when Anna swooped down to jerk off the quilts, exposing his bare chest and underdrawers. When she grabbed his ear, pinched it painfully then dragged him from bed, Eaton came to his feet. It was that or risk having his right earlobe ripped off the side of his head.

"While you head north I will hire private detectives," she insisted. "Nothing but the best. The Pinkertons, of course. Until they arrive *you* will be at Fort Griffin to keep *me* updated daily."

"I'm sure your husband will mount a posse so—"

"So nothing!" she railed furiously. "If you expect Roland money to support your campaign for U.S. Senator then you will get off your duff and get on that train!"

Eaton stared at the pompous banshee for a long moment, trying to decide if he should arrange to have *her* abducted, too. It was an exceptionally pleasing thought.

Anna shook her bejeweled finger in his face. "I will give you one hour to prepare for your trip. If you aren't packed and ready to board the train, I will let it be known that you are personally to blame for Gabrielle's disappearance."

He was but he'd cut out his tongue before he confided that to the raving banshee.

"Indeed, how do you expect to oversee the needs of the citizens of this state and this country if you can't keep track of your fiancée?" She bared her teeth and snarled, "I promise you, Eaton, I will ruin your chances of being elected for anything if you don't return to Fort Griffin immediately."

She flashed him another hateful sneer. "If you don't find my daughter you are finished. Do you understand me?"

"Completely." He massaged his throbbing earlobe.

Flinging her nose in the air, she stamped out.

Eaton glared at her parting back and said, "I had the wrong woman kidnapped, Anna. I should have started with *you*."

Chapter Nine

The next day dawned cold, cloudy and windy. Hud saddled Rambler and the sorrel gelding while Bri walked to the pool to freshen up. When she returned, he handed her hardtack.

"I usually travel light. This is all I have to offer."

She fished into her saddlebag to retrieve a half a loaf of bread, then handed Hud two pieces and took one for herself. "I stopped by the bakery before I left The Flat."

He arched a curious brow as he munched on the bread.

"I had planned to survive on bread and water after I left the boys with the caravan and found another Ranger at the nearby camp to guide me cross-country to join my father." She frowned in concern. "I hope the boys are all right."

"They'll manage until you rejoin them. However, things might become complicated since all of them are hopelessly infatuated with you. Don't trounce on their young hearts."

She chuckled lightly. "Ah, finally, suitors who meet my approval. They are several steps above Eaton Powell."

"Don't take their feelings for you too lightly," Hud cautioned. "Male pride is a delicate thing, especially at their impressionable age."

She cocked her head, smiled and studied him while munching on her bread. "Then what's your excuse for being stone-hearted? Did a woman betray you and trample on your feelings until you built rock walls around them?"

Hud loved that impish grin that made her blue-violet eyes glisten with playful spirit. Bri was sassy, lively and extremely appealing to him, no matter how hard he tried to deny it. "No, you're the first woman to hurt my feelings and trample on my pride."

"Really? I'm honored."

Hud handed over the reins to the sorrel. "Save your torment tactics until later. It's time to ride. *Now* we are burning daylight." He gestured toward the gloomy clouds. "The approaching storm might cut traveling short today."

"I want to hear more about how I've injured your pride when no other woman has accomplished the deed," she teased as she pulled herself effortlessly into the saddle.

"For starters, your vanishing act was an embarrassing blow to my pride," he admitted as he left the box canyon. "I was sure the stunt was designed specifically to make me look the fool after I strongly urged you to turn around and go home."

"You give me too much credit. You don't need my help looking like a fool."

Hud slanted her a sideways glance to note the playful smile was still intact. Hud couldn't get used to Bri. For the most part, his life was serious business. Chasing outlaws and marauding Indians put him in life-threatening situations constantly. There had been little time for amusement. He had hoped to live an *un*eventful lifestyle when he retired from service with the Rangers. He and Speck had planned to enjoy life rather than fight their way through it....

His expression must have given him away because she said, "Hud? I'm sorry. I was only teasing you."

"I was just thinking of Speck and the life we planned when we resigned and accepted our land grants. I bequeathed my land to Speck and vice versa, just in case one of us didn't survive. It's hollow consolation to have twice as much property coming to me."

She didn't speak for a long moment. "I'm sure your best friend would want you to make the most of the land you have risked your lives to earn. I know I would."

Hud knew he felt the same way, but the guilt of not being there to back up Speck on that fateful day still haunted him. Moreover, it drove him to hunt down Speck's murderer.

"Yesterday, before the interruption of the panther attack, I asked you about the two men responsible for your friend's death," Bri reminded him. "What do they look like?"

"Mad Joe Jarvis has stringy brown hair, gray eyes, bad teeth and a lean build. Pete Spaulding is heavyset, bow-legged with auburn hair and hazel eyes."

Bri jerked upright and stared attentively at him. "Joe has gray eyes? Pete has hazel eyes? Both of them are somewhere near your age or slightly younger?"

Hud pulled Rambler to a halt, his senses on high alert. "You've seen them? Where?"

"The first night at the hotel, when I was walking

down the hall to confront Eaton and found him with Sylvia. Joe propositioned me. His friend, Pete, held him at bay when I threatened to scream down the walls of the hotel if he came near me. It *had* to be them. They are in The Flat!"

Hud glanced east, longing to reverse direction and race hell-for-leather back to town.

"Go after them," Bri encouraged. "I can make it to your Ranger camp if you give me directions."

Hud sat in the saddle, wishing he could be at two places at once. The thirst for revenge was so strong he could almost taste it. Yet, leaving Bri to fend for herself might spell disaster, just as it had when Speck volunteered to ride off to investigate the robbery alone.

Hud hadn't been there to guard Speck's back and he might not be there if Bri needed him. Yet, if Hud delayed in pursuing the promising lead there was no telling where Joe and Pete might turn up next, no telling who might become their next victim.

"I'm serious, Hud," Bri said, breaking into his conflicting thoughts. She reached over to clutch his clenched fist and stared intently at him. "Continuing on my own will be a good test for me. I plan to take the boys with me to explore the mountains of Colorado and then venture all the way to the Pacific Ocean."

He snorted at that. "Surely you plan to travel by train or stagecoach, not rough it in the wilderness."

She lifted her shoulder nonchalantly. "This isn't the first time I've traveled the frontier. I visited my father while he was inspecting Ranger camps near El Paso. I charaded as a boy and made part of my trip on horseback."

"The colonel knew about it and approved?" Hud questioned, incredulous.

A mischievous smile quirked her lips. "I didn't say that. I simply tested the skills Papa and Benji taught me. I survived on bread and water during that trip, too."

"I'm not leaving you unattended," he declared firmly. "And if you hightail it off without informing me, I won't go easy on you this time. Count on it."

Bri thrust back her shoulders and lifted her chin. "Your comment implies that you still don't believe that I didn't stage my own abduction. If you don't trust me then this conversation is over."

She nudged her horse into a trot, but then she pulled back on the reins abruptly. She swiveled her head around to stare wide-eyed at Hud. "You don't suppose Joe and Pete planned to abduct me after they discovered who I was, do you? Then again, maybe it wasn't intended as abduction. Perhaps Joe decided to act on his insulting proposition then tore up my room for spite since I wasn't there."

Hud frowned pensively. "It's possible."

The prospect of Joe and Pete raping and kidnapping Bri sent cold chills down his spine. "They might have been prowling the hotel, looking for an easy mark to rob."

"You might be right," she murmured thoughtfully. "They might have been looking for hidden money when they trashed my room." She focused solemnly on Hud. "They might still be in town. You should go back."

"Not without you."

"I have a time schedule," she reminded him. "After I visit Papa for a few days I have to circle back to pick up the boys."

"They'll manage just fine. They prowled the alleys of The Flat for months, after all."

"I *promised* them," she said emphatically. "They

believe they can count on me to do exactly what I say when they can count on no one else. I refuse to disappoint them." She flicked her wrist at him. "Now go, Hud. This is as important to you as fulfilling my promises to the boys is to me."

"And have your death on my conscience, same as Speck's?" he snorted. "No thank you." He urged Rambler into a trot. "This is not negotiable. We'll ride west and that's that."

"Did anyone ever tell you that you're infuriatingly stubborn and exasperatingly mule-headed?" she muttered as she kept his accelerated pace.

"You forgot to mention delightfully charming," he said, and glared at her.

Not to be outdone, she glared right back. "I left that out on purpose, Captain Attila."

On that parting shot, she gouged the sorrel in the flanks, sending it cantering through the valley where low-scraping gray clouds threatened to rain down on her head any minute.

Hud cast one longing glance eastward then picked up his pace. With luck, Joe Jarvis and Pete Spaulding would still be somewhere near The Flat after Hud delivered Bri to her father.

Learning that the two renegades had confronted Bri and might have been responsible for trashing her hotel room unnerved him. The thought of Bri becoming a victim of Joe's brutality would be his worst nightmare.

Determined of purpose, Hud took every shortcut across the rugged terrain. He hoped to outrun the storm that loomed on the northern horizon so he could deliver Bri safely to the Ranger camp. Then and only then would he find Speck's killer.

The bastard would get his first taste of what hell was like before he reached the flaming gates, Hud promised himself vengefully.

Bri ducked instinctively when the first crack of thunder resounded overhead. The sky had been dark and threatening most of the day, but by early evening, it looked downright ominous. She peered apprehensively at the green-tinged clouds that foretold of hail and turbulent winds. She wondered where she and Hud might find shelter when the storm unleashed its fury.

"How much farther are we riding?" Bri called above the sound of the whistling wind.

"There's a small cave on the far side of the canyon that Speck and I used when we passed through here."

He gestured around the monolithic rock formation that rose up on the canyon floor like a stalagmite. Bri surveyed their surroundings, noting the deep, eroded gorges and V-shaped ravines that dropped off the escarpment that towered fifty feet above them. She could imagine all sorts of disaster befalling them in this place where two-legged and four-legged predators might be lurking.

As if the threat of the storm wasn't foreboding enough.

This was the most unforgiving terrain they'd encountered, she mused. It was also the last place she preferred to be if the sky opened up before they found shelter.

The thought no sooner crossed her mind than lightning streaked across the horizon like bony fingers reaching out to snare wayward souls and drag them into hell. The deafening clap of thunder startled the sorrel gelding. He ducked his head between his front legs and kicked up his back heels.

Bri yelped, unprepared for a high-flying buck. The

horse's momentum launched her forward. She flung her arm around his neck to prevent being catapulted over his head. Her attempt to keep her seat alarmed the sorrel gelding. He whinnied, darted sideways and tossed his head. The sudden movement thrust Bri backward abruptly.

Then the cloudburst unleashed its fury, drenching Bri in less than a minute. Her horse was still prancing skittishly when hail the size of hen eggs bombarded them.

"Get off your horse!" Hud yelled from behind her. "Keep hold of his reins. If we loose him during this storm he might run until he drops."

Bri slid off the saddle and swore mightily when the sorrel tried to break and run from the hail that hammered at his head. Pain pulsated through her skull when a hailstone bounced off her forehead. She could barely see where she was going because the rain came in torrents, driven by such fierce winds that it was difficult to keep her feet.

Never once had Bri endured the force of a storm without the comfort of shelter. *So much for living the adventure,* she mused cynically.

Hud snaked his arm around her waist to steady her against the gale-force wind then he gestured his head to the west. "I'd ask what else could go wrong today but I'm not sure I want to know. This is plenty to deal with."

Bri blinked water from her eyes and held her arm over her head to protect her from the hail as she followed the direction of Hud's grim stare. She watched in fiendish fascination as the churning cloud dropped a tornado a quarter of a mile west of their location.

An eerie sensation slithered down her spine when the fierce south wind died abruptly then picked up to come at them from all directions at once. The powerful storm sucked up the air, feeding itself, intensifying with each passing second. Bri's ears popped and her breath stalled in her chest. Still she stood, as if hypnotized, as the twister whipped up dirt and rumbled toward them like an oncoming freight train.

"Come on, damn it!" Hud practically jerked her arm from its socket in his haste to get her moving again.

Bri yelped when another hailstone slashed across her cheek. She tried to protest when Hud pulled her against his chest to take the brunt of the downpour and protect her from a brain-scrambling blow.

He was the one who needed to be in command of his senses, she thought to herself. He knew where they were and where to find shelter. Her previous survival training had not included enduring tornadoes, hailstorms and cloudbursts.

Rain poured off the brim of Hud's hat as he hugged her against him and took the reins to both frightened horses. He tried to move steadily toward the cave but it might as well have been ten miles away for all the good it was doing them when they found themselves in another circle of hell.

"Hold on to me," Hud told her as he rested his chin on the crown of her wet head. "And watch your footing."

She glanced down to see water stacking up on the ground. The rain was coming too fast to drain off. When the relentless deluge filled the steep-sided gorges to overflowing, the canyon floor would flood—and that spelled disaster.

"Damn!" Hud roared when the first wave of flash flood waters slammed into his knees, knocking him off balance.

When Hud toppled over, Bri lurched toward her horse to regain control of the reins. The sorrel gelding screamed in terror and reared up as cold water swirled around him. The wild-eyed animal dragged Bri with him as he scrabbled uphill to avoid the rushing water that flowed from dozens of twisting gullies at once.

Bri groaned when another hailstone thumped her between the eyes, dazing her momentarily. She could hear the roar of the approaching twister and feel the icy rain soaking her skin. The whirling wind threatened to knock her off her feet and she staggered unsteadily. At the worst of all possible moments, the sorrel collided with her, sending her reeling backward.

Rushing water slapped her in the face. She heard Hud bellowing at her before she went under. The fierce current tossed her around like driftwood. It was impossible to determine which way was up. She swore her lungs were about to burst from lack of air. When she realized she still had a death grip on the reins, she pulled herself hand over hand toward her horse. Surging upward, Bri thrust her head above water long enough to grab a much-needed breath.

Hail pelted the rushing water that swirled like an eddy as the forceful winds of the twister engulfed them. Bri floundered to gain her feet, fighting the floodwater that rushed through the gulches and ravines and threatened to wash her away. She had no clue what had happened to Hud and Rambler. She called out to Hud, but she doubted he could hear her over the roaring wind and churning water.

Bri yelped when something—driftwood perhaps—slammed her broadside. She swallowed a mouthful of water when the force of the flash flood towed her under. She realized she could die in this watery grave, swept away to only God knew where.

The reins that anchored her to her horse slipped through her fingers as she tumbled helplessly with the fierce current. Pain exploded through her head and shoulder when she banged into a boulder or tree—she had no idea which. She lost consciousness as the cold, black silence swamped her…

"Bri!" Hud bellowed when he lost sight of her in the frothy water.

The sorrel scrambled from the swirling water and clambered onto high ground. Hud held his breath, hoping Bri would magically appear. No such luck, damn it.

He wiped the muddy water from his eyes and stared frantically downhill. Even though Rambler was tugging painfully on the reins that Hud had wrapped around his wrist, he refused to let go. It was all that steadied him against the powerful rush of water. He supposed he should feel fortunate because it had stopped hailing and they had missed the tornado's direct hit by a scant fifty yards. That was still close enough to make his ears pop and leave him with a suffocating sensation as the air flowed into the twister.

Hud had weathered dozens of violent storms. He'd barely missed being struck by lightning twice. However, having a twister descend in the middle of a hailstorm and being swallowed up in a flash flood was a new experience. He never wanted to repeat it. There was too much happening at once.

Swearing foully, Hud glanced every which way, trying to determine where Bri had gone down and where she might resurface—if she hadn't drowned already. The unsettling thought galvanized him into action. He waded toward the canyon wall to reach a place where the floodwaters weren't so swift and deep. Once he found solid footing—more or less—he released Rambler's reins so the horse could bound onto higher ground.

Hud became more anxious by the second. He saw nothing of Bri in the frothy water. If darkness descended before he located her, he feared she wouldn't survive. The thought rattled him to the extreme. He had accepted the possibility of his own death years ago. He'd dodged bullets, flying arrows, knives, bayonets and cannon-balls. Yet, the prospect of losing the commander's daughter, a woman so bewitching, vibrant and full of life, was unthinkable.

She had too much living left to do, he reminded himself. She had planned her grand adventure and Hud didn't want her dream of exploring the West to end in a flash flood. He didn't want to lose the woman who had slipped past his carefully guarded defenses and appealed to him in ways no other woman ever had. *Especially not* while he was still dealing with the guilt and grief of losing his childhood friend.

His thoughts scattered when he lost his footing and slid down the slick embankment to take another dunking in the icy water. Cursing, Hud scratched and clawed his way above water.

His knees slammed into an object that appeared to be jammed against a partially submerged tree stump. Hud thrust his arm into the swirling water and realized it was a body. Hurriedly he lifted Bri above the surface, praying frantically that she hadn't been underwater too long to recover. He tossed her lifeless body over his shoulder and shuffled through the water. Despite the slippery incline, he managed to crawl uphill on his hands and knees—but it wasn't easy.

Floodwater was still rushing through the gullies at an alarming speed, even after the rain slacked off and the storm shifted east. Hud sent a prayer of thanks winging heavenward as he huffed and puffed to reach level ground. He eased Bri facedown and shoved the heels of his hands against her ribs and shoulders. He wasn't sure if she was breathing on her own and he sure as hell wasn't going to waste time checking when every second could mean the difference between life and death.

Straddling her hips, he attempted to force water from her lungs. When she didn't respond he jackknifed her unresponsive body over his knee and whacked her between the shoulder blades repeatedly.

After what seemed an eternity, her body shuddered. Then she sputtered and gagged. Hud wanted to shout to high heaven when she gasped for breath and coughed her head off. Upended though she was, she braced her forearms on the muddy ground and raised her soggy head.

"Am I dead yet?" she rasped.

"You were, but you're better now… No, stay where you are," he ordered when she tried to rock back to her knees. "Keep coughing to expel water. You must've swallowed a couple of gallons of the nasty stuff."

She did as he instructed. After a few minutes of sputtering and wheezing, she breathed normally—to some extent at least. Hud hooked his arm around her waist and tugged her onto his lap. When she snuggled up against him and shivered, he breathed a gigantic sigh of relief.

"I suppose now that you've saved my life you're never going to let me hear the end of it," she croaked like a waterlogged bullfrog.

"Damn straight. Now what was that silly nonsense

about how you could make this trip solo?" he teased gently. "Admit it, you couldn't have survived without me."

"Obviously not… Hud…?"

"Yeah?" he murmured as he nuzzled his cheek against the side of her neck and rubbed his arms over her quivering body.

"I wouldn't have held you responsible if I had died," she assured him as she linked her arms around him and buried her head against his chest.

"But *I* would have."

And he would have. Maybe it wasn't his fault that flash floods, hailstones and a twister tested their abilities to survive. But if he hadn't decided to take this shortcut through one gully-riddled canyon after another, she wouldn't be forced to endure a difficult journey at a relentless pace. She wouldn't have been swept off her feet and washed away by the rushing water. Her ordeal was his fault. He'd been anxious to get her off his hands before temptation got the better of him and he did something they both might regret later.

Even now, after all they'd been through, hungry need tormented him. He held Bri close. Their wet clothes clung to their bodies like second skin. He could feel her luscious curves and swells meshed tightly to his body. He ached to touch her as familiarly as before. He wanted to yield to the maddening desire that had hounded him for days on end.

Before he became hopelessly sidetracked by the kind of forbidden need and churning emotion that could sweep him away like floodwaters, he set Bri to her feet then stood up beside her. She wobbled unsteadily so he slid a supporting arm around her.

"Let's find the cave and hope it remained above water level," he suggested.

She raked the wet mop of hair from her face and looked around. "Where are the horses?"

"Hell and gone most likely," he replied as he shepherded her along the rim of the caprock.

"I'm sorry. It's my fault we're on foot."

"Rambler will come back," he assured her. "With luck, your horse will follow mine. But the sorrel was pretty spooked the last time I saw him."

"Without saddlebags and bedrolls it will be a cold night and we'll have to go without supper," she reminded him.

He smiled crookedly. "Can't imagine how you could be hungry after you swallowed so much muddy water."

"I'm not. I was thinking of you," she murmured.

"This isn't the first meal I've missed."

He didn't add that his appetite had reached the point that it couldn't be satisfied with food. He wanted to peel off their wet clothing and make a feast of her. He'd come dangerously close to losing her and the urge to celebrate being alive by savoring every hour of pleasure the night had to offer nearly overwhelmed him.

He wondered what Bri would say if he told her that. Wisely, he kept his mouth shut and escorted her along the narrow trail.

Joe Jarvis swore foully when the ominous storm clouds rolled toward him. Thus far, he'd had no trouble following the two sets of hoofprints that led west. He knew the woman and the Ranger weren't too many hours ahead of him because he'd found their overnight campsite at noon. If they were in the path of the approaching storm, their tracks would be obliterated and he might have trouble trailing them.

"Damn the luck," Joe grumbled as he fished into his saddlebag to retrieve the food he'd stolen from the caravan.

He decided to tuck in and eat his meal before the storm hit. He unsaddled his horse and ducked beneath the outcropping of rock. And none too soon. Thunder rolled through the canyon and echoed around the eroded walls. The rain came down in sheets and the wind swirled and howled. Despite the overhang, Joe became drenched in nothing flat.

Swearing a blue streak, he huddled against the wall and waited out the storm. Remembering the whiskey bottle, he grabbed his saddlebag. While the wind roared and hail thudded around him, he drank heavily. Groggy, he slid down the wall and sprawled on the wet pebbles. As was his custom, he didn't fall asleep; he passed out.

Chapter Ten

Bri blinked in surprise when she spotted the two horses grazing on the spring grass covering the mesa of caprock above them. "There's a stroke of luck," she said. "We can change into dry clothing."

Hud flashed a scampish grin. "Damn, I already pictured you lounging naked in the cave while your clothes dried out."

A warm blush rose up her neck to stain her cheeks. Exhausted though she was, the suggestive remark had the power to incite her secret fantasy of an unhindered view of Hud's muscular physique. She had seen enough of him to arouse her feminine curiosity. But the prospect of being naked with him…

Stop that! she scolded herself.

Bri concentrated on listening to Hud call to Rambler. The midnight-colored gelding lifted his broad head and waited for Hud to approach. The sorrel kept his distance for a few moments, but he eventually followed Rambler when Hud led his horse back to Bri.

"Busy yourself with removing my bedroll and saddlebags," Hud instructed quietly. "I'll unsaddle Rambler and maybe your skittish mount will wander close enough for me to grab his reins."

Bri cooed softly to Rambler while she retrieved Hud's gear. When the sorrel finally ventured close enough Hud placed his foot on the trailing reins. He glanced between her and the horse and grinned rakishly.

She smirked as she ambled over to wrap her hand around the sorrel's bridle and give him a comforting pat on the neck. "If you were considering letting my horse run off again so I'd be without a change of clothing, it wouldn't have mattered. I would have commandeered *your* clothing and you would have been tramping around naked."

Hud shrugged lackadaisically. "It was an intriguing thought nonetheless." He removed his rifle from the sling to inspect it carefully. "Although our pistols are waterlogged the rifle should be all right."

"My pocket watch!" Bri yelped, startling the sorrel. She soothed the horse with one hand and dug into her pocket with the other. Her shoulders slumped in disappointment when she realized Benji's watch had stopped working. "Oh, damn."

The playful expression faded from Hud's rugged features. "I'll see what I can find to eat for supper," he commented while she brushed her thumb sentimentally over the pocket watch. "There should be some displaced game after the flood."

Bri tucked the watch in her pocket and glanced this way and that. "Where is this cave you boasted about?"

Hud wrapped Rambler's reins around a scrub bush then gestured for her to follow him. After she tethered the sorrel gelding, she grabbed her gear then followed

Hud down the narrow footpath that wrapped around the side of the bluff. She gaped in amazement when he ducked into a cave about the size of her hotel room in The Flat. To her astonishment, provisions had been stacked neatly in one corner.

"Speck and I used the cave last winter when a blue norther blew in and left us stranded for two days. We decided to leave behind dry firewood, a tinderbox and a quilt for any other Rangers who found themselves stranded while on patrol."

"Very considerate of you," she praised. "I can't wait to snuggle up to a warm fire and shed these wet clothes."

Hub ambled over to grab a few logs. "I'll start the—"

"I'll take care of it," she volunteered, anxious to have the privacy to strip from her wet clothes. She shooed him on his way. "Find food, great white hunter."

Her teasing smile faded when Hud strode over to brush her damp hair from her face. He inspected the bruise on her cheek. For a moment, she thought he was going to kiss her and she would have let him. It had become a daily ritual, after all. Instead, he brushed his thumb lightly over the bruise.

Bri gave way to impulse, flung her arms around his neck and kissed him full on the mouth. "Thanks for saving my life."

"Glad to help." He pressed a kiss to the tip of her nose before he backed away.

She noted that he wasn't as playful and responsive as he had been before she became distressed about her waterlogged pocket watch. She couldn't fathom why it bothered him so much that she wanted to preserve the keepsake.

When he exited, Bri stacked wood near the mouth of

the cavern to prevent smoke from forming a choking cloud inside. She was still recovering from a near drowning and she refused to inhale unnecessary smoke. In a few minutes, she had a small fire crackling. The welcome warmth made her smile in relief. Now if only she could find a place to wash away the mud that clung to her, she could sprawl on her pallet and recuperate.

Venturing onto the ledge that overlooked the craggy canyon, she surveyed the receding floodwaters. She smiled appreciatively when she noticed a hollowed out basin twenty feet below her. The rainwater had pooled and the sediment had settled to the bottom. It looked reasonably clear so she hiked downhill to peel off her grimy clothes.

After a quick bath, she washed her hair then rinsed out her clothes. She muttered at herself when she realized she had been in such a hurry to bathe that she had forgotten to bring clean clothes with her. She clamped the wet garments to her torso and climbed uphill to the cave.

"Bri? Where are you?"

Hud's concerned voice echoed around the stone walls and Bri flattened herself against the rock when Hud looked over the ledge.

"I found a place to bathe and wash my clothes," she called up to him. "Go away. I'm not dressed."

"Damn, another fantasy shot to hell," he said before he disappeared from sight.

Bri scampered up the trail but she stumbled to a halt when she entered the cave to see Hud cleaning the prairie chicken he'd snared. He didn't glance up—gentleman that he was—when she inched past him and backed modestly toward her satchels and saddlebags.

Then she wondered if she should be insulted that he

hadn't peeked, not even once. Although he teased her occasionally about his supposed fantasy, he hadn't tried to seduce her. In addition, the mention of Benji was enough to make him back away emotionally.

Come to think of it, she was usually the one who instigated kissing. The thought made her frown pensively.

"Hud, can I ask you something?"

"Sure. What is it?"

"If I was someone else besides who I am, would you be the least bit interested in me?"

She watched his hands stall as he prepared the meat for cooking, but he didn't glance over his shoulder at her.

"Someone besides my commander's daughter and the love of Benji's life, you mean?"

"Yes." She didn't correct Hud's erroneous assumption that she and Benji were more than the closest of friends and confidants. She simply stepped into a pair of dry breeches then shrugged on her shirt while he kept his back to her.

"Now that I know you, I'm surprised to hear you fishing for a compliment," he teased. "You aren't the shallow socialite I mistook you for before we met."

The comment pleased her enormously. "You aren't the mean-spirited Ranger who introduced himself to me at the first of the week, either. I'm finding several qualities I admire and respect about you."

He chuckled as he went back to his chore. "You're just feeling generous because I plucked you from a flash flood and revived you."

She noticed that he hadn't answered her direct question, which implied that he felt more responsibility than affection for her. The realization disappointed her.

"You're right. I'm not myself at the moment," she

said. "I'm not usually the sappy, sentimental sort. I spent too many years standing up to my mother's constant pressure and defying her attempts to mold me in her image."

Bri hunkered down beside Hud to take the knife from his hand. "Your turn to bathe and change, Captain Stone, I'll get the meat on to cook while you're gone."

He rose agilely to his feet. "Are you going to spy on me while I'm bathing, like you usually do?"

She grinned impishly at him. "Why break a perfectly enjoyable habit, I always say."

He doubled at the waist, his bronzed face level with hers. "Careful, Bri, we are playing with fire."

She stared into his amber eyes, lost to the flames reflecting from the campfire. "*We* are? Since you dodged my question, I assume the answer is no. You aren't interested."

"I didn't say that."

"Then what *are* you saying?"

He expelled an audible sigh. "We're alone in the middle of nowhere," he reminded her solemnly. "You are a beautiful woman, no doubt about that. My willpower will only stretch so far. Which is why I've been taking shortcuts through canyon country in an all-fired rush to reach camp so I can turn you over to your father in the same condition I found you."

She wondered if that was as close to an out-and-out compliment as she would receive from Hudson Stone. Impulsively, she reached up to limn his high cheekbones and trace the crow's feet at the corners of his eyes. "Tell me the truth, *for once*. Do you *like* me in the least? Or is it only that I'm female and convenient that poses a slight temptation for you?"

She wanted to whack him in the knees when he

smiled enigmatically and he rose to full stature. Then he pivoted on his heels and walked off without answering her question.

"Don't forget to take dry clothes with you," she reminded him. "Unless you want to walk back to the cave naked."

He reversed direction to rummage through his saddlebags. He didn't say a word until he stepped outside the cave. "I like you, Gabrielle Price," he admitted in what sounded like a begrudging tone. "If you weren't the commander's daughter and you weren't tied to a memory, things might be different."

A warm flood of pleasure cascaded over Bri and she grinned as she returned to her chore. Apparently, if she wanted Hud to overstep the boundaries he had established for himself, *she* would have to be the one to seduce him.

He was too blasted honorable.

Who would've thought she'd see that as a fault in a man?

For the first time in her life, Bri longed to cast aside her inhibitions and experiment with passion. If she had learned nothing else from Benji it was to live in the moment and to be satisfied with every scrap of good fortune. She didn't hold with her mother's philosophy of focusing on appearance and pedigrees and surrounding herself with prestige symbols. She wanted to live an adventure and face challenge.

She also wanted Hudson Stone in a way she had never wanted any other man. Having come within a hairbreadth of dying in the flash flood this afternoon drove home the point that tomorrow was uncertain and happiness was fleeting.

Frowning pensively, Bri skewered the meat and set it above the fire. Then she stood up to survey the cave. Tonight would be her first and last chance to take her fierce attraction to Hud to the most intimate level. They would arrive in the Ranger camp the next day. Their accommodations were a far cry from the luxurious hotel suites in Austin, but they would have to make do.

Bri decided, then and there, that she wanted to share one night of intimacy with Hud.

Hud sank into the improvised tub Bri had discovered and he scrubbed his arms and chest with soap. He glanced up at the ledge at regular intervals to see if she planned to interrupt his bath again. He was sorry to say that he was disappointed that her red-gold head didn't appear on the outcropping of rock and that she didn't flash him that mischievous smile that did funny things to his pulse and made him ache with lust.

He shouldn't have flirted with her earlier, he scolded himself. But at the time, he'd been trying to lighten the grim mood after she nearly drowned. In addition, he should have kept his trap shut and refused to admit he was attracted to her. But it had been impossible to continue dodging her question when he stared into those mesmerizing indigo eyes surrounded by a fringe of thick lashes. Impossible when he focused on those dewy lips and wanted to kiss her until he'd had his fill of her. Which would be *never* because every kiss they had shared thus far left him craving more, not less.

The arousing thought made Hud scowl. He was weak and vulnerable where Bri was concerned, he realized. Hand-to-hand combat against Indian raiders and bloodthirsty outlaws he could handle. Battling inclement weather was commonplace in his life. However, resisting a woman who would never be a part of his future, but couldn't be cast off as a meaningless one-night tryst, was tormenting the living hell out of him.

Plus, Hud wondered if the man Bri eventually took as her lover or husband would be a substitute for Benji, her adolescent sweetheart who had died protecting the expensive gift she presented to him. Hud hated to admit it, but it stung his pride when she became so upset about the damaged watch.

Hud sighed heavily, dunked his head in the water, then climbed from the pool to dress. He was going to march himself up to the cave, eat his supper and crawl into his bedroll—alone. First thing tomorrow, he'd escort Bri to her father. He might escape temptation by the skin of his teeth, but at least he'd escape without shaming Bri or outraging her father.

Resolved to keeping a respectable distance and giving Bri time to recover from her harrowing ordeal, Hud gathered his wet garments and strode uphill. The instant he ducked into the cavern, his jaw dropped open wide enough for a meadowlark to roost and he silently cursed the inviting scene that awaited him. He knew immediately what impossible temptation looked like— and this was it.

The campfire cast dancing shadows and flickering light around the cave. Bri had rolled out both pallets side by side in the back corner. She sat with her arms wrapped around her bent knees. Her curly hair tumbled over her bare shoulders and played hide-and-seek with the peaks of her breasts.

Hud couldn't draw breath. Seeing this forbidden

siren naked hit him like a rockslide. He staggered back a step and bumped his head on the outcropping of rock near the entrance of the cavern.

"If you're playing mischievous mind games with me, Bri, this isn't a damn bit amusing," he grumbled, massaging his temple.

She shook her head. The mass of reddish-gold curls skimmed over the full swells of her breasts. Hud nearly swallowed his tongue. Indeed, the fistful of clothing he carried with him dropped beside his feet before he realized he'd let go.

"I didn't ask for your escort service, Captain Stone," she said softly. "But I am asking for lessons in passion. Eaton didn't inspire me to experiment, but *you* do."

He wanted to ask if she had experimented with her beloved Benji, but he was having too much trouble stringing words together. He was all eyes and lusty anticipation, even though the voice of reason was shouting at him to turn around and run for his life before he crossed the line of no return.

While he stood frozen to the spot, battling his most formidable enemy—*himself*—she cocked her head slightly. He inwardly groaned when he caught a glimpse of her rosy nipple. Need delivered such a devastating blow that Hud felt like doubling over and howling in exasperated torment.

"Would the offer be more appealing if I *paid* for services rendered?" she asked.

"You don't want to do this, Bri," he said, startled that his voice sounded as if it had rusted.

Too much floodwater. Or too much exposed feminine flesh had choked him up. Hud was pretty sure it was the latter.

"I don't? As it happens, seducing you is exactly what I want to do. Unfortunately, you aren't very cooperative."

She leaned back, bracing herself up on her arms, exposing her creamy breasts to his devouring gaze. He could tell by her expression that it required considerable nerve to offer herself to him. She wasn't trying to tease and torment him. She was trying to prove to him that she wanted him.

Damn it! He wanted to be noble and sensible and turn her down for her own good, as well as for his own. And sure, he knew this had everything to do with her brush with death and a compelling desire to reaffirm life. But what hot-blooded man would reject a woman with Bri's beauty, intelligence and irrepressible spirit? She was every man's fantasy, after all.

She had been *his* secret fantasy since the night she stole into his room, kissed him senseless and left him craving more.

"Hud?"

Her voice quivered slightly as she gazed at him with growing uncertainty. Hud caved in because disappointing her was unacceptable. He walked toward her, never taking his eyes off her as he peeled off his shirt and then his breeches. He almost smiled when her gaze widened at the sight of him completely naked—and fully aroused.

Hud sank to his knees in front of her. He reached out to trail his forefinger around one pebbled nipple and then the other. He watched her lips part on a shuddering breath, saw her blue-violet eyes smolder with desire. Then he bent his head to flick his tongue against her nipple and suckled her gently.

"Sweet mercy," she rasped as she arched toward his kisses and caresses.

"Last chance," he whispered against her silky flesh. "Tell me to stop and I will. In a few more minutes you'll have to shoot me to get me to walk away from you."

"I might shoot you if you do," she murmured as she curled her arm around his neck to hold his head against her breasts. "Now, how much is this lesson in passion going to cost?"

"I don't work cheap," he teased as he took her nipple between thumb and forefinger to tug lightly, playfully.

"Wouldn't expect you to," she said on a ragged breath. "No strings, Hud. I want it all. I want everything you can teach me. I'm only asking for tonight…"

When she kissed him with the same hungry urgency that gnawed at him, he was ready to agree to any terms. If she wanted the moon in exchange for one night of learning her exquisite body by taste and touch, he'd find a way to get it for her.

Hud told himself repeatedly to take his time with Bri, to relish every wandering caress, each white-hot kiss. He even forgot his concern about becoming a substitute for Benji when desire seized control of his mind and body. All he knew was that he wanted to make a thorough study of her satiny skin and discover what pleasured her most.

He smiled in satisfaction when his lingering touch drew breathless gasps and husky moans from her lips. While she sat with her back against the wall, cushioned by his discarded shirt, he nudged her knees apart and propped himself between her legs. He delighted in watching her flush furiously. He wanted her to watch him touch her intimately, wanted to memorize every changing expression on her enchanting face, wanted to see the flare-up of need flashing in her blue-violet eyes while he pleasured her in every way imaginable.

Fascinated, he drew an invisible line from her lips, down her breastbone to her belly. When his forefinger trailed lower to sketch the soft flesh of her inner thighs, she sagged against the rock wall and closed her eyes on a ragged sigh.

"Look at me, Bri," he commanded as he rubbed his thumb over the moist bud between her legs.

Hud had never devoted so much time to seducing a woman. He'd eased basic needs...until now, with Bri. He craved all the passion she could offer him for as long as this secret moment lasted in this remote canyon in the middle of nowhere.

When her eyes fluttered open and her chest heaved on a shattered breath, he angled his head to flick his tongue against her softest flesh. He tasted her desire for him and the incredible intimacy between them made him burn with such feverish need that he shuddered uncontrollably.

"Hud," she gasped. "I—"

Her voice fizzled out when he stroked her with his thumb and eased his finger inside her, arousing her to the limits of her sanity. When he bent his head again, his gaze was still locked with hers as he tasted her. Bri felt immeasurable heat coiling tightly in her body. She ached to have him inside her as sensation upon insatiable sensation assailed her.

She struggled to draw breath as he stroked and suckled her intimately, destroying what little composure she had left. She came unraveled beneath his compelling kisses and caresses and she gasped when buffeted with the kind of erotic pleasure she never realized existed until Hud revealed to her a world of sensual ecstasy. Her responsive body quivered beneath his lips and fingertips and she knew that he knew how hot he made her burn with desire. When he cupped her hips in his hands and lifted her to him, Bri felt the first wave of rapturous spasms rippling through every fiber of her being.

Her breath broke as she clamped her hand around his wrist, anchoring herself against the bombardment of fiery sensations that turned her wrong side out. She dug her nails into his flesh and held on for dear life as he caressed her over and over until she swore she was going to die from the onslaught of overwhelming sensations. His name tumbled from her lips in a hoarse litany as exquisite pleasure pulsated through her. For the very first time in her life she knew what wild, maddening desperation and the blind rush of ardent passion felt like.

"Come here!" she panted urgently. "Hud…Please… Now!"

"You're sure?" he whispered against her heated flesh.

"Yes," she groaned mindlessly.

"If you insist…"

Hud couldn't name another moment in his life when anyone wanted him as frantically as Bri did. He smiled in masculine satisfaction as he rose to his knees and wrapped her slender legs around his hips. He pressed gently against her and became instantly aware that she hadn't been with another man. Knowing he was her first experiment with passion, he watched for the slightest sign that he hurt or frightened her. But she didn't recoil; she responded to him with reckless abandon.

When she curled upward to link her hands around his neck and slanted her lips over his, he forgot to proceed slowly. She kissed him until he couldn't think, only feel himself gliding into her moist heat. And then he was hopelessly and completely lost in rapturous oblivion. A firestorm of sensations blazed through his body, consuming him in the unbelievable passion they had ignited in each other.

He rocked urgently against her, unable to slow his frantic pace. He savored every heart-racing instant of ecstasy he shared with her. He could feel the mind-boggling crescendo building inside him, expanding until he shook with the intensity of it.

When Bri cried out his name, besieged by another climax, Hud drove into her, over and over again. His body throbbed in frantic rhythm with his thundering heart as passion seared him from inside out. He clutched her to him and surrendered to the inexpressible pleasure that sent him plummeting into an abyss of swirling sensations. He wondered if he'd ever find his way back—and didn't really care if he did.

Hud swore the flash flood, hailstorm and tornado they had endured earlier was no match for the devastation that racked his body and emotions. His strength and energy were zapped. Gasping for breath, he tucked his head against her shoulder and waited for his pulse rate to return to normal.

When he realized he was probably crushing her into the rock floor of the cavern, he propped himself on his forearms and peered down at her. Bri was giving him the strangest look and he couldn't begin to interpret it. It alarmed him. Had he hurt her? Was she instantly regretting her recklessness?

"You are very thorough, Captain," she murmured a moment later. "It was worth the price."

"You get what you pay for, Princess," he teased huskily.

He tried to gauge her mood, but that quick second of vulnerability he'd noticed a moment earlier vanished and he didn't understand what it meant. Then she flashed him that mischievous smile she wore so well. He really wanted to know what she was thinking and feeling, yet he didn't ask.

"I do believe your goose is cooked," she remarked.

"Prairie chicken," he corrected—and wondered if it truly was *his* goose she was referring to.

If so, she was right. He had given entirely too much of himself when instructing Bri through her first intimate encounter with passion. But damn if he didn't feel supremely pleased that he was the first man she had known, not Benji.

Hud couldn't say why, but he felt the overwhelming need to seal their erotic tryst with a kiss before he eased away to check on their supper. And so he kissed her with penetrating thoroughness then playfully nipped at her lips before he made himself get up, don his breeches and move away.

The prairie chicken, he noticed, looked singed on the outside, while *he* felt scorched clear through. Sharing Bri's passionate embrace left not a single nerve, muscle or emotion untouched and that rattled him to the extreme.

He glanced back at Bri after he removed the meat from the fire. "I'll be back in a minute, and then we'll eat."

He ambled outside to see that it was half past dark. In the wake of the ominous storm, the sky sparkled with stars. Wasting no time, he strode down to the pool for a refreshing dip. Yet, the bath didn't smother the smoldering flame still burning inside him. He had hoped that what had to be his one and only downfall into forbidden temptation with Bri had been appeased completely. Apparently not. Every time the vision of Bri arching instinctively toward him in the throes of reckless desire flashed across his mind's eye he became aroused all over again.

Hud stepped from the pool and sighed heavily. He predicted that surrendering to impossible passion was going to haunt him the rest of his days. Of course, if Commander Price found out about this, Hud wouldn't have all that many days left. He had committed the cardinal sin of betrayal and his commander would be out for his blood.

No doubt about it, he mused as he walked off, his days were definitely numbered. He had traded his unblemished record and his future for one incredible moment of ecstasy with Bri.

Hud smiled to himself and said, "It was worth it."

Chapter Eleven

When Hud returned to the cave, Bri brushed past him on her way out to freshen up. She wasn't sure what she expected to feel after the most intimately personal moment of her life. But the emotions and sensations were still so intense they alarmed her. She realized she was falling in love with Hud, despite her good judgment, in spite of her dream of following her adventurous heart and exploring the frontier.

"What are you worried about?" she mumbled to herself as she plunked into the pool. "Hud isn't interested in commitment and you told him you wanted no strings. You lived in the moment and discovered you like passion. A lot. With him."

Idiot that she was, she found herself wondering if she measured up to the other women who had come and gone from his bed. Well, it didn't matter, she convinced herself. She was living in the moment, taking pleasure where she found it. Certainly, Hudson Stone was an honorable man who wouldn't boast about his conquest so she wasn't afraid he'd embarrass her at the Ranger camp. Besides, *she'd* made the decision to seduce him and she'd initiated the tryst. *She* had conquered *him.*

Bri splashed water on her face when she blushed profusely, remembering the amazing intimacy between them. By damned, she was not going to face him, acting awkward and self-conscious. She might *feel* awkward and self-conscious but she didn't want him to know it. Hadn't she managed to cover up that revelation the moment she acknowledged she'd fallen in love with Hud? She'd recovered in time to toss out a teasing remark about paying for lessons learned. She could pretend to be as nonchalant and self-assured as Hud if she put her mind to it.

Resolved to remaining nonchalant in his presence, she donned her clothes and returned to the cavern. Hud was sitting cross-legged by the fire, waiting to dine with her. She murmured her thanks when he offered her the tender meat and she ate hungrily. Apparently, passionate lovemaking stimulated all sorts of appetites, she mused.

"How much longer before we reach your camp?" she asked between bites. Small talk would conceal any uncomfortable feelings of embarrassment, she assured herself. She had honed the skill in ballrooms from Austin to Houston.

"About four hours. We're camped on Angel Mesa. From there, you can see for miles in every direction."

"Are there interesting landmarks to view along the way?"

Hud shrugged a broad shoulder, and then mentioned a few rock formations and creeks that provided spectacular scenery.

"How often does your battalion break camp and change locations?" she asked interestedly.

"Depends on the amount of criminal activity in the area. We've been camped on Angel Mesa for six months. Several bands of Mexican banditos and white outlaws are roaming the area, preying on thousands of head of cattle driven to Dodge City. Occasionally, thieves strike army supply wagons and stagecoaches headed to New Mexico. We've also investigated thefts against ranchers and sheepherders."

"You have a lot of territory to cover with only a few men," she remarked then took a swig of water from the canteen.

"Minus one good man," Hud murmured somberly.

"I suppose you'll be teamed up with someone else now."

He nodded his raven head. "I've never worked with anyone else. It will take some getting used to."

For certain, Hud faced not only guilt and grief from the recent loss of his best friend, but he'd also require a period of adjustment while working with someone else. He had been comfortable with Speck. Now he had to accept the ways and the habits of another man.

Hud glanced at her. A wry smile quirked his lips. "Is all this chitchat your way of pretending what happened between us didn't happen?"

The perceptive question took her aback momentarily, but she recovered quickly and displayed what she hoped was a casual smile. "I am very much aware of what happened. I enjoyed it thoroughly and I'm not in denial. Are you?"

"I know your emotions were in upheaval after your near-death experience in the flood."

"You do?" His attempt to tell her how she felt and

what she thought while she was doing her best to appear detached aggravated her.

He bobbed his head. "Yes, I do. Sometimes people do things in a reckless moment they regret later."

"You speak from personal experience?"

"After a difficult foray against lopsided odds, I have on occasion cast caution to the wind," he admitted.

She was the most recent occasion, she presumed. Bri stared at him, not knowing what she wanted from him. Was it for him to say he loved her, too? Maybe so. But she knew he didn't and she'd be crushed if he tried to lie to her.

Ultimately, what she wanted to hear was that *he* couldn't resist her any easier than she could resist him, even if he felt nothing more than lust and physical attraction.

She decided to test her theory, here and now. This night was far from over and she yearned to become as familiar with Hud's incredibly masculine body as he was with hers. She wanted him to understand how it felt to be so desperate that need obliterated all other thoughts and emotions.

What she lacked in experience, she vowed to compensate with creative ingenuity because her feminine pride demanded that he remember her in the years to come. She was definitely going to remember him and she couldn't bear the thought of being one of those occasions when he recklessly cast caution to the wind, then couldn't remember her name a month later.

Playing with fire, he'd said. Indeed. They would see how hot passion burned when you struck a match to it. Keeping that in mind, Bri removed her blouse and reminded herself that she shouldn't be embarrassed because it was too late for modesty.

"What are you doing?" Hud croaked, frog-eyed.

"Conducting an experiment."

She swallowed a chuckle when he stared at her breasts, her face, then her breasts again. His eyes turned a darker shade of gold. When she leaned forward to unbutton his shirt, he glanced warily at her.

"Bri—" he choked out, gaping wide-eyed at her.

She tossed his shirt toward his saddlebags then kissed him into silence. Rising, she clutched his hand and led him to the pallet. She noticed he didn't put up much of a fight. However, he did try to forestall her when she reached down to unfasten the placket on his buckskin breeches. Not to be deterred, she moved his hands out of her way.

"This is not a good idea," he rasped as she pushed his breeches over his hips and left them pooling around his feet.

She was pleased to note that he was already aroused. "No? Why not?"

"Because I—"

His voice dried up when she curled her fingers around his erection then glided her hand from base to tip. Steel sheathed in satin, she thought as she caressed him. Fascinated by the rumbling purr she drew from him, she stroked him repeatedly.

She urged him to the pallet then directed him to prop his back against the wall, the same way he had done when he worked his phenomenal magic on her body. Still holding his pulsating flesh in her hands, she knelt beside him to trail a row of featherlight kisses from his lips to his chin and down his muscular chest.

His hand slid around her neck to bring her head back to his devouring kiss. He brushed his fingers over the rigid crest of her breasts, making her burn with pleasure. But she was determined not to become sidetracked. This time she would know him by sight, by taste, by touch and by heart.

She broke the scalding kiss and angled her head to brush her lips over the dark furring of hair that descended over his washboarded belly to his abdomen. Hud growled hoarsely and wrapped his hand around her hair like a rope to bring her head back to his.

"I can't take much more of this erotic torment," he rasped against her lips.

"Don't sell yourself short." She smiled impishly as she stroked his throbbing length. "That would be inaccurate. A big strong Ranger captain like you? You *can* endure. *Challenge* yourself."

She pulled her long hair from his hand and leaned down to take him into her mouth. Hearing his ragged groan of pleasure wasn't enough to satisfy her. She wanted to watch him surrender to her intimate touch as helplessly as she had surrendered to him.

Bri nudged his muscled legs apart then she looked up to see that he was watching her suckle him. His long-lashed eyes glowed like molten lava. His jaw clenched, as if he was battling for hard-won control and he was on the brink of losing the fight. She flicked her tongue at him and heard his breath rush out on a hiss. She saw his chest expand then shudder and she reveled in the power she held over him.

"You're killing me," he whispered raggedly. "Aw… damn…"

His voice trailed off when Bri nipped at him with her teeth. She delighted in hearing the growls of pleasure that tumbled from his lips each time she stroked him provocatively with her hand, her lips and her tongue.

When a silvery drop of need escaped his control, she caressed her way up the masculine contours of his body to offer him a taste of his desire for her in a scorching kiss. Suddenly she found herself flat on her back while Hud hovered over her like a powerful mountain lion pinning down its prey.

"I've reached my limit," he rumbled as he peeled off her breeches then nudged her legs apart with his knees. "What is it that you want to hear, temptress? That I can't resist you, no matter how hard I try? Is that what your experiment is all about?" He pressed intimately against her, filling her with his throbbing length. "You're right. I can't resist you, Bri. You utterly defeat me because I can't see past my obsessive need for you."

Bri realized that was what she longed to hear. She needed to know that he couldn't resist this ardent passion that billowed between them any better than she could. She needed to know that she could make him want her to the same maddeningly desperate degree that she had ached for him earlier that evening. For her, the feelings and sensations transcended mindless lust, even if that's all she had wanted in the beginning. Now it delved deeper and burned brighter than any emotion she'd ever experienced.

Yet, she couldn't bring herself to make demands on Hud. She had to be satisfied with his compelling passion for her and to expect nothing more. At least he acknowledged that they were drawn inexplicably together by the kind of desire that defied their fierce will.

"I want you like hell blazing, Bri," he whispered as he moved urgently inside her.

"I want you the same way." She looped her arms around his neck and matched him thrust for penetrating thrust.

The world went completely out of focus as they moved in frantic rhythm, chasing the erotic sensations that built one upon the other until intense pleasure burst like a shooting star that scattered flames across the night sky. Hud couldn't breathe, couldn't think. All that mattered was that he had become a living breathing part of her as they held on to each other, spiraling through vibrant sensations that left him spinning helplessly out of control.

The dizzying freefall of ecstasy depleted every ounce of his strength. He shuddered then collapsed beside her on the pallet, exhausted but completely sated.

"No more experiments," he whispered breathlessly against her ear. "That one damn near did me in."

She smiled drowsily as she cuddled up against his laboring chest. "Whatever you say, Captain Ranger."

"Whatever *I* say?" he murmured, and realized that he could speak freely now because she had faded off to sleep. "I lost control of the situation when I stepped into this cavern after my first bath. I've been battling this tormenting conflict of wanting you when I know I can't keep you since the day I met you. Now look what's happened."

So much for the higher standard he'd set for himself, he thought with a self-deprecating snort. He'd shot it all to hell. He eased away, cursing his insatiable weakness for her all the while. Then he picked up his pallet and moved it to the far side of the cave so he'd keep his hands off her luscious body. She needed uninterrupted sleep and she wouldn't get it if he remained within touching distance.

It shook him to the core that he'd allowed her to

touch him in the most intimate ways imaginable—in ways he'd never permitted another woman to know him. She'd made him lose complete control—and not even care. She had shredded his willpower as if it never existed and assured him that his noble restraint was nowhere near as invincible as he previously thought.

The moment she'd placed her hands on his body, he'd melted like lard in a hot skillet. He'd become a willing slave to the kind of obsessive passion he'd never experienced.

Now there was a tidbit of information he could have done without, he mused as he spread out his pallet. Even if he had never known such incredible pleasure, he *did* know their wild forbidden tryst began and ended this evening within the shadowy confines of this cavern in the middle of nowhere. That's where the memory of this erotic interlude had to remain, too, he reminded himself as he tiptoed outside to check on the horses and clean his waterlogged pistols.

When something cold and wet nudged his cheek, Joe Jarvis groaned groggily. He pried open one blood-shot eye to see his horse standing over him. Joe yawned broadly and scratched his aching belly. He'd ridden out the violent storm in a drunken stupor and the sun was still hours away from rising.

Levering himself up on one elbow, he stared into the darkness. He tried to remember the last time he'd been awake this early. Never, he decided. This was usually the time he staggered to bed and collapsed after a bout with whiskey.

Ray Novak, the rancher who'd hired him and Pete, had ordered him to drag himself up at sunrise to steal cattle from his neighbors. But Joe preferred to prowl the darkness, drink his fill and sleep until noon.

Today he had good reason to get up and get moving. As soon as he captured that female who was worth a double ransom, he could head to Montana or Idaho or wherever he wanted with a fortune stuffed in his saddlebags.

The thought prompted Joe to climb to his feet. His head throbbed but he grabbed the reins and led his horse from the makeshift shelter. All he needed was a drink to get his juices flowing.

"Hell," he muttered when he realized he'd finished off his last bottle of whiskey.

Well, he could buy all the liquor he wanted if he succeeded in snatching up that female who couldn't be more than a few hours ahead of him.

This time he was going to have some fun with that woman who had sharply rejected him that night in the hall of the hotel. She wouldn't deny him this time, he promised himself.

Bri awakened shortly after dawn to see that Hud had moved his pallet a noticeable distance away from her. The implication of the wide space he had placed between them stung her pride. He might as well have come right out and announced that once the passion between them fizzled out it was back to business as usual. Any sentimental attachment he felt for her lasted no longer than their reckless trysts.

Well, two could play that game, she mused as she dug into her satchel to retrieve several large bank notes. While Hud slept soundly, she walked over to place the money on his chest. She had paid him in full for his lessons in passion. If that insulted him as much as the implication of the distance he had placed between them insulted her, then all the better.

Satchels in hand, Bri exited the cave to bathe. She descended the slope to take a chilly dip in the make-shift pool then donned her clothes. Since Hud still hadn't exited from the cave, Bri decided to check on the horses.

Bri saddled the sorrel gelding and led him across the grass-covered mesa. She noticed the clump of willow and cottonwood trees that overlooked another scenic canyon. She decided to gather up some tree limbs to leave behind in the cavern for the next hapless travelers who needed to make use of the shelter.

She ambled into the underbrush that encircled the buffalo wallow to pick up branches. She tensed appre-hensively when she saw a horse tied to a tree on the far side of the hollowed-out basin that stood full of water after the downpour. Whoever owned the mount was around here somewhere and he could dash through the shallow water to attack her. Hurriedly, Bri turned back to her horse, hoping to retrieve from her satchel the pistol Hud had given to her. She froze to the spot when a familiar face, embedded with slate-gray eyes and sur-rounded by straggly hair, rose like a demon from the scrub bushes. To her dismay, she didn't have time to grab the handgun before she found herself staring at the speaking end of the outlaw's six-shooter.

She shifted her gaze to the left, trying to calculate her chances of diving for cover before Mad Joe Jarvis, who had gunned down Speck Horton in cold blood, shot her, too. Damn it, how did he know where to find her? And where, she'd like to know, was his sidekick? She looked around discreetly, wondering if Pete Spaulding had a pistol trained on her, also.

"Don't try it, lady," Jarvis growled menacingly.

Bri thought it over and decided she *would* try to escape. If nothing else, the discharging pistol would alert Hud that unwanted company had arrived. Even better if Hud confronted the man he'd been chasing all over creation, here and now.

When she launched herself toward the bushes and rolled sideways, she expected to hear a gunshot. To her frustration, Jarvis didn't fire at her. Instead, he pounced from the underbrush and raised his arm to strike her. Bri shoved the heel of her hand into his chin, then kicked with her legs, knocking Jarvis off balance.

He landed with a thud and spouted the foulest curse she'd ever heard. Then he hurled himself on top of her before she could crawl to her hands and knees. Bri chastised herself for leaving her dagger in her satchel after bathing the previous evening. The one time she had ignored her rule of carrying a concealed weapon had come back to haunt her. All she had for protection was her wits. Considering his strength and violent temperament, she would have preferred to be holding a loaded pistol and a very large, very sharp knife.

When Jarvis backhanded her, her head whiplashed and her senses reeled. By the time she could think straight again, he'd shoved the barrel of his six-shooter between her eyes and smiled victoriously, displaying his discolored teeth.

"Good to know that you learned how to fight back, hellion. Yer daddy must've taught you," he sneered at her. "I'll remember that."

Icy dread slithered down her spine. This ruthless

desperado knew who she was. That was not a good thing. He looked entirely too pleased with himself for capturing her. If she didn't escape immediately, she'd be in serious trouble.

Knowing that, Bri shoved the barrel of his pistol away from her face abruptly and simultaneously jerked up her leg. She kicked Jarvis in the side of the head then slammed her boot heel into his ribs. When he yelped and swayed sideways, momentarily dazed by the blow, she rolled away and scrambled onto her hands and knees.

But she didn't get far before she heard his enraged snarl fill the air. He leveled a hard blow to the back of her head with the butt of his pistol. Pain exploded through her skull. Nonetheless, she crawled forward, hoping to startle her horse and send it trotting back to Rambler.

Her attempt to alert Hud was a wasted effort. Jarvis delivered another brain-scrambling blow to her head. She collapsed facedown in the water that filled the buffalo wallow. The last thing she remembered was the sound of wicked laughter accompanying her into the wet, swirling darkness.

Chapter Twelve

Hud sighed heavily as he rolled to his side on the pallet. He opened his eyes to see blinding light slanting into the mouth of the cavern. Scrubbing his hand over his face, he bemoaned the hours he'd lain awake in the middle of the night, trying to convince himself not to disturb Bri's sleep, even if depriving himself had tormented him beyond measure.

He levered onto his elbow to glance toward the corner where he'd left Bri sleeping peacefully. He wasn't alarmed when he noticed her empty pallet. No doubt, she'd awakened and had walked down to the pool to bathe. Rising, he plucked up his shirt then shrugged it on. He walked outside to retrieve the leather vest he had draped over a scrub bush to dry out.

When he looked over the ledge, he didn't see Bri at the pool. "Where the hell is that woman?" he asked himself.

He strode around the corner of the rock wall to see that she had taken the sorrel gelding. Frowning, Hud retraced his footsteps to the cave. The first thing he saw was the bank notes that were tangled in his bedroll. He scowled as he scooped them up. When he remembered Bri saying that she'd pay him for services rendered, he scowled again.

The next thing he noticed was that her satchels were missing. He swore furiously when he recalled that she had asked him about the location of Ranger camp, the length of time to reach it and identifying landmarks along the way.

"Damn her ornery hide!" he roared. His voice echoed around the cave and bombarded him from everywhere at once.

Bri hadn't made idle chitchat; she'd been getting directions so she could leave without him! Stomping mad, Hud jerked up the two bedrolls and grabbed his gear. That infuriating female must have decided to make him look bad by arriving in camp ahead of him. When he caught up with her this time he *would* strangle her for this stunt.

Even if she was capable of taking reasonably good care of herself, this was no Sunday stroll in the park. If she encountered trouble, he'd never forgive her and Winston Price would not only have Hud plugged full of holes, but his head would also be roasting on a spit over a blazing campfire.

Hud's footsteps stalled when another thought occurred to him. Maybe she had been too ashamed to face him in broad daylight after their two wildly intimate encounters. Or perhaps leaving money behind and sneaking off without him was her way of assuring him that she had no expectations or any real sentiment for him. She had been quick to insist that their trysts came with no strings attached, he reminded himself. Although he knew damn well that was for the best, it still stung his pride that she dismissed him so easily.

Mumbling oaths to the tormenting vision hovering above him, he saddled Rambler then stared into the distance. Even though he should be greatly relieved that Bri didn't appear to be a clingy, sentimental female it still annoyed him that he felt the same way he had as a child—discarded and rejected and left behind as if he was unworthy of affection.

He kept reminding himself that Gabrielle Price was considered royalty in the eyes of the elite family hierarchy of Texas. He, on the other hand, was just an unwanted kid from the backstreets who'd gained respect and recognition because he'd learned how to fight with every weapon he could lay his hands on.

Hell, he knew he was a worse mismatch for Bri than that haughty politician. But she still didn't have to toss money at him then trot on her merry way.

Growling in frustration—and not knowing how much of a head start Bri had on him—Hud cantered Rambler westward. He kept expecting to spot Bri in the distance, but winding canyons and deep ravines hindered his view. Damnation, she might've become lost in the labyrinth of chasms and gullies. Roving bandits might've overtaken her.

It's what she deserved, of course, but even his spiteful anger couldn't override his concern for her welfare.

"This is the second time you've left me behind," Hud muttered at the beguiling image floating in his mind.

He'd fretted about Bri's whereabouts and safety when he thought she'd been kidnapped from The Flat. If she didn't stop riding off without him, he'd *tie* her to her horse and bid her a hearty good riddance when he delivered her to her father.

How was it possible, he wondered, that he could

become so completely lost in that spirited woman one moment and so eager to choke the life out of her the next?

"Damn good thing you have more sense than to fall in love with that firebrand," he congratulated himself. "She has too much independent spirit for any man to handle. Hats off to any fool who tries! Not me, of course, but some other fool!"

Two hours later, Hud frowned warily when he saw four riders approaching from the west. His apprehension doubled when he recognized Commander Price, Major Ketter and two fellow Rangers—Marcus Yeager and Floyd Lambert.

"Where the devil is Gabrielle?" Price demanded without preamble. "Didn't she make the journey from Austin?"

"You haven't crossed paths with her this morning?" Hud questioned the question.

The commander's brows swooped down in a sharp *V.* "What are you talking about? She's *supposed* to be with you. I expected you yesterday afternoon. We became concerned and came looking for you. Did you get caught in the storm?"

"Yes." Hud glanced every which way, trying to figure out how he and the Ranger scout patrol could've missed Bri. The only explanation that came to mind spelled trouble. Damn it, where was she?

"Well, *what?*" Commander Price barked sharply. "Confound it, Hud, what happened?"

"We were caught in a flash flood and I rescued her from high water—"

"Dear God!" Price howled in dismay.

"But we found shelter in the cave where Speck and I weathered the blizzard last winter." Now for the difficult part, thought Hud. He was going to look like every kind of fool when he finished his explanation. "When I woke up this morning Bri was gone."

"Bri?" Price's face scrunched up in a disapproving frown.

Hud shifted awkwardly in the saddle. "She insisted that I call her Bri rather than Mizz Price," he said hastily. "I assumed that she walked down to the pool to bathe before we rode off this morning. Naturally, I didn't want to disturb her and I kept waiting for her to return to the cave."

Hud noticed that Ketter and the other two Rangers were biting back grins. They were probably thanking their lucky stars that they hadn't been sent to escort the commander's daughter and somehow misplaced her. Hell's bells, Hud didn't have a single blemish on his service record—until now. Gabrielle Price had turned his world on its ear and made him look like a bungling tool.

"After I gathered our gear and walked uphill to saddle the horses I found her sorrel gelding gone." Hud inwardly winced when the commander glared murderously at him. "I don't have to tell you how strong-minded and independent your daughter is, sir."

"No, you don't. But thank you so much for bringing it to my attention," Price growled sarcastically.

"She kept insisting for two days that she could reach the camp without my assistance. When I described the man who killed Speck, she realized she had seen him in The Flat. She encouraged me to reverse direction and track him down. I thought maybe she left without me this morning, hoping I'd go looking for Mad Joe Jarvis."

"We didn't cross paths with Bri," Price muttered as

he twisted in the saddle to scan the canyons that dropped off the wide mesa to the north.

"As for Mad Joe Jarvis, word came down the pike that he was killed by the same marauding Indians who tried to attack a theater caravan," Major Ketter reported.

Hud jerked upright. "Jarvis is dead? Who verified it?"

"Lieutenant Davis from Fort Griffin. He said he encountered Pete Spaulding while he was escorting the theater troupe north."

"Pete Spaulding!" Hud howled. "That's Joe's cohort."

"So I've been told," Price remarked. "But the army lieutenant wasn't aware of that. He didn't know until after the fact that the men were on the Rangers' Most Wanted list. He was simply relaying information about the raiding party to the two Ranger scouts he encountered when he turned the caravan over to the military escort from Fort Elliot. Davis and his men spotted another raiding party and decided to drive them north to the state border."

Hud's head was spinning like a windmill. Joe Jarvis was dead? The manhunt to avenge Speck's senseless murder was over? Lieutenant Davis was chasing Comanche renegades so he hadn't delivered the message to Marshal Long that Bri had been found?

"Where was Pete Spaulding headed?" Hud wanted to know. "We still need to apprehend him and question him about the extent of his involvement in Speck's death."

"Lieutenant Davis said Spaulding spent the night with the caravan then headed west," Major Ketter reported.

"Did Davis give a description of Spaulding?" Hud asked.

"No, I'm afraid not," Ketter replied. "The Rangers I

talked to two days ago were simply glad that one of their own men had been avenged, even if Indian raiders delivered the death blow."

Commander Price waved his arms in expansive gestures. "I don't wish to sound insensitive about the loss of your close friend and compatriot, Stone. But my immediate concern is locating Bri."

"We didn't notice the tracks of any riders," Major Ketter declared. "Do you think Mizz Price might have simply drifted off course?"

Hud shook his head. "She asked me about interesting landmarks between here and Angel Mesa. I mentioned the sandstone Alter of the Gods and the Trio of Comanche Spires." He swiveled in the saddle to glance back in the direction he had come. "I pushed Rambler to the limits, hoping to overtake Bri. I can't imagine how I could have overlooked her."

"Why not?" Price snorted caustically. "You managed to lose her first thing this morning, didn't you?"

This is what happens when you let a beguiling, spirited, infuriating woman distract you, Hud reminded himself sourly. He looked the fool because he'd behaved like a fool. He had no excuse except that he'd allowed fierce physical attraction to overshadow his common sense. If Commander Price didn't dishonorably discharge him on the spot, he'd be surprised.

Despite Price's disdainful glare, Hud reversed direction and trotted east. Unease settled over him with each passing minute. Hud was greatly troubled to learn that Pete Spaulding had crossed paths with the theater troupe and had ridden west. The outlaw might have figured out that Bri had been traveling with the troupe. Hell, the boys might have unwittingly alerted him that Bri had joined the caravan. If she was right in speculating that the two thugs trashed her room…

Another eerie sensation skittered down Hud's spine. He had *presumed* Bri had left him behind, either because she felt self-conscious about facing him the morning after or because she'd wanted to play a mischievous trick on him. While *he* was feeling rejected, insulted and outraged someone might have abducted *her*.

Damn it to hell, he hadn't bothered to check for suspicious tracks in the area. No, he'd been too sensitive and too emotionally involved to react rationally. He'd simply assumed that she'd performed a vanishing act and he'd charged off to overtake her before she reached camp alone and made him look like the incompetent idiot he was turning out to be.

And it's no one's fault but my own, he reminded himself harshly. *I wasn't there to guard Speck's back, and now Bri might be in terrible danger, too.*

The tormenting thought urged Hud to nudge Rambler in the flanks, while the other men fell in line behind him. I'm going to find Bri, he vowed resolutely. And she had better not be in the same condition I found Speck.

He couldn't bear to lose them both in the same month. That was more anguish than he could tolerate.

Bri regained consciousness to find herself draped over her horse. Her hands were bound around the sorrel's neck and her feet were lashed to the stirrups. Her splitting headache throbbed in rhythm with her pulse and made her nauseous. Worse, Joe Jarvis was leading her horse east, not west.

Without alerting Jarvis that she had roused, Bri surveyed her surroundings discreetly. She had no clue where Jarvis was taking her, but he wasn't following the same path Hud had used. Hud knew the shortcuts through canyon country like the back of his hand, but Jarvis was avoiding the deep canyons—which took more time.

Bri berated herself for being caught by this murdering bastard. Ordinarily she paid close attention to her surroundings. This morning she had been wrestling with myriad emotions and conflicting feelings toward Hud. She had been hopelessly distracted and preoccupied.

Now it didn't matter that Hud had moved his pallet as far away from her as he could get or that her affection for him was one-sided. She had fallen into the hands of a known killer and her future—or lack thereof—was grim.

When Jarvis glanced over to check on her, Bri kept her head down so he couldn't see her eyes. He huffed out an agitated breath then veered north. Thirty minutes later Bri noticed the adobe ranch house that served as a stagecoach station. The sign over the door boasted a small general store alongside the café to feed passengers. A large barn, surrounded with corrals, sat a short distance away. The pens were filled with horses, sheep and a few head of cattle.

Bri presumed Jarvis planned to parallel the east-west stage route that followed the Mountain Fork of the Brazos River. He might be planning to stock up on supplies at one of the station houses along the way to wherever the blazes he was taking her.

When Jarvis halted in a clump of cottonwood trees near the river and tied up her sorrel, she remained perfectly still. Since she was hanging over her horse like a rag doll, he didn't pay much attention to her. Leaving her behind, Jarvis trotted his horse toward the squatty stage station.

Bri sprang into action the instant Jarvis was out of sight. She stretched out as far as she could, hoping to unhook her bound arms from the horse's neck. The contrary mount tossed his head, making it difficult for her to get loose. Finally, she managed to get him to hold his head down long enough for her to raise her arms. Even though her hands were tied in front of her, she managed to unwrap the reins that Jarvis secured to a tree branch.

Casting apprehensive glances at the station, she tried to untie her bound wrists with her teeth. She had to abort the attempt when Jarvis sauntered from the station, carrying two bottles of whiskey, hardtack and canned food.

Gouging her horse, Bri thundered away from the concealment of the winding river channel and commenced screaming at the top of her lungs as she blazed past the stagecoach station. Her cry for help startled the sheep and cattle. She hoped the choir of alarmed livestock didn't drown her out completely. She held the hope that the stationmaster would become concerned and notify the guard and driver on the next incoming stage.

Anything to call attention to her plight and encourage someone to search for her!

Bri grunted uncomfortably when the sorrel jumped a ditch while she was looking over her shoulder, watching Jarvis clamber onto his horse. Hot-tempered and ruthless as he was, he began firing his six-shooter at her immediately. Bri reined her horse back to the river, hoping to use saplings and underbrush as protection from the rapid-fire gunshots.

Although she didn't know how far she was from The Flat and the soldiers stationed at Fort Griffin, she decided that riding east was her best bet. At least now she could see the rutted trail that coaches and wagons used to cross the High Plains. If she headed west, she might become lost in the labyrinth of canyons.

"Come back here," Jarvis bellowed then punctuated his demand by blasting away at her with his rifle.

Bri didn't look back to calculate how much head start she had on that scraggly-haired brute. She concentrated on guiding her horse down the muddy slope of the riverbank and crossing at a shallow point so Jarvis couldn't follow her tracks easily. She needed to buy some time so she could stop to work loose the knotted ropes around her wrists and ankles.

She gasped in alarm when the sorrel slipped sideways in the mud as he came ashore downstream. Fortunately, he didn't lose his footing completely and fall on top of her. The sorrel couldn't eject her from the saddle because her feet were anchored to the stirrups, she reminded herself. As the horse floundered, Bri shifted her weight in the saddle and encouraged him to lunge up the steep slope to reach level ground.

She spared a glance over her shoulder before she urged the gelding into his fastest gait. She was relieved that she saw nothing of Jarvis for the next few minutes. She'd be delighted to no end if he slipped in the mud, banged his greasy head against a tree trunk and knocked himself out. With any luck, he'd pitch sideways and drown in midstream, too.

"Damn the luck," she mumbled when she saw a flash of color among the trees that skirted the river. Jarvis had picked up the tracks where her horse had faltered and now he was firing wildly at her again. The furious criminal showed no signs of abandoning the chase.

Bri doubted her sorrel could keep the frantic pace all

the way to the next stage station so she veered back to the river channel to let the gelding catch his breath. Her skull throbbed painfully, compliments of the two blows Jarvis had delivered to the back of her head. However, she had no time to rest because Jarvis was hot on her heels.

"This is where we camped last night after the storm." Hud directed his four companions' attention to the winding path that led to the cave. "There should be tracks around here to tell us something about Bri's disappearance."

"They already have told us something." Winston Price flashed Hud the evil eye. "You were careless."

No matter how many snide remarks Winston hurled at him, Hud couldn't have felt worse than he did already. He'd broken two of his hard-and-fast rules—never presume anything and never become emotionally involved in an assignment.

While Marc and Floyd combed the area, looking for clues, Winston rode his horse alongside Hud's. "I trust that you remembered that Bri is my daughter and that she is an engaged woman," he said with a pointed stare.

"I assure you, Commander, I am very aware of who she is."

Nevertheless, it hadn't stopped him from yielding to forbidden temptation, but he'd never forgotten. Except during two encounters with incredible ecstasy when he couldn't think past his wild desperation for Bri.

"However, you need to know that Bri called off her engagement after she walked in on Powell, who was in bed with an actress from the theater troupe."

Winston gaped at him then muttered a foul oath to Powell's name. Hud silently seconded it.

"There are other complications I didn't mention in front of everyone else," Hud explained solemnly. "Also, Bri rescued three young boys from the back alleys—"

"Not that again," Winston groaned. "I suppose it's because I disapproved of her odd friendship with that urchin in Houston. She wanted to bring him home and hire him to work on the estate, but her mother pitched a conniption fit and, for once, I sided with Anna."

That pretty much said what Winston and Anna Price would think of Hud if they knew his background. Not that he'd dare to express an interest in Bri. Hell, he'd tried not to like her, impossible as that turned out to be. But Hud was sensible enough to know he had no future with Bri. Her family wouldn't approve of him any more than Benji Dunlop.

"Bri gathered up the boys and rode off with the theater group. She arranged with the owners to give the youngsters a new start. However, she didn't consult me first," Hud added.

Winston frowned, puzzled. "Why the devil not? You were sent to escort her to me."

Hud shifted uneasily in the saddle. "I made it perfectly clear at our first meeting that I thought this was a foolhardy cross-country trip and that my services could be put to better use on the manhunt."

Hud expected the commander to rant and rave furiously. Instead, he blew out his breath. "You never challenge Bri. She can't resist a dare, Captain. You might as well have waved a red flag in her face."

"I found that out the hard way," Hud mumbled. "But most disturbing of all is that when Bri left the evening before I planned to escort her to camp, someone ransacked her room."

"Good God!" Winston hooted, owl-eyed. "What do you think they wanted with Bri?"

"We can only speculate. But when I described the man responsible for Speck's death, Bri claimed that she had encountered Jarvis and Spaulding in the hotel hallway. We wondered if they might've conspired to rob or kidnap her."

"Well, hell," he said, scowling. "I guess it was a stroke of luck that she left town when she did." He stared intently at Hud. "Is it possible that, after Jarvis died, Spaulding learned where Bri was headed and captured her for ransom?"

"It is a possibility," Hud agreed grimly.

"Commander! Over here!"

Hud jerked up his head when Major Ketter called out unexpectedly, then gestured for them to trot over to the buffalo wallow that was surrounded by trees and underbrush.

"Hoofprints," Marcus Yeager, the thickset Ranger who was five years Hud's junior, pointed out.

Floyd Lambert, the rail-thin Ranger, squatted down on his haunches. "Do these belong to Mizz Price's horse?" He looked up at Hud with somber brown eyes.

Hud dismounted to survey the prints then bolted back to his feet. "This is the same horse, the one with a cracked hoof, that I tracked through the alley the morning after Bri's room was ransacked and she disappeared from The Flat."

"What!" Major Ketter crowed. "Damn it, you left out a few important details. You should have—"

Winston flapped his arms to silence the major. "Hud briefed me on the incident. Much as I hate to say it, part of this is Bri's fault. She was trying to save the less fortunate again and it might have gotten her into trouble."

"There are more prints on the south side of the wallow," Marc pointed out.

Hud took a quick look. "These tracks belong to Bri's sorrel gelding…"

His voice fizzled out when he saw signs of a struggle, then noticed the pocket watch in the grass. Hud knew Bri would never willingly discard the treasured keepsake. Cursing himself up one side and down the other, he tucked away the watch then bounded into the saddle. He followed the prints northeast. The knowledge that Bri had fallen into dangerous hands and the outlaw was miles ahead tormented him to no end.

All because sensitive emotions clouded your thinking at the worst of all possible moments, he criticized himself. Lord, how could he have been so careless, so negligent? If his mistakes—and he'd been making a lot of them lately—cost Bri her life, Hud would never forgive himself.

"I have the inescapable feeling that Pete Spaulding caught up with Bri this morning," Hud predicted in a grim tone. "My guess is that he plans to hold her for ransom."

All four men cursed sourly as they mounted their horses to follow Hud. He didn't look back to see how many accusing stares drilled into his back. He picked up the trail of one horse following closely behind another, indicating Bri had been led away unwillingly. Damn it, if he'd made a thorough search for Bri this morning he would've known foul play was involved. He was personally responsible for her plight and that knowledge tortured him every step of the way.

Bri slowed the laboring sorrel as she zigzagged through the trees skirting the river. Jarvis was still on her trail. He paced his horse so he could continue to stay close enough to keep her in his sights without pushing his mount and risk losing track of her altogether.

Casting another apprehensive glance over her shoulder, she halted long enough to grant her horse a much-needed drink. Meanwhile, she grabbed her canteen and sipped freely. Then she stared into the distance, noting that another crude stage station lay a mile ahead.

Although there was no sign of an arriving coach, Bri hoped to warn the proprietor and seek refuge in the station. At the very least, she might be able to get someone to untie her from the saddle.

She stared in frustration at the rope that bound her feet. If she took time to free her hands and feet herself, Jarvis would be within shooting distance. Bri nudged the sorrel and climbed the embankment. She picked up her pace, hoping to reach the station well ahead of Jarvis.

"Help! A killer is chasing me!" she yelled at the top of her lungs.

The moment she commenced shouting for assistance the report of Jarvis's rifle overrode her. He intended to scare off anyone who tried to come to her rescue. Bri ducked away from the whizzing bullets then muttered in disappointment when she saw a little girl toddling across the yard. The child's mother dashed out to scoop her up then ducked inside.

Bri couldn't bring down Jarvis's wrath on the family who ran the stage station. She'd never forgive herself if someone were hurt because of her. Given no choice, Bri reined back to the river to make sure no stray gunshots hit the family huddling inside the house.

Another shot rang out when she was twenty yards

from the protection of the trees. She gasped when searing pain blazed down her left arm. Since her wrists were bound together, she couldn't clamp her hand around the seeping wound to stem the flow of blood. The best she could do was pause briefly to press her arm against a tree truck.

The red stain spread over her shirtsleeve and the coppery scent filled her nostrils. Bri desperately needed to rest and eat, but that was impossible with Jarvis barking at her heels like the hound from hell that he was.

If she could get loose she might be able to send her horse racing off as a decoy then double back to overtake Jarvis. But she was virtually helpless with her bound hands and feet and a painful wound on her arm.

Bri gave the sorrel his head while she used her teeth to attempt to untie the rope on her wrists. She heard Jarvis's horse thrashing through the underbrush behind her, but she forced herself to focus on the task of getting loose. The seeping wound and lack of nourishment were making her light-headed. It required fierce determination to tug at the ropes.

"You might as well give up, you troublesome minx," Jarvis shouted. "Nobody is gonna help you. I'll shoot anyone who tries. You're my ticket to a new life and I ain't backin' off. It's too damn bad you sneaked off that night in town when I came to get you. I could've saved myself a lot of time."

In other words, he *was* planning to ransom her, she realized as she struggled with the rope. She'd like to strangle whoever had given away her identity while she was in The Flat. It could have been Eaton, Hud or the stagecoach depot agent who had mentioned her name in passing. The information could have been overheard and unwittingly fallen into the wrong hands. Bri had tried to keep a low profile and she couldn't imagine how she could have been recognized when she made herself inconspicuous in her drab gray dress, shawl and bonnet.

No matter what, she wouldn't make it easy for Jarvis to collect his money, she vowed. The worthless scoundrel was going to earn every blasted penny trying to capture her.

Bri sent a silent prayer of thanks heavenward when she finally managed to untie the rope with her teeth. With her hands free she leaned over to untie her right foot. The report of Jarvis's rifle broke the silence. The bullet whistled past the place where her head had been a second earlier.

The sorrel bolted when the gunshot nicked his ear.

"Whoa!" Bri shouted when the frightened horse reared up then lunged off, splattering water around them as he raced through the stream.

Bri worked furiously to loosen her foot from the stirrup while her horse unintentionally dowsed her with water.

"Come back here, damn it!" Jarvis fired off another shot.

He missed, thank God.

Bri freed her right foot then made a wild grab for the derringer and knife she had stashed in her satchels after her bath the previous night. No matter what else happened she would have concealed weapons strapped to her legs. Even if the derringer had clogged during her fall into the floodwaters, it was still a good deterrent if she had to bluff her way through a confrontation. But she decided to keep Hud's spare pistol in her saddlebag. If she tucked it in her waistband and Jarvis somehow managed to overtake her he'd check her person for other weapons. The pistol wasn't much use to her against a long-range rifle anyway.

Bri grunted uncomfortably when the sorrel scrabbled up the steep riverbank while she was jackknifed sideways, trying to free her left ankle. Finally, she managed to loosen her foot from the rope then sat upright in the saddle. Pain shot down her left arm and dizziness circled like a vulture. Determinedly, she took control of the sorrel and urged him onto level ground so he could run for all he was worth, for as long as he could.

She didn't look back again, not even when Jarvis fired off two more wild shots. She clamped hold of her injured arm and told herself that she would apply an improvised tourniquet the first chance she got. Right now, she needed to place more distance between herself and the trigger-happy lunatic who was trying to shoot her out of the saddle.

Chapter Thirteen

Eaton Powell gnashed his teeth in irritation while waiting for Ray Novak to meet him after dark in the foul-smelling alley beside the hide yard in The Flat. Thanks to the stagecoach robbery that left Eaton flat broke and without the fashionable clothes in his stolen luggage he was feeling desperate and out of sorts. Not to mention his frustration with Anna Roland Price who demanded that he return to this godforsaken outpost of society to find Bri. Being without his usual supply of funds was damn inconvenient. Here he was, counting on the rancher to loan him enough money to cover his mounting expenses. Plus, he needed to have Gabrielle returned promptly. He refused to spend the rest of his life with Anna the Hag breathing down his neck, issuing threats.

Eaton pivoted on his heels when he heard muffled footsteps behind him. He saw Novak's bulky silhouette emerging from the shadows. Thankfully, he had come alone. The fewer people who knew about "the arrangement" the better.

"Powell," Novak said, inclining his head slightly.

Eaton didn't care for the self-made rancher's arrogance. It wasn't as if the corrupt shyster came from old money like the Powell dynasty in Austin. Novak had nothing to be cocky about, as far as Eaton was concerned.

"Thank you for coming," Eaton said, pouring on the charm. "I'm hoping you can float me a loan for a few days."

"Certainly…with interest. I'm willing to help, in exchange for a few favors when we get you elected." Novak smiled and his white teeth flashed in the darkness.

"With interest, of course," Eaton managed to say without scowling. "I was robbed during my stagecoach ride and had to ask for credit to buy more clothing. I can repay you as soon as my father wires the money from Austin."

Novak counted out several large bank notes then placed them in Eaton's hand. Then he added a few more for good measure. "You have a problem," he mumbled.

Eaton tucked the money in the pocket of his breeches. "Besides being robbed at gunpoint, you mean?" he said, smirking.

"It's more complicated than that," Novak said.

"Everything will be fine after your men release Gabrielle. A nice walk back to town won't hurt that little snip, either. She needs to be put in her place often enough to break her independent spirit."

"It's about that. The two men hired to abduct your fiancée quit their jobs on my ranch without notice."

Alarm trickled down Eaton's backbone. "They decided to strike off on their own with my hostage?"

Novak shrugged. "Can't say. All I know is that the new cowboy I hired two days ago said he crossed paths with a caravan and its military escort. They reported that a Comanche raiding party killed Joe Jarvis. Pete Spaulding headed west."

"Alone?" Eaton crowed in dismay.

"That's the story I was told." Novak pulled a cigar from his pocket then lit it. Light flared over his weatherbeaten features and bushy brows. "Things don't look good for your fiancée."

Never mind her. Things don't look good for me!

If raiding Comanches captured or killed Gabrielle then Anna Roland Price would be out for blood—his. In addition, she'd probably want his scalp, too. That spiteful woman carried a grudge longer than anyone he knew.

Eaton's campaign would be in jeopardy if he couldn't produce Gabrielle. He'd have to drag out the supposed search as long as possible and hope Gabrielle turned up eventually. Damn it, everything had gone to hell with the kidnapping.

"It is understood that you will favor large ranchers and convince your associates to pass legislation that discourages those pesky small farmers from squatting on public land," Novak said pointedly.

"Yes, yes, of course," Eaton mumbled, distracted. His immediate problem was finding a way to forestall Anna the Hag.

Novak snapped his fingers in Eaton's face. "I'm serious, Powell. If you don't come through, as promised, then the good citizens of Texas might get word of your kidnapping scheme. It could prove costly in more ways than one."

In other words, he'd be blackmailed and scandalized. Eaton silently swore as he stared into Novak's shadowy face.

"You do understand what I'm saying, don't you?"

Novak puffed on his cigar so he could blow smoke in Eaton's face.

"Perfectly," Eaton muttered, and choked.

"Good. I'm always dismayed when my associates aren't perfectly clear on how I want our transactions handled." He turned to walk off then halted to glance back at Eaton. "Buy you a drink, my friend?"

"Thank you, but no," Eaton said as civilly as he knew how. "I have to recover my fiancée quickly."

"Good luck with that. You'll be lucky if the Comanches didn't take her across the border to Indian Territory."

The Comanche were welcome to Gabrielle, if not for the inevitable wrath of Anna Roland Price, thought Eaton.

When Novak disappeared into the shadows, Eaton burst out with a salty oath that had Novak's name attached to it. "Nothing worse than making a deal with the devil." If he'd known then what he knew now about Novak's widespread underhanded dealings and his enthusiasm for blackmail threats he'd never have taken a campaign donation from the bastard.

Scowling, Eaton stalked off. He decided to use some of the money in his pocket to pay for a visit to a bordello. He desperately needed to distract himself from his festering problems. Then he'd try to locate Gabrielle before Anna the Hag sent the Pinkertons— and they uncovered too much information about the staged-kidnapping-turned-sour.

Hud led the way cross-country, paying particular attention to the double set of tracks. He halted when he noticed the prints with the cracked hoof veered to the stage station that was housed in a squatty adobe building.

"Marc, would you and Floyd check for the sorrel's

prints by the river," Hud requested. "We'll see if the stage agent can provide helpful information."

Dismounting, Hud and his two superior officers strode inside to see the planked tables and shelves, filled with traveling supplies. Hud nodded a silent greeting to the stationmaster, whose wrinkled face was concealed partially by a long beard and thick mustache.

"Our Ranger search party is looking for a man who kidnapped a young woman early this morning," Winston Price announced.

The proprietor bobbed his head. "He was here earlier this afternoon," he reported. "He *robbed* me of whiskey and food at gunpoint. I heard a woman scream for help and I looked out the window to see her racing down the road on horseback."

Hud inwardly winced. He could only imagine the anger and fear Bri endured because of his carelessness and lack of attention to his surroundings.

"It looked as if she was tied to the saddle," the stationmaster went on to say. "She was wearing breeches and a shirt but her long reddish-blond hair was flying out behind her. The thief bounded onto his horse with his stolen goods and fired shots at her as she rode off."

Winston gasped then swore mightily.

"Can you describe the bandit?" Hud requested.

"Long greasy hair. Gray eyes. Tall and thin. Bad teeth."

Tormenting dread skittered down Hud's backbone. "Joe Jarvis," he growled sourly.

"Jarvis? He's supposed to be dead," Major Ketter burst out. "Then who—?"

"Pete Spaulding," Hud interrupted quickly. "I suspect Jarvis assumed Spaulding's name and identity. There's a helluva lot of difference between killing a Ranger and robbing a relay station than for being an *un*participating accessory."

While Major Ketter bought supplies and food for their journey, Hud stalked outside to mount Rambler. Cold fury froze in his veins. Pete Spaulding as Bri's abductor would've been bad enough, he mused. But Mad Joe Jarvis? Hell! Hud doubted Jarvis had a conscience or a compassionate bone in his body.

According to the stationmaster, Bri was bound up and she was trying to outrun her captor. How long could she elude Jarvis and how would he react if he caught her? The bleak speculations caused Hud's heart to squeeze painfully in his chest.

"Damn it to hell," Winston snarled as he rode up beside Hud. "This just keeps getting worse." He tossed Hud a stony glare that held him responsible for every traumatic ordeal Bri endured. "I hope my daughter can hold out until we overtake that murdering thief."

Hud looked up when Marc and Floyd approached. "Did you find any tracks?"

Floyd nodded somberly. "Looks like Spaulding tied Mizz Price to a tree but she managed to get loose and take off without him. Her tracks led back to the road."

"The station owner said Bri screamed for help as she rode away, but Jarvis took potshots at her after he robbed the store," Winston reported grimly.

Floyd glanced up sharply and frowned. *"Jarvis?"*

"He's using Spaulding as his alias?" Marc asked and Hud nodded. "I picked up some empty shell casings for evidence."

"I hope he didn't hit what he was aiming at," Floyd mused aloud then glanced apologetically at Commander Price.

Hud noticed the commander's face turned peaked and he scowled at the careless comment.

Major Ketter trotted up and tossed hardtack and bread to each man. "We'll save time and eat on the go."

Bleak scenarios chased each other around Hud's head and robbed him of his appetite. Nonetheless, he choked down his meal. Not knowing Bri's fate and imagining everything that could go wrong was driving him a dozen kinds of crazy. *If* Bri managed to stay a step ahead of Jarvis without being shot it would be a miracle.

Hud hadn't prayed for a miracle since his mother abandoned him and he foolishly thought he wanted her back. But he was praying for a miracle to save the vibrant, spirited female that mattered more to him than he dared to say.

Bri was becoming desperate. She had spared time to rip a ruffle off the petticoat crammed in her satchel and tie off the wound. But the jarring pain drained her stamina. That and the fact that she hadn't eaten since the previous evening. She wasn't sure how much longer she could remain upright in the saddle without pitching headfirst into the dirt.

Wearily, she dug into the saddlebag to retrieve what was left of the stale bread she had purchased in The Flat days earlier. While she choked down the dry bread, she glanced skyward, trying to estimate the time of day. She looked forward to darkness and the chance to slip away from Jarvis when he couldn't spot her easily.

She reminded herself that Jarvis might become desperate again and resort to trying to shoot her horse out from under her. With that in mind, Bri quickened her pace, hoping to make good time and increase the distance between her and Jarvis.

Then, from out of nowhere, Jarvis topped the rise of ground and thundered toward her. He fired his rifle twice, forcing Bri to veer toward the protection of the underbrush near the river. She flattened herself over the sorrel that had become gun-shy after having the tip of its ear blown off. The horse ran in fits and starts as she guided him through the underbrush and he struggled to keep his footing. More than once, she feared she'd be catapulted over the gelding's head when he bolted at the sound of reeds crackling around him and bullets whizzing past his head.

Bri clamped her right hand on the pommel to anchor herself as the sorrel gathered his hindquarters beneath him to bound down the steep embankment. She gave him time to drink from the shallows before reining him downstream. She heard a low growl and twisted in the saddle to see Jarvis perched on the cliff, taking careful aim with his rifle.

"Go!" Bri shouted at her horse and dug in her heels. The sorrel skittered sideways then plunged forward in the nick of time. The whistling bullet plugged a nearby tree limb and it dropped to the ground, missing her by mere inches.

Jarvis swore foully as he forced his horse down the embankment in hasty pursuit. "Next time I'm shootin' to kill!" he roared at her.

Bri thought he had been all along, but she refrained from tossing out the comment. Instead, she concentrated on plastering herself against the gelding's neck as he crossed the stream to scrabble uphill. She yelped in dismay when the gelding lost his footing and stumbled to his knees, very nearly catapulting her to the ground. She tried desperately to upright herself, but when the floundering horse staggered sideways, her injured shoulder collided with a tree trunk.

Pain sizzled down her arm and stars circled in front of her eyes. Frantic, she reached for Hud's pistol that was still stashed in her satchel. She wished she'd stuffed it in her waistband.

When the gelding tried to lunge uphill, Bri lost her balance. Before she could get her hands on the six-shooter, she somersaulted backward and landed with a thud that knocked the breath out of her. Gasping for air, she scrambled to her hands and knees, hoping to catch her horse and grab the gun.

She howled in outraged fury when Jarvis tossed the loop of his lasso around her shoulders. Before she could pull it over her head, Jarvis jerked hard and sent her sprawling again. Refusing to give up the fight, she lashed out with her feet to kick his horse in the rump. Jarvis cursed furiously when his mount reared up and tried to bolt uphill.

To Bri's dismay, Jarvis managed to control the horse before it ran away with him. She screeched in pain when Jarvis dragged her along behind him until she no longer had the energy and strength to fight back.

"Gotcha," he sniggered as he stared smugly at her from atop his horse.

Later that afternoon, after riding hard for several hours, Hud dismounted at the next stage station along the eastern route. His four companions followed him inside to greet the husband and wife—a young couple that looked to be in their mid-twenties—and their blond-haired toddler, who was sitting on her mother's lap.

After a round of polite how-do-you-dos and introductions, Hud got down to business.

"We're trailing an outlaw named Jarvis who took a young woman captive," he reported to Jacob and Sally Murphy.

Sally hugged her daughter, Hallie, close then nodded solemnly. "They passed by here not too long ago. We felt so helpless. But there was nothing we could do for the woman."

Hud tensed, wondering what that meant.

"When the woman shouted for assistance, Sally dashed outside to grab Hallie," Jacob explained. "The outlaw was blasting away with his rifle, but the woman veered from the station when she spotted Hallie. I think she spared us from the brutal bandit."

That sounded like something Bri would do, Hud thought. She had jeopardized her own life to spare someone else, just as she had rescued the three boys from poverty and starvation. She definitely wasn't the self-centered, self-indulgent socialite he'd expected to meet. He'd been completely wrong about Gabrielle Price and he regretted every critical thought and comment he'd made at their first encounter.

"What is her name, this woman who risked disaster to save my wife and child?" Jacob asked as he curled his arm possessively around his family.

Hud wondered what it felt like to have a family who needed his care and protection. He had no experience whatsoever with family connections. Suddenly he felt deprived.

"Gabrielle Price is my daughter," Winston spoke up. "I assure you that Bri wouldn't place a child in harm's way, even if it meant she had to run for her life."

"She's in our prayers," Sally murmured as she gave Hallie a hug. "All we could do for Gabrielle was alert the guard and driver on the eastbound stagecoach to keep a sharp lookout."

"When did the coach pass through here?" Hud asked.

"We hitched up a new team to the coach an hour ago," Jacob replied. "It's the coach from Tascosa that connects with the east-and-westbound stage line to The Flat."

While the other Rangers posed a few more questions, Hud exited the station to follow Bri's tracks. The prints veered back to the trees skirting the river again. If he didn't scout the area right now, it would be difficult to find prints when darkness settled over the countryside.

Hud let loose a furious curse when he saw several more empty rifle shells littering the path leading to the river. The smeared tracks indicated that Bri's horse had scrabbled downhill. He fought to draw breath when he saw the dried blood on the bark of a willow tree near the hoofprints.

The grim implication tormented the hell out of him. He could visualize Bri battling to free herself from the ropes while she raced ahead of Jarvis. He could only imagine her frustration at having to abort her attempt to take shelter at the stage station so she wouldn't involve an innocent family.

Hud knew she must have been suffering after being shot. From firsthand experience, he knew what it felt like to be jarred painfully and continue to stay in the saddle.

Damn Mad Joe Jarvis, he seethed. He wished that heartless bastard as deep in hell as a buzzard could fly in a week. Jarvis had killed Speck. Now he'd shot Bri and Hud had no idea how severe her injuries were.

Before losing daylight completely, Hud focused on

the tracks. He stared grimly at the site where Bri's horse had floundered a second time before regaining its footing and bounding uphill to race down the open road.

He paused to pick up a few more empty cartridges then stuffed them in his vest pocket. The thought of shoving the shells down Jarvis's throat and letting him choke on them held tremendous appeal.

He hoped Bri would still be alive so she could watch.

Bri chewed herself up one side and down the other for falling off her horse—and into Jarvis's ruthless hands. Her cheek stung like fire where he had backhanded her to punish her for leading him on a merry chase for half the day.

"You can bet you're gonna pay dearly for runnin' me ragged," Jarvis snarled as he dragged Bri by the feet and tied her to a tree.

Casting Bri another venomous glower, Jarvis gathered up fallen limbs to build a campfire. Once he had the fire going, he stomped off to grab a bottle of whiskey. He guzzled several drinks then wiped his mouth on his grimy shirtsleeve. Then he made a big production of leering at her, in case she hadn't figured out that she was the main attraction this evening.

"Me and you are gonna have a go at it later," he promised, flashing another lecherous smile.

Although the prospect sickened her, she refused to let her trepidation show. She stared steadily at the black-hearted villain without changing expression.

"Think you're brave, do ya?" he taunted then guzzled an amazing amount of liquor in three swallows. "You'll be beggin' 'fore I'm through with you."

"Where's your partner?" she asked abruptly.

"Dead," he said without a hint of remorse. "He didn't have the stomach for this line of work." He chugged more whiskey. "I had to shut Pete up permanently, in case he decided to go straight and sold me out for bounty."

Knowing that Jarvis had deliberately killed the closest thing he had to a friend drove home the point that he had no heart, no soul and no conscience.

The realization made her swallow hard. "I'm thirsty. Can I at least have a drink?"

Jarvis grinned nastily as he swaggered over to scoop water from the river into his hat. Then he dumped it on her head. He laughed uproariously at his spiteful prank then tipped back the bottle to chug more whiskey.

Mercy, the man was a lush, Bri noted as she blinked water from her eyes. She vowed to use his addiction to her advantage, if possible. For certain, if Jarvis was falling-down drunk it would be easier for her to escape him.

"You're going to have to feed me," she demanded, mimicking her mother's peevish tone. "I've gone hungry all day and I won't be of any use to you if I pass out."

Jarvis's reply was a defiant snort. "No wonder that dandy was itching to have you hauled off."

Bri went perfectly still as she watched Jarvis down another drink. "Are you referring to Eaton Powell?"

Jarvis plopped down to stretch out his long skinny legs. "That fancy-talkin' politician who cozied up to Ray Novak."

"Who's Ray Novak?" she demanded in a dominating voice that would have done her mother proud.

Jarvis was beginning to show the effects of guzzling whiskey at amazing speed. He slung his arm sideways in a reckless gesture. "My former boss," he mumbled. "He had Pete and me out at all hours of the night gatherin' the neighbor's weanin'-size calves and placin' them in his herd so he can drive them to the railhead in Dodge City. Novak and Powell are doin' each other favors to help win the election. I was s'posed to take you captive at the hotel, but you sneaked off and fouled up everything."

"You're saying Powell *hired* you to kidnap me?" she asked, incensed by Powell's ruthless treachery.

His smile displayed a full set of rotten teeth. "Yep, but we skipped town with the money he paid us and he don't know you've been runnin' loose all this time."

He took another drink. Whiskey dribbled through his scruffy whiskers. "Now I got big plans that'll set me up for life. Between sendin' a ransom to yer daddy and blackmailin' that snooty politician I'm gonna have more money than God."

Bri silently consigned Eaton Powell to Hades. "Powell told you and your partner to hold me in captivity?"

Jarvis nodded his head and his stringy hair flopped over his bony features.

"For how long?"

His shoulder lifted in a negligent shrug. "He was gonna wait and decide if and when to release you, dependin' on how much publicity he got out of it for his campaign."

Bri clenched her fingers, wishing she could wrap them around Powell's neck and pinch off his head. He was using the political stunt for sympathy votes and making it *appear* that he was distraught about her abduction.

She sat smoldering in frustrated fury, vowing all sorts of retribution for that conniving scoundrel. No doubt, canceling their betrothal had provoked Powell's vicious retaliation. Then he'd turned the situation to his advantage to promote his campaign…

Her angry speculations trailed off when Jarvis staggered toward her. He cast aside the empty bottle and leered at her. But Powell's cruel betrayal outraged her to such extremes that it was difficult to switch mental gears and concentrate on the imminent threat looming over her.

When Jarvis chuckled devilishly, she focused on him. He smelled of whiskey, reeked of sweat and looked like something Satan had dragged from the river Styx. Now that he had Bri's absolute attention, she tried to figure out how to avoid the disgusting vermin. She reminded herself that first he'd have to untie her from the tree trunk. She'd have a small amount of time to escape. Unfortunately, Jarvis knew she was a scrappy fighter, after their encounter at the buffalo wallow, and he'd be expecting her to attack.

Bri knew she'd have to be more creative. She remembered her passionate trysts with Hud and she loathed the prospect of having those magical moments tarnished by nightmares of this drunken bully ravaging her.

She also wondered where Hud was. How long had it taken him to realize that she had been abducted? Was he tracking her because he considered her an assignment and a responsibility? Did he hold any affection for her? She'd like to think he cared a little. Was that asking so much?

Bri glanced this way and that, wishing Hud would miraculously appear to rescue her from this tight scrape. But she knew better than to hope for someone to save her. She was responsible for her own fate. Benji had taught her that.

"Never mind about that dandy who hired me to

kidnap you," Jarvis slurred out. "I'm done talkin' 'bout him now." He swayed slightly as he unfastened his holsters then reached for the top button on the placket of his filthy breeches. "It's time you learned what purpose a woman serves and I'm gonna be the one who teaches you…"

Chapter Fourteen

Hounded by a fierce sense of urgency, Hud pushed himself and Rambler to the limits. The sturdy black gelding possessed the kind of stamina the other horses couldn't match so Hud forged ahead of the pack, hoping to overtake Jarvis and rescue Bri by nightfall.

He knew that age and fearful concern for Bri was wearing on Winston Price. Hud had specifically asked Major Ketter to lag behind, in case the rescue brigade happened onto a gruesome scene. The bleak prospect of Mad Joe Jarvis's intentions for Bri had Hud swearing one blue streak after another. He *had* to find her before disaster stuck.

This was his best chance, he told himself. Jarvis probably wasn't planning to travel at night. He'd have other things on his mind. Things that Hud didn't want Bri to endure—but were a very real possibility.

When Hud picked up the scent of smoke in the air, he noticed a campfire flickering in the gathering darkness near the river. Anticipation rose inside him, though he reminded himself that anyone—military troops, freighters, outlaws or bounty hunters—could be camped beside the river.

He glanced over his shoulder at the silhouettes of the Ranger patrol trailing a half mile behind him then quickened his pace once again. A few minutes later, he dismounted and tied Rambler to a tree. Pistol drawn, he moved silently on foot toward the campfire.

Hud pricked his ears when he overheard voices in the distance. He crept closer, praying for all he was worth that it was Bri and her captor and that he wasn't too late to save her from hellish torment. Sure enough, there she was, tied to a tree while Jarvis towered over her. Her hands were bound behind her back and he could see bloodstains on her shirtsleeve. Apparently, the injury wasn't life-threatening because she was staring defiantly at Jarvis.

"It's about time you learned what purpose a woman serves," Jarvis mumbled drunkenly, "and I'm gonna be the one who teaches you."

"I'm not serving anyone's purpose, especially yours until you bathe," Bri snapped back. "After all, I should get something enjoyable out of this. And I damn well intend to."

Despite his concern, a smile quirked his lips. He really had to hand it to that fiery female. She was a warrior and refused to be intimidated, even if she was scared to death. And if she had any sense she *was* scared, because Mad Joe Jarvis was as dangerous and heartless as they came.

Hud stuffed his pistol in his holster and inched quietly toward the campsite. He wanted to drop that murdering bastard in his tracks, but he needed a better angle. If his aim was off the mark and he missed Jarvis, he might shoot Bri accidentally.

"I don't give a damn what you git and don't git," Jarvis snorted hatefully. "I'm takin' what I want and that's that."

Drunk though Jarvis was, he swooped down to untie Bri from the tree then dragged her across the ground by her boot heels. She wormed and squirmed and kicked until he released her left leg then she slammed her heel into his hip.

It demanded all the self-control Hud could muster to hold his position. Forced to watch and wait for the right moment to strike was one of the most difficult challenges he'd ever undertaken. His fierce need to protect Bri and to vent his fury on the man who had killed Speck tormented the living hell out of him. But Hud didn't have a clear shot and he couldn't reach Bri quickly—without making a racket in the underbrush.

When Jarvis tried to tie Bri's left ankle to another tree and force her flat on her back she lashed out with her leg and caught him squarely in the crotch. He howled like a dying coyote and dropped to his knees. Snarling, he lunged forward to strike her across the cheek and she yelped in pain.

Much as Hud hated to admit it, he found himself thanking Benji, who'd trained Bri to be resourceful when it came to self-defense. Hud wished *he*'d had that much influence on Bri, but at least she was putting up a fight that distracted Jarvis so Hud could sneak up to overtake him.

While Jarvis huffed and puffed for breath, Hud came to his feet. He wanted to take Jarvis apart with his bare hands for mistreating Bri. Growling viciously, he plowed through the underbrush while Jarvis rocked forward in an attempt to stand. Bri recoiled her legs, and then struck out with her feet, catching Jarvis on the chin and sending him somersaulting backward into the campfire. While he screamed bloody murder and rolled on the ground to smother the flames on his shirt, Bri bounded up to snap-kick Jarvis upside the head.

Hud skidded to a halt to watch Bri in action. She brought Jarvis under control single-handedly. As much as he wanted his turn at the murdering thug, he stayed where he was so he wouldn't distract her while she vented her fury on Jarvis.

Again, Hud begrudgingly thanked Benji for teaching Bri hand-to-hand combat maneuvers. She lashed out with her feet, elbows and bound fists then retreated before Jarvis could lay a hand on her. It was impressive really. She was agile and quick on her feet and she made Jarvis look like a bungling fool…until the rascal managed to grab his discarded gun.

Bri glared angrily at Jarvis, who grinned victoriously as he sat up and held her at gunpoint. This time, however, Hud was in a better position to fire his weapon without endangering Bri. His six-shooter cleared leather with practiced ease and his shot sent Jarvis's pistol flipping through the air and out of his reach.

Jarvis yelped when blood spurted from the wound on his hand. Bri made certain he felt every ounce of pain by kicking his injured fingers for good measure. She was still pelting his hand with the toe of her boot when Hud strode up to her.

"You want me to untie your hands so you can scratch his eyes out?" Hud asked, noting Jarvis had slumped into a stupor.

When she finally focused on him, he noticed she still had murder in her eyes and several bruises on her face. She was so intent on taking out her fury on Jarvis that Hud wondered if she registered that he had arrived on the scene.

"Bri?" he prompted as he reached around to untie her wrists. "Sweetheart, are you okay?"

He could see that she wasn't. Emotion was ripping through her like a tornado. Her upper arm was wrapped in a makeshift tourniquet and the wound needed attention. Her hair was wet. So were her clothes. She was quivering with fury.

"No, I'm not okay," she muttered, her teeth clenched, her breasts heaving. "I want to kill him."

"We all do," Hud assured her as he cupped her face in his hands. "Everything is going to be fine now. Look at me. Take a deep breath, Bri."

Although it was completely inappropriate to kiss her, given that Commander Price could arrive at any moment. Given that Bri had paid him for last night's love lessons. Given that he was still steamed about that, even if he had discovered later that she hadn't left camp of her own accord. Nevertheless, the overwhelming need to kiss her consumed him and he gave in to it wholeheartedly.

At first Bri didn't respond to his gentle kiss. It was as if she was still trapped in a furious red haze of anger. Emotions and survival instincts were still spurting through her, making her body vibrate. However, little by little, she melted beneath his kiss. Then she arched toward him and he wrapped her protectively in his arms. He held on tight to compensate for the hellish day he'd spent worrying about her and berating himself for letting this happen to her.

A quiet moan rose from her throat and he sighed in relief when she looped her arms over his shoulders. For the first time since sunrise, the fear and apprehension that tormented him mercilessly drained away. Raw need and volatile emotion billowed between them. Hud instinctively fit her lush body against his and deepened the kiss, his tongue fencing with hers as they shared the same panting breath.

"I was worried as hell about you," he murmured when he finally marshaled the willpower to break their kiss.

"I was a little worried myself," she said shakily.

Bri shook her head, as if to clear her dazed thoughts. Then she looked down to see that she still had her foot on Jarvis's throat and that he'd finally passed out.

When Hud stepped back to examine her arm, she brushed his hands away. "I'm fine."

What she really wanted to do was to hurl herself back into Hud's arms and remain there all night—and the rest of her life. But she doubted Hud wanted a simpering female clinging possessively to him. She wanted to earn his admiration and respect, not draw his pity by bawling her head off and decomposing before his eyes.

"You are *not* fine," Hud contradicted. "You've had a really bad day. I don't know why you can't admit it."

He didn't know the half of it. She'd been starved and terrorized and she was exhausted, but there were things Jarvis had told her that Hud needed to know. "Listen, Joe said—"

"Bri! Thank God!"

She half turned to see her father dashing through the underbrush in his eagerness to reach her. She groaned when he scooped her up in his arms and squeezed her overzealously. Every injury, throbbing pain and sore muscle complained when he practically hugged the stuffing out of her.

"You might want to ease off, Commander," Hud advised. "One look at your daughter testifies that she's had a horrendous day and looks the worse for wear."

"No thanks to you, Captain," her father muttered in a resentful tone as he reared back to inspect Bri closely.

He brushed his fingertips lightly over her bruised chin and cheek then stared at her injured arm in concern. Then he focused his furious glare on Jarvis, who was still out cold and lay on the ground like a displaced doormat.

"That murderer is going to pay for abusing my daughter," he growled vindictively.

"You've got that right," Hud affirmed. "I know a few Comanche torture techniques that I plan to practice on him."

"I get first crack at him," her father demanded. "I outrank you, Stone."

"Don't pull rank on him, Papa," Bri protested. "Hud lost a longtime friend and companion. I am only scuffed up a bit."

When Hud cast her an appreciative smile for siding with him, Bri returned his grin. When she heard the rustling of underbrush again she glanced left to see three men scurrying toward her. She wasn't sure what her father and the Rangers were doing here, but she was glad they were.

"I went the wrong direction this morning," Hud said in answer to her unspoken question. "I thought you had ridden off alone to reach Ranger camp. It was two hours before I realized my mistake. I'm sorry."

She predicted that Hud had been furious with her...until he realized that she hadn't left the cave on her own accord.

"I was worried about you after that damaging storm

blew through," her father remarked as he plucked leaves from her tangled hair. "So we rode east, hoping to locate you and the captain."

"Bri, this is Major John Ketter," Hud introduced the bowlegged Ranger, who tipped his hat politely to her.

"This is Marcus Yeager and Floyd Lambert," he said, gesturing toward the younger men.

Bri smiled a greeting at the men, who seemed a mite bashful around her.

"This is Joe Jarvis," he muttered as he glared at the man who was sprawled, unconscious, as his feet. "He shot Speck in the back and, as you can see, he's been abusive to Bri."

"Jarvis didn't confess to the killing." Bri finished what she'd started to say earlier as she rubbed the raw skin on her wrists. "He admitted he killed Pete Spaulding, who didn't have the stomach for murder and became a risk to Jarvis."

She watched Hud's expression turn to granite as he swooped down to grab Jarvis by the nape of his shirt. No one said a word or tried to interfere when Hud placed Jarvis in shackles then dragged him away. Whatever Hud had planned for the murdering outlaw was long overdo— as far as she and everyone else on hand was concerned.

"Your father was really worried about you, Mizz Price," Major Ketter confided.

Her father smiled affectionately as he retrieved his pipe and lit it. "If you'd like to freshen up while we fetch the horses and put together a meal, go ahead, hon. Just don't wander too far away."

Bri nodded, grateful for a warm meal and the opportunity to bathe and change clothes. Retrieving her satchel from her horse, she strode off in the direction

Hud had taken. In the moonlight, she saw Hud toss Jarvis into the shallows of the stream and dunk him repeatedly until he regained consciousness.

Jarvis gasped and sputtered but Hud was relentless in forcing the outlaw's head underwater until he panicked and squealed. Only when Jarvis begged for mercy did Hud haul him ashore and bind his shackled hands and feet with rope.

"You killed the closest thing *you* had to a friend," Hud growled as he got right in Jarvis's peaked face. "And you shot the closest thing *I* had to family."

Even at a distance, Bri saw the flicker of recognition in Jarvis's facial expression. It wasn't a confession but it was a telling reaction.

"I'll be downstream while the men prepare supper," she informed Hud as she walked past him.

He didn't glance in her direction, just continued to glare daggers at Jarvis.

Bri walked off, leaving Hud to vent his fury on Jarvis, who definitely deserved slow death by torture. She would have to make a point to learn a few techniques because she intended to apply them to Eaton Powell. Just wait until she got her hands on that devious sidewinder politician!

Scowling, Hud stared at Jarvis, who was too drunk to remain awake for more than a few seconds at a time. He bound up Jarvis good and tight to a tree then left him to sleep off his recent bout with whiskey.

Hud was far from feeling vindicated just because Jarvis was in custody. Yet, as much as he wanted to wring a confession from Jarvis, his compulsive need to be with Bri demanded that he follow her. He'd spent a maddening day trying to catch up to her and make sure she was safe. It didn't seem to matter that her father was upstream, rustling up a meal for his daughter and that three other men were nearby. He needed to be with Bri and he needed to be with her *now*.

"You're fighting an uphill battle and you're a hopeless cause," he criticized himself as he trailed after her.

How could he need to be with her more than he needed revenge for Speck? he asked himself. There were a hundred and one good reasons to leave Bri to herself and to rejoin his fellow Rangers. Every reason was rational and sensible, but none of them prevented him from running the risk of being discovered alone with Bri. Not even the possibility of facing her father's outrage and wrath.

Which said a hell of a lot about the intensity of his forbidden feelings for her. Too much in fact.

His footsteps stalled when he saw Bri swimming in midstream. Moonbeams sparkled around her like diamonds on the rippling water. The tempting scene drew him ever closer. Nothing seemed as important as holding her in his arms and assuring himself that his carelessness hadn't caused her excessive pain and irreparable harm.

He heard Bri gasp and saw her cover herself when she noticed him standing on the riverbank. He stared straight at her as he doffed his shirt and vest.

"If you don't want me to join you then say so now." He unbuckled his holsters and let them drop at his feet. "I'll turn and walk away if that's what you want. But my need to be with you is driving me crazy, Bri."

When she met his gaze directly, the remembered heat of the passion they ignited in each other flared to life.

"I thought you'd never get here," she told him with an impish grin. "It certainly took you long enough."

He smiled rakishly as he made fast work of shedding his boots and breeches. For this moment in time, it didn't matter that he had been aggravated at her this morning and terrified all the livelong day that his neglect might cost her life. Despite every obstacle between them, despite good judgment, obsessive desire drew them together and held them fast.

That and scads of other tender emotions that Hud refused to delve into too deeply, for fear that he might not want to face the real reason he couldn't keep his distance from Bri.

"What about Jarvis?" she asked.

He walked toward her, oblivious to the cool water swirling around him. "He'll keep. Right now all I need is to be with you."

Hud slid his arms around her hips and drew her voluptuous body against his. He savored the mind-boggling pleasure that sent the world and all its troubles drifting away in a fog. He kissed Bri, as if it had been weeks instead of minutes since he had tasted the honeyed softness of her lips and inhaled her enticing scent.

His hands moved on their own accord, rediscovering every silky inch of her shapely body, offering pleasure to soothe away her aches and pains. He laid her over his arm, letting her float on the water, watching her red-gold hair drift around her beguiling features. Mesmerized, he grazed his lips over the pebbled peaks of her breasts. Her soft moan echoed around them as he flicked his tongue at her then suckled her nipple lightly. He caressed her repeatedly, unable to get enough of touching her. He relished the quiet moans of pleasure that he drew from her as she arched toward his kisses and caresses and whispered his name like a chant.

Bewitched, bedazzled by the kaleidoscope of emotions she stirred inside him, he kissed her again. He touched her intimately then inhaled her tantalizing scent and got lost in the haze of heady pleasure swirling around him. He smiled in satisfaction when she playfully accused him of withholding what she wanted more than she wanted her next breath.

"Come here," she demanded raggedly. "I need you now and you damn well know it."

He came to her then and glided her legs around his hips. Bri surrendered the instant she felt his hard arousal pressing intimately against her. She desperately needed him to erase from her mind the horrors of the day. She needed him to remind her how gentle and caring he could be, where Jarvis was rough and abusive.

It didn't matter that Hud had hurt her feelings by moving his pallet away from her the previous night so she wouldn't throw herself shamelessly at him a third time. It didn't matter that passion for the sake of passion brought him to her tonight. She wanted him under any circumstance and pride be damned.

It thrilled her that he'd come to join her, despite the risk of discovery. He *wanted* her—badly—and she craved all the wild, reckless pleasure she knew awaited her in his brawny arms. She ached to share whatever Hud could offer, even if it didn't include his heart. She had his passion for the moment and it was enough.

When he surged toward her, filling her, driving urgently against her, she arched eagerly into him. She rocked against him, wanting to hold him deep inside her, to feel that white-hot crescendo building until it exploded over her like a volcanic eruption.

She could feel the rapturous intensity of their union expanding in all directions. Desire billowed and burned through every fiber of her being. Her breath broke when rippling spasms of ecstasy consumed her. She gasped and clutched Hud to her, absorbing him into her, quivering helplessly around him. She bit back a wild cry that ached to fly free and held on for dear life as pleasure roiled through her, leaving no part of her body and soul untouched.

Bri looked up into his shadowed face, watching his golden eyes flare, watching his jaw clench as he thrust against her one last time to satisfy the same mindless need that rippled through her. Clasping her hands on the sides of his face, she kissed him—hard, hungrily. She wanted to convey what was in her heart without expressing the words he didn't want to hear. If she made him uncomfortable with a confession of affection, he'd put a mental and physical distance between them again, as he'd done at the cavern.

She kissed him with all that she was, all that she felt for him as she shivered in the riveting pleasure that cascaded over her. She heard Hud groan, felt him clutch her tightly to him as he shuddered in helpless release.

When he tucked his head against her shoulder and nuzzled her neck, she smiled in supreme satisfaction. She doubted that Hudson Stone, hard-hearted, rough-and-tough Ranger that he was, would ever come to love her as deeply as she loved him, but there was no question that he desired her as desperately as she desired him. She had that, at least.

"I must be out of my mind," he mumbled as his

sensuous lips skimmed over the pulsating column of her throat and his hands glided possessively over her hips.

"Why's that?" she asked as she snuggled up to him.

"Your father might catch us together. And my fellow Rangers might figure out that I'm hopelessly addicted to you. But none of that matters right now. Holding a gun to my head wouldn't have kept me away from you tonight."

The comment pleased her immensely. However, the remark also prompted her to ease away to bathe and dress quickly. After all, her father *was* one hundred yards upstream visiting with three other Rangers. Which proved that *she* couldn't keep her hands off Hud, either.

"Wait," he whispered before she could swim away. "Let me see your arm."

Bri waited while he gently inspected the wound. "It's only a scratch," she assured him.

"Nevertheless, we will treat it when we return to camp," he insisted before he let her go.

She watched him wade ashore, knowing this would be the last time she would share the incredible passion and soul-deep intimacy she'd discovered with him. Hud would transport Jarvis to jail to await trial and then return to his battalion. She would ride to The Flat to confront Powell with his treachery—if he was still in town. More than likely, he'd headed south to lounge in his lap of luxury—the devious cad.

The thought of never seeing Hud again left a hollow ache in the pit of her belly and a hole the size of Texas in her heart.

"Something wrong?" he asked perceptively.

Bri glanced up to watch him fasten his breeches. Yes,

something was wrong. She had become too attached to this brawny Ranger in such a short time that it amazed and tormented her. "I'm fine," she lied convincingly.

Damn it, of all the men who had courted her money and her family connections these past few years, she had fallen recklessly in love with a man who needed no more than the temporary pleasure of passion before getting on with his life.

The disheartening thought made her gnash her teeth. Damn it, she wanted to matter to him—a lot.

"You're in pain," he diagnosed.

"Yes," she muttered. Her feminine pride was smarting like nobody's business.

"I'll go into camp first and I'll tend to your arm as soon as you arrive," he insisted.

"You can't cure heart trouble," she mumbled.

"Pardon?" He arched a curious brow as he picked up his holsters and strapped them around his lean hips.

"Nothing. I'll be along in a few minutes."

Bri watched him walk away and told herself this was good practice for his final fare-thee-well in the morning. She tried to convince herself that nursing her grudge toward Eaton Powell would distract her from suffering the hurt of one-sided love. But she knew Captain Hudson Stone was going to be a hard man to forget. Impossible, in fact.

"Where's Jarvis? Or rather, what condition did you leave him in?" Major Ketter asked the moment Hud returned to camp.

All three men glanced expectantly at him.

"He blacked out." Hud ambled over to pour himself a cup of coffee. "Torturing Jarvis while he's drunk isn't any fun. I'll take my fury out on his hangover, bright and early in the morning."

Marcus Yeager strode over to grab Hud's hand and placed a tarnished badge in his palm. "I found this in Jarvis's saddlebags," he said somberly. "I thought you'd like to have it."

Hud brushed his fingers affectionately over Speck's badge—one that he'd hammered from a Spanish coin. Now he understood Bri's sentimental attachment to Benji's pocket watch because he felt the same connection to Speck's badge. Fierce emotion hit Hud like a tidal wave. He was tempted to storm back to Jarvis and pulverize him, even if he was too drunk to remember Hud beating the living hell out of him.

"We also found several hundred dollars of bank notes," Floyd Lambert added. "How much money did the station manager say had been stolen before you found Speck?"

"Only forty dollars," Hud recalled.

"There's a helluva lot more than that tied to Jarvis's horse," Major Ketter confirmed. "I wonder where it came from."

Frowning pensively, Hud sipped his coffee, and then stared with remorse at the badge. He also tried to pretend that he hadn't been with Bri, whose astounding passion practically turned the river to steam and had definitely fried his brain.

Hud felt like a damn schoolboy. He was afraid to look Commander Price in the eye for more than ten seconds, for fear the father of the woman he had ravished for the third time in two days could tell by looking at him what he'd been doing—and with whom.

Damn, what had he been thinking? Hud asked

himself incredulously. He *hadn't* been thinking. That was the problem. He'd wanted to be as intimately close to Bri as he could get and he hadn't had enough willpower to deny himself, no matter who could have seen them together and what consequences might await him.

"Did you see anything of Bri?" Winston questioned anxiously.

He'd seen a lot of her, but he wasn't about to tell Winston that! "She walked past me while I was trying to rouse Jarvis. She said she was going downstream to bathe."

"I hope she's all right," Winston said worriedly. "She's resilient and spirited but she's had a harrowing day."

"I'm fine, Papa," Bri declared as she emerged from the darkness to pass a reassuring smile around camp. She rolled up her shirtsleeve as she walked over to Hud. "Do you have some poultice...?" Her voice trailed off when she noticed the badge in his hand. "Speck's?"

Hud nodded. "Marc found it. Circumstantial evidence at best, but it does connect the two of them."

"Jarvis didn't admit to you that he shot your friend?" she asked gently.

"No, he passed out before I could get a confession."

"There's always tomorrow," she said confidently. "Deprive him of whiskey and that obnoxious drunk might tell you what you want to know. He has a serious addiction."

"Let me tend your arm, sweetheart," Winston insisted as he strode over to fish into his saddlebag. "Are you feeling better after your bath?"

Hud cast her a discreet glance and noted the enigmatic sparkle in those luminous indigo eyes. No one else could interpret that certain glimmer, but Hud knew exactly what she meant when she said, "My bath was amazingly invigorating and I'm more relaxed than I've been all day."

"Good to hear." Winston led her closer to the campfire to shed light on her injury. "Maybe you can have another bath before we ride off in the morning."

"I'd like that," she said with a cryptic smile.

Hud bit back a grin. He'd like that, too. One last phenomenal tryst to tide him over for, oh, say, the next fifty years. He'd give all of his tomorrows to spend a few more hours with Bri in breathless ecstasy.

To his dismay, the other men demanded Bri's attention during supper. Hud was left to eat in silence. When Winston insisted on a detailed report of her ordeal, Hud held his breath. He wondered how she would explain what happened this morning when he lost track of her. Thankfully, her story coincided with his explanation that she had gone down to the pool to bathe then ambled to the buffalo wallow, where Jarvis had launched his surprise attack and she had no opportunity to alert Hud.

Bri had covered for him and he was grateful. However, he still didn't know if she had originally planned to head west without him after she'd paid him for her first experiment with passion. She hadn't said and he hadn't asked. Of course, he'd been too busy lusting after her this evening to get around to asking questions.

Hud ate his meal and told himself that he'd return the money she'd tossed at him, first thing tomorrow morning. For now, he sat back and watched Winston Price dote on his daughter while she practically charmed the pants off Hud's fellow Rangers.

She had charmed the pants off him—literally—the past few days and made him relish every wild, reckless, uncontrollable moment.

The erotic thought made Hud grin. He looked the other way so the Rangers wouldn't notice that he was smiling for no reason the present conversation could possibly explain.

Chapter Fifteen

"Now that you've had a decent night's sleep and I've checked your wound again, we are going to have a private talk, young lady," Bri's father said firmly the next morning.

While the Rangers prepared coffee and breakfast, and Hud strode off to rouse Jarvis, her father shepherded Bri away from camp. He halted when he was out of earshot of the other men then pivoted to frown at her in disapproval.

"Hud tells me that you left The Flat without him. Yesterday morning when he woke up you were gone. He thought you were headed west without him. Why was that?"

"Captain Stone is a tattletale," she replied, smiling playfully. "I wouldn't have thought it."

Her father wasn't to be cajoled out of spouting his lecture. His brows flattered over his narrowed brown eyes and he stared sternly at her. "I respect and appreciate your independent and self-reliant nature, you know that, Bri. Unfortunately, this is wild, unforgiving country. Ruthless heathens run loose, as you found out yesterday. Captain Stone also told me that he felt responsible for your striking off alone from The Flat because he was impolite and judgmental when you two first met."

"I—" She tried to wedge in a comment but her father talked over her.

"However," he added, using the commanding tone he usually saved for his army troops and Ranger battalion, "he assured me that you felt justified and that you were on a crusade to rescue three young orphans."

Bri huffed out a breath. "Goodness, Captain Stone did spill his guts to you, didn't he?"

"Hud is a former soldier and now a highly regarded Texas Ranger," he reminded her. "He wanted me to have all the facts to explain how he managed to lose you *twice.* And do not think for one minute that I didn't express my displeasure to him. I most certainly did. He is one of our best men, but even he can't keep track of my strong-willed daughter, who has to take responsibility for her part in this rescue-party fiasco."

Bri wisely kept her trap shut while her father clasped his hands behind his back and paced along the riverbank. "Since we are closer to The Flat than Angel Mesa, I have decided to escort you to town," he announced.

"Good, I have a few matters to attend while we're there."

"The boys?" he guessed correctly.

She nodded. "I'm taking them with me on a sightseeing trip west." She was also going to have Powell arrested for kidnapping if he was still in town.

"I'm not in favor of your traipsing off to explore the west with only three young boys for protection," he objected. "I also know about the incident with Powell that prompted you to cancel your engagement."

Bri rolled her eyes and sighed. "Captain Stone has a loose tongue, indeed."

Her father flung up both hands. "Now don't go stomping off to chew on his ear for offering me explanations for your behavior and actions. Actually, he defended you to me and shouldered all the blame."

Hud had defended her?

"I learned from Jarvis yesterday that he and his partner were *paid* to kidnap me as retaliation for rejecting Powell's engagement," she reported. "Fortunately for me, I left town earlier than planned. Otherwise, I might still be stashed out of sight and at the mercy of Jarvis."

"What?" her father howled in outrage, his eyes popping.

Bri nodded sharply. "In fact, if not for the bungled abduction in The Flat, Jarvis wouldn't have known who I was. He captured me yesterday, planning to ransom me to *you* and to blackmail *Powell,* who arranged my abduction."

"What!" her father roared furiously.

"Is everything all right?"

At the unexpected sound of Hud's voice, Bri lurched around to see him striding toward her.

"Everything is fine," she insisted.

"No, it is not!" her father boomed like a cannon.

Bri clamped her hand over her father's mouth to shush him. "It isn't anything I can't handle," she told Hud.

Hud's amber-colored gaze bore into her. "I've heard that before from you and it always makes me nervous."

"Did you have something to report, Captain Stone?" Bri asked, sounding as military-like as her father.

The faintest hint of a smile quirked Hud's lips. He

glanced from Bri to her father. "As a matter of fact I do, *Commander Price*. After serving Jarvis a breakfast of empty shells that he used to blast away at Bri, I applied a few tried-and-true methods of persuasion. Jarvis admitted that he shot Speck Horton." His expression became very serious. "Also, Jarvis had planned to use the confiscated badge to pass himself off as a Ranger, if the situation presented itself in the future."

"Conniving rascal," her father muttered sourly.

"I request permission to escort Jarvis to Tascosa and see that he is bound over for trial immediately. Marshal Vickers can hold him in custody and we can set a court date quickly since the circuit judge resides in town."

"Very well," her father replied. "I'm escorting Bri to The Flat to—" He glanced at her curiously when she shook her head in warning. "So we can visit before I return to duty."

Bri stared at Hud, knowing this was likely the last time she would see him, knowing she could never bring herself to confide her feelings for him because he didn't intend to be a part of her future. It broke her heart to know that of all the men she could have had, because of her wealth and social connections, she couldn't have the only man she wanted.

What had Hud told her? Ah, yes, he had said that sometimes you had to let go of the very thing you treasure most—or something to that effect.

The thought prompted her to reach for the water-logged pocket watch. Her heart twisted in her chest when she realized she had lost that, too. It must be somewhere between here and the buffalo wallow, where Jarvis had jackknifed her over her horse and led her away. Her link to Benji was gone and her soul-deep affection for Hud would become a bittersweet memory very soon, too.

"Papa, would you mind if I thanked Captain Stone in private for escorting me cross-country? As you reminded me, I need to apologize for causing him so much frustration and distress this past week."

Her father bobbed his head then stared sternly at Hud. "In return, Captain, you can apologize, *again,* for your wrongful assumptions about my daughter and for your neglect that left her in a killer's hands yesterday."

On that parting remark, Commander Price strode off to rejoin the other Rangers.

Hud watched until Winston was out of earshot before turning his full attention to Bri. There was something going on here. For some reason Bri was withholding information from him and he wanted to know *what*—and *why.*

"Mind telling me why you shushed your father when he was trying to explain something to me?"

"Yes, I mind. Unlike you, who tells everything he knows to his commanding officer—"

"Not everything," he interrupted with a pointed stare.

She blushed but she added, "I prefer discretion."

Hud snorted at that. "I call it withholding valuable information in most instances."

"For instance?" She elevated a challenging brow.

"Like the time you left The Flat without bothering to tell me. Like throwing money at me for giving you lessons in passion and then wandering off without alerting me."

"Surely you're smart enough to figure out why I did it," she sniped, tilting her chin to a defiant angle. "I was certainly astute enough to deduce why you moved your pallet to the far side of the cavern after I seduced you twice."

Hud gaped at her. She thought he had rejected her? Hell, he had tried to be courteous and considerate and she had misunderstood. If she'd taken it the wrong way, was that why she'd tossed money at him? Had she felt insulted, as he had?

"Listen, Bri—"

"Never mind. It doesn't matter now," she interrupted.

Hud grunted uncomfortably when she launched herself in his arms unexpectedly and kissed the breath clean out of him. His brain broke down in the time it took to blink. He forgot what he intended to say, just kissed her ravenously, urgently. He knew this was the last moment of privacy they'd share—ever. He wasn't about to waste precious time talking when he could hold Bri in his arms, inhale her tantalizing scent and commit every treasured moment with her to everlasting memory.

Sometimes you have to let go of the priceless treasure you want to keep in order to survive, the sensible voice in his head said. *Don't hold onto impossible dreams. You aren't good enough for her and you damn well know it.*

Hud clutched Bri to him and devoured her lips. His hands roamed over her lush curves and swells, savoring the feel of her shapely body beneath his fingertips. He held her possessively against him, letting her feel the dramatic and immediate effect she had on him.

"I'm going to miss you like crazy, despite everything," she whispered when she broke the heated kiss. "I'm sorry for worrying you."

"You were worth it." He brushed his thumb over the rigid peak of her breast and watched her expressive eyes darken with desire.

"So were you," she rasped. "No hard feelings?"

Hud grinned rakishly as he glided familiarly against her. "I wouldn't go so far as to say that."

Her impish laughter filled all the empty crevices in his soul. She reached up to smooth his tousled hair away from his forehead then pushed up on tiptoe to place one last kiss to his lips. "I wish—"

She sighed audibly then stepped away. He wondered what a woman who had everything she could possibly want—and then some—might possibly wish for. As for him, he'd like to share one last uninterrupted moment of pleasure with her. But that had been impossible this morning because she had strode off to bathe while he used *un*friendly persuasion on Jarvis.

"Goodbye, Hud," she murmured before she walked away.

"Goodbye, Bri. Tell the boys hello for me."

She glanced back and smiled at him. Then she disappeared from sight like a shimmering dream swallowed up in shadows.

Hud watched Winston Price and Bri ride down the road. An uncomfortable twinge clamped around his chest. He'd felt as if there was more he needed to say to Bri, but he wasn't sure what it was. Now it didn't matter because he hadn't been able to speak privately with her before she rode away.

Marcus Yeager whistled appreciatively as he saddled his horse. "That is one gorgeous woman."

"That she is," Hud agreed.

"Some men get all the easy duties."

Hud grinned good-naturedly when Marc chuckled teasingly.

"If she wasn't the commander's only daughter and

entirely too bold and independent for her own good, I'd say she'd be the perfect female," Floyd Lambert remarked as he strapped his saddlebags in place.

"She's also the kind of woman who could get a man discharged from duty if he overstepped propriety," Major Ketter said with a meaningful glance in Hud's direction.

Hud tightened Rambler's cinch and kept his expression carefully blank because all eyes were on him. "I'm relieved Commander Price is here to take Bri off my hands." *Liar!* "I want to make certain Jarvis is locked up tight."

His companions' taunting smiles faded as they nodded in solemn agreement.

"As soon as you hand over your prisoner to Marshal Vickers in Tascosa and fill out the paperwork, you'll need to ride to The Flat," the major declared.

Hud glanced up and frowned. "Why?"

"Our new recruit will be arriving soon and you're breaking him in."

He supposed that's just what he needed to preoccupy him from bittersweet thoughts of that indigo-eyed siren.

Hud waved farewell when the Rangers rode west. Then he walked his horse over to order Jarvis to mount up. The drunken outlaw was still groggy and surly from his hangover. Hud set a swift pace, anxious to have Jarvis behind bars, awaiting a trial.

Bri settled more comfortably on the padded seat of the stagecoach that rolled toward The Flat. She and her father had been fortunate to arrive at one of the stage stations minutes before the eastbound stage pulled in to hitch up fresh horses.

She had quickly changed into her drab gray dress and

bonnet while her father tied their mounts to the back of the coach. Since the only passenger stepped down to wait for the southbound stage, they had the coach to themselves for the last leg of the journey. They were making excellent time that afternoon and the driver predicted they'd reach The Flat in time for a late supper.

"Now about those orphans," her father commented as he sprawled out on the seat across from her.

"You'll have the chance to meet the boys this evening," she declared. "The theater troupe is due to arrive back in town today and set up for tomorrow's performance."

Her father pulled a face. "Is this because I sided with your mother about your friend in Houston? How many orphans do you plan to save on your way to the west coast?"

"How many innocent victims do you plan to save by placing Ranger battalions on the frontier to control lawlessness?"

Her father sighed audibly then slumped back on the seat. "Touché. I understand your need to rescue orphans to compensate for your friend who didn't survive. But taking in *all* of them isn't feasible, Bri."

She shrugged casually. "I will be satisfied if I can place abandoned children in caring homes or find them jobs to support themselves. It is my way of honoring Benji, who taught me how the other half lived."

Her father finally nodded his approval. "I made a mistake with your friend Benji," he admitted. "I was afraid your friendship might become more than your mother could tolerate. She can make a person's life miserable when she really tries."

Bri smiled wryly. "You're right. Mother doesn't

relate to anyone beneath her elevated station. She would have put great effort into making Benji feel unwanted and unaccepted at our estate. I should have tried to place him elsewhere so I could visit him on occasion."

She thought of the lost pocket watch that she had carried faithfully for years. A reminder of a lost friend. Then she thought of Hud's priceless heirloom necklace that belonged to his grandmother. He had sacrificed the keepsake to feed himself and Speck. Now her watch had gone the same way as Hud's family heirloom.

"When we reach The Flat, I'm heading directly to Powell's room, if he's still in town," her father insisted. "I will delight in placing that conniving scoundrel in chains and having him transported to Austin in disgrace to face scandal and prosecution."

Bri flung up her hand. "Powell *paid* to have *me* abducted. I intend to have my say and my revenge first," she demanded emphatically. "After that you can drag him through the street in chains. Drag him all the way to Austin if you want. But I want to see the look on his face when he realizes I survived and that his own treachery will cause the downfall of his reputation and his political ambitions."

"That reminds me," her father said, staring curiously at her. "Why didn't you want Hud to know that Powell paid Jarvis to abduct you?"

"Because I have detained and frustrated him long enough. He is anxious to put *his* obligation to his dearest friend to rest by incarcerating Jarvis," Bri explained. "It is *my* mission to repay Powell personally."

She stared earnestly at her father. "When I detoured north with the boys so they could become acquainted with the theater troupe, I cost Hud a day of traveling.

When we realized Jarvis was in The Flat I urged him to backtrack, but he refused to abandon me. I don't want him to think it's his responsibility to deal with Powell. Hud is the kind of man who honors obligations and I don't want to be his obligation. I refuse for Hud to put his important trip to Tascosa on hold for me."

Her father was watching her so closely that she felt the need to fill the stilted silence. She chose her words carefully. "The time I've spent with Hud has…endeared him to me. I respect and admire him greatly and I don't want to waylay him from arraigning Mad Joe Jarvis."

There, that didn't sound so serious that it might alert her father to her deep-felt affection for Hud. She wasn't about to confide to her father that she had fallen in lust and then hopelessly in love with a man she had known less than a week, a man who only wanted to appease his needs with her when the situation presented itself.

Couldn't have her father storming off in a blind rage to gun down Hud because *she* had seduced *him,* now could she?

"I saw how upset and worried Hud was when you were captured," her father replied. "He cares about you, too, and he would want to know that Powell set you up."

Hud *desired* her, but she couldn't tell that to her father, either. "His reputation was at stake because you gave him a direct order and he had yet to carry it out," she said.

Her father smiled. "I think there's more to it than that."

So did she. *Lust.*

"The point is that we said our official goodbye and I thanked Hud for his time and his effort in keeping me safe. Now it's time to let go."

You have to know when to let go, she reminded herself.

"I still don't see why—"

Bri ran out of patience and made a slashing gesture with her hand to forestall another probing question. "I don't need some big, strong Texas Ranger to fight my battles for me. I don't need him to come riding in to save my day. I can deal effectively with Powell. I *want* to deal with him. I *relish* the opportunity. If anyone is going to punch Powell in the mouth it's going to be me."

Her father chuckled. "Fair enough, sweetheart. You can rant and rave at him and smack him around a few times. Then I'll barge in to put him in shackles. We'll both have our fun with the worthless fiancé your mother handpicked for you. Deal?"

"Deal," she confirmed. "The only thing that devious, backstabbing politician will be *running for* is his *life*."

Chapter Sixteen

Hud's stomach was growling something fierce so he reached into his saddlebag to retrieve hardtack to tide him over until they reached the next stage station along the route. The past hour had been uneventful. Jarvis had dozed off and awakened only to demand whiskey or to relieve himself. Hud didn't give him a drop of liquor, though the hopeless drunk had the shakes so bad he was a mass of twitches.

"You're a heartless bastard," Jarvis snarled while they went down the road.

"And you'd know, being one yourself," Hud retorted.

Jarvis squinted at him. "How far to Tascosa?"

"Hours away. We're closer to The Flat, but you'll go to trial faster if I take you all the way to Tascosa."

Jarvis pushed himself upright in the saddle. "How 'bout if we veer to The Flat and I cut you in on the deal. I can arrange to set up both of us for life."

"Not interested. I've been offered deals by the likes of you before, Jarvis."

"I'm not talkin' about a small-time bribe," he insisted. "I'm talkin' plenty of money to live in luxury."

Hud eyed him curiously. "I'm listening."

Jarvis grinned, exposing his jagged yellow teeth. "Double blackmail. We split it right down the middle. You go your way and I'll go mine."

"Go on," Hud encouraged, unsure where Jarvis was going with his unexpected offer.

"First off, Ray Novak, the rancher I worked for, sends out his men to steal weanin'-size calves from his neighbors. Then we brand them and he drives them up the trail to sell at Dodge City."

"So we're going to blackmail Novak for rustling?"

Jarvis nodded and his stringy hair brushed over his angular features. "That should bring in good money. Besides that, Novak has been paddin' that politician's pocket for favors. Then we blackmail the politician, too."

"For accepting the bribes?"

Jarvis frowned, bemused. "She didn't tell you? Go figure."

An uneasy sensation dribbled down Hud's spine. She, he presumed, was *Bri*. What the hell had she kept from him?

"What else do we have on the politician that will set us up for life?" Hud prodded.

"He paid me to kidnap his fiancée from The Flat."

Cold fury settled in the pit of Hud's belly and his hand curled into a tight fist. He itched to break a few of Powell's teeth and bash in his arrogant smile.

"Powell was debatin' which would get him more votes, havin' his fiancée temporarily disappear then return or just lose her completely."

When Hud snarled ferociously, Jarvis cocked a bushy brow. "You sweet on that hellion? Don't know why. She fights like a wildcat… Hey!"

Jarvis yelped when Hud gouged Rambler and took off east. The outlaw's horse bolted sideways, flinging him around like a rag doll.

"What's the matter with you? Are you takin' the deal or not?" Jarvis wanted to know as he settled himself upright on the saddle.

"No deal," Hud muttered as he veered straight east toward the valley that led to Government Hill and The Flat. "I'm leaving you with Marshal Long. You can rot in jail, waiting for the circuit judge to make his rounds. Powell and Novak can keep you company."

While Jarvis swore foully then complained about the furious pace, Hud silently cursed Bri for neglecting to tell him that Powell had paid to have her spirited off so he could add a dramatic flair to his campaign.

How dare she keep that from him! She knew he'd want to break that haughty dandy into bite-sized pieces then feed his sorry carcass to the wolves…

Which was why she didn't tell me, Hud realized insightfully. *She* wanted to confront him, damn that fiery little imp. *She* wanted to see the look of shock on Powell's face when she accused him of paying for her abduction. She thought Hud would steal her thunder and she wanted to prove that she was capable of handling the situation herself.

He wondered if Commander Price would be allowed to witness the confrontation. Her father maybe, but not Hud. Well to hell with being left out! he thought indignantly. The least he could do was be there to hold Powell down while Bri took out her outraged fury on him.

If Hud was good enough to share a secret tryst, why wasn't he special enough to be included in the reckoning?

Maybe I should blackmail Gabrielle Price, he thought spitefully, his pride smarting something fierce. Maybe she should have to pay good money for his silence about their steamy, passionate trysts. That'd show her.

Hud huffed out his breath and told himself to calm down and think rationally. He had to accept that Bri wasn't interested in an ongoing affair or even a lasting friendship. Their time had come and gone, so that was that. Period. End of story.

Let her go, said the sensible voice in his head. *Let her have her revenge in her own way. She doesn't need you and you don't need her, either.*

Yet, the thought of never holding Bri again made his heart twist so tightly in his chest that it hurt to breathe.

He knew he couldn't match her formal education, her social connections or her financial status. There was nothing whatsoever that he could give Gabrielle Price that she didn't have already. They were as far apart on the social pendulum as two people could get.

Nonetheless, he refused to switch direction and head to Tascosa. Instead, he took a grueling shortcut to The Flat because he had to see for himself that nothing went wrong during Bri's confrontation with Powell.

There was always the chance that the cocky dandy might try to make a run for it. Hud could shoot his legs out from under him so Bri wouldn't have to exert much effort to overtake him. Even if it hurt Hud's feelings that

Bri didn't think enough of him to confide in him, blasting Powell until he leaked like a sieve held tremendous appeal.

"Eaton Powell's poor fiancée has finally been rescued from her terrifying ordeal! Isn't that wonderful news?"

Bri looked up from beneath the floppy brim of her gray bonnet to stare blankly at the young clerk who was manning the hotel counter. While he beamed with excitement, she wondered what devious scheme Powell had devised this time.

"That is good to know," she murmured as she retrieved money from her pocket. She couldn't check in using the name of Price, she mused. That would draw curiosity and she wanted nothing to spoil the surprise she had planned for her sinister ex-fiancé. "I would like two rooms please…for Bri and Hud Stone."

When she handed over the money, the clerk presented her with two keys. "Naturally, Mizz Price is completely exhausted," he added conversationally. "She's resting in the suite."

Bri silently fumed. There was no end to Powell's manipulation and cunning. *Until now,* she promised herself. Very soon, Powell would be behind bars and in the midst of a firestorm of scandal. When her side of the story hit the newspapers, she would bury his political campaign in a grave of bad publicity.

While her father was stabling their horses at the livery, Bri carried her satchels upstairs to enter the same room she had used during her first trip to The Flat. Originally, she had planned to bathe and dine before she lowered the boom on Powell, but the urge to confront him, after hearing about his latest publicity stunt, overwhelmed her. She was mad as hell at him and she wanted revenge—now!

"He'll rue the day," Bri muttered as she tossed aside her bags.

Wheeling around, she pelted down the hall. She didn't bother to knock on the door of the suite, just turned the knob—and found it locked. Muttering at the inconvenient delay, she reached beneath her bonnet to retrieve a hairpin.

"Thank you, Benji," she murmured as she used the skill he'd taught her to pick the lock.

When she opened the door, she looked into the mirror that hung over the dresser in the bedroom. She saw Powell's naked back and a bare-chested woman and thought, *Isn't this where I came in?*

She squinted to get a closer look at the woman, whose hair was the exact color of hers. When she recognized Sylvia Ford's facial features, surrounded by a red-gold wig, Bri understood Powell's clever scheme.

It was a damn shame that he couldn't use his cunning for the benefit of the good citizens of this state and the nation. He might have made a fine senator—if you overlooked his multiple flaws of character and personality.

Oh, well, she thought as she tiptoed across the sitting room. Maybe Powell could organize a political society while he was doing time in the penitentiary.

"Hello, darling, I'm back," she announced in a mocking tone. "Did you miss me?"

Powell yowled in surprise and ceased groping Sylvia. He twisted around to see Bri standing in the doorway.

"You!" he snarled furiously.

Powell shot off the bed like a discharging bullet and plowed into her. Before Bri could latch on to the dagger or defective derringer strapped to her thigh, he slammed into her. It was a stroke of bad luck that the tender knot on her head hit the edge of the doorjamb. Pain shot through her skull and stars exploded in front of her eyes.

She thought she heard Powell shouting curses at her from a long winding tunnel a second before the world turned black as pitch and she collapsed in a crumpled heap on the floor.

Hud towed his reluctant prisoner inside the jail to see Marshal Long sitting behind his desk that was stacked with papers. He had his feet propped up and his beefy hands clasped behind his head. He bounded up to grab the keys to the cells when Hud gestured to the door at the back of the office.

"This is the man who shot a Ranger and robbed at least two stagecoach stations," Hud said hurriedly.

"I didn't do nothin' wrong!" Jarvis hooted. "I'm innocent and I need a damn drink!"

Hud cast him a withering glance and marched him into the cell to slam the barred door in his face. "Jarvis also worked for a rancher named Ray Novak. Have you heard of him?"

The marshal nodded in recognition. "Yep. He owns a big spread north of here. There have been rumors and accusations circulating for years, but no conclusive evidence that he rustles his neighbors' cattle then drives them to Dodge."

"For a drink or two, Jarvis might share his incriminating information with you." Hud slammed the door to the outer office when Jarvis commenced shouting and rattling the bars in outrage. "How long before the circuit judge passes through here?"

"End of next week," Sparrow replied as he plunked down in his chair to fill out the paperwork for his new prisoner.

"I plan to be here to testify against him for charges of murder, robbery, kidnapping and assault," Hud declared.

"This is turning out to be a good day," Sparrow remarked with a smile. "First the politician finds his missing fiancée and now you've captured that murdering thief."

Hud frowned, bemused. "Powell found Gabrielle Price? What the hell does that mean? Didn't you receive my note?" He smacked himself on the forehead when he remembered that Lieutenant Davis had been detained because he was chasing renegades back to the reservation.

"What note?" Sparrow asked.

"Never mind. What about Powell?" Hud prodded impatiently.

Sparrow's shoulder lifted in a shrug. "All I know is that he rode out of town to check a couple of abandoned shacks. He returned with Mizz Price, who claimed she'd been blindfolded, bound up and detained for several days."

"That isn't right," Hud protested. "I know that for a fact because *I* located Bri several days ago. She should have arrived with Commander Price a few hours earlier."

"What?" The marshal bolted to his feet. "Then who was that woman riding in the wagon with Powell? He escorted her to the hotel so she could rest and recuperate."

Hud didn't know the answer to that question, but he sure as hell intended to find out what was going on. And where the blazes were Bri and Winston Price? Damn it, they better not have met with trouble during their journey to town.

He burst from the office and jogged toward Brazos Hotel. Marshal Long was two steps behind him.

"What the blazes do you think is going on?" the marshal panted as he scurried to keep up with Hud's long, impatient strides.

"I think maybe the politician *hired* someone to portray his missing fiancée," Hud said over his shoulder.

"Why would he do that?"

"Besides taking advantage of free publicity for his campaign and drawing sympathy votes, you mean?"

"Damn, I even bought him a meal after he returned to town from Austin. The stagecoach he was riding in was robbed," Marshal Long muttered, thoroughly disgusted.

"I know for a fact that Powell hired Jarvis and his former partner to abduct Mizz Price. She canceled their engagement against his wishes and he retaliated."

"Well, hell," the marshal said, scowling. "He's been playing one dirty trick after another."

"You said it, Sparrow. I'm in favor of shooting him and putting him out of our misery," Hud grumbled spitefully.

"It's what he deserves. He had this whole town feeling sorry for him. He played the role of a desperate, forlorn fiancé to the hilt."

"That's it!" Hud erupted abruptly.

The marshal angled his head in a birdlike manner. "What's it?"

"Powell was playing his role like an actor. He probably hired someone from the theater troupe to impersonate Gabrielle Price. Probably the redhead that Gabrielle caught Powell rolling around with in bed."

"Damn, I'm the marshal of this town and I'm supposed

to know all and see all," he complained. "Why didn't I know this?"

Hud didn't bother to comment. He broke into a run when he saw Commander Price striding across the street, laden down with saddlebags and puffing on his pipe. Winston frowned, befuddled, when he recognized Hud.

"What are you doing here? I thought you were headed to Tascosa so Jarvis could go to trial immediately."

"Change of plans. I double-timed it here when Jarvis told me that Powell had arranged to have Bri kidnapped. Nice of her to tell me," he muttered, disgruntled.

"She claimed she didn't want you to feel obligated to sort all this out," said Winston. "Plus, she wanted to handle this herself."

Obligated? After all they'd been through together this week? He felt a damn sight more than obligation. Didn't she know that? "Why are you so late getting here?" Hud asked curiously.

Winston puffed on his pipe. "Had to delay to repair a broken wheel."

Remembering his manners, Hud hitched his thumb over his shoulder. "Commander Price, this is Marshal Long, or Sparrow as he's affectionately known."

"Glad to meet you," the marshal panted, still trying to catch his breath.

"Where's Bri?" Hud demanded.

"She's renting our rooms." Winston took off toward the hotel. "We decided to freshen up before she confronted Powell. Then I plan to swoop in to take him into custody."

"I'm betting she decided to confront him immediately, if she heard the news that Powell rescued his missing fiancée this afternoon and brought her to the hotel to recuperate."

"What the hell—?" Winston choked on his pipe smoke and practically coughed his head off.

Hud left Sparrow to whack Winston between the shoulder blades until his throat and lungs cleared of smoke. Not knowing precisely where Bri was worried the hell out of Hud.

She had better be in her room, lounging in her bath, waiting for her father to arrive, damn it.

The moment he entered the hotel lobby he veered to the counter. "Did a woman check in here this evening?"

The young man nodded and smiled. "Yes. Two rooms for Bri and Hud Stone," he reported.

Bri and Hud Stone? he mused. Interesting.

"She rented the two rooms at the west end of the upstairs hall," said the clerk. "And isn't it grand that Mr. Powell found his fiancée this afternoon?"

"Did you tell Bri that?" Hud demanded curtly.

The clerk's smile fizzled out and he frowned, puzzled by Hud's sharp tone. "Yes, sir. I've told everyone who's checked in. The whole town has been worried about the poor woman."

Muttering a foul oath, Hud took the steps two at a time. The clatter behind him indicated that Sparrow and the commander were bringing up the rear. Hud veered toward the west end of the hall. He rapped his knuckles impatiently on the door but received no immediate response.

"Where could she be?" Winston asked from behind him.

As if he didn't know. Hud scowled as he spun around then brushed past Winston and Sparrow to stride quickly toward the spacious suite at the far end of the hall. He pounded on the door but no one answered.

Since the door was locked and he was worried as hell

about Bri, Hud hiked up his leg and kicked the knob with his boot heel. Then he rammed the door with his shoulder. Wood splintered and dust dribbled from the woodwork as the door wobbled open.

He charged inside to see the mirror hanging above the dresser. As Bri had mentioned, it provided a clear view of the bed in the adjoining room. The sheets were rumpled and the bedspread was missing.

That was not a good omen for Bri, Hud decided.

"Where is that deceitful bastard?" Winston growled as he barged past Hud to check the bedroom. "His luggage is here."

Hud reversed direction and headed for the stairs. "I'm betting Bri was here and she didn't leave of her own accord."

"God! I know better than to leave her unsupervised," Winston howled in frustration. "How could I let her disappear without double-checking on her?"

Hud glanced over his shoulder and said, "Welcome to the club, Commander."

Bri came to and found herself bound, gagged and rolled in a bedspread. She hung over Powell's shoulder like a feed sack and she took special pains not to move so he wouldn't know she had regained consciousness.

"You are such a nuisance," Powell complained as he tossed Bri into what she presumed to be the bed of a wagon.

She bit back a groan when the knot on the back of her head collided with the wooden planks.

"I'm not sure about this," Sylvia Ford said uneasily. "I agreed to pretend to be your missing fiancée for a certain price. And I will accompany you down the stagecoach line as you requested, to pretend to die in an unfortunate accident. But I don't want anyone's death on my conscience, Eaton."

Bri sighed inwardly. Not only had Powell hired Sylvia to pose as his missing fiancée, but he also had planned to pretend to kill her—somewhere between here and Austin. Damn, was there no end to the extremes Powell was willing to go to protect himself?

Honestly, she could see little difference between him and Mad Joe Jarvis. They were both rotten to the core. The only difference was that Powell dressed in the latest fashion and Jarvis didn't. Other than that…

"I don't have a choice," Powell insisted. "If she speaks out now, my life and my political career will be ruined. It's she or I. I choose *me*, so climb up on the damn seat and let's get rolling before someone sees us and starts posing incriminating questions I don't want to have to answer."

Bri felt the wagon shift as Powell piled onto the seat and Sylvia joined him a moment later.

"I recognized your fiancée," Sylvia declared in a voice filled with nervous apprehension. "I know for a fact that she was with a Texas Ranger. They joined our traveling caravan for a day. If he comes around, asking questions—"

"Stop worrying," he interrupted sharply. "You'll be in Austin by then. I'll make sure you have a blossoming career in a reputable theater troupe, not that roaming band of gypsies and bad actors you're sharing a stage with now. You have real potential, Sylvia," he praised to win her over. "If you help me then I'll help you. That's the way the game is played."

"I don't know—"

"Shut up!" Powell snapped, dropping his coaxing tone—which didn't seem to be working with Sylvia. "If you don't keep quiet about this, you won't last the night and your career in theater will be over before it gets started!"

While wrapped in the bedspread, Bri contorted her body and reached down with her bound hands to retrieve the knife strapped to her thigh. The motion of the wagon jostled her sideways as it picked up speed. She heard the clatter of hooves and the rattle of other wagons that indicated Powell had left the alley and pulled onto the street.

She wished she could rip off the gag and scream her head off. Instead, she grabbed her knife and sawed on the ropes that secured her wrists.

Mercy, was it only yesterday that she'd had to free herself from confining ropes to escape from Jarvis? She was getting far more experience as an escape artist than she preferred. Maybe she should work up an act and take it on the road with the theater troupe.

She allowed herself a wry smile, thinking her new career would infuriate her snobbish mother to no end— which made it tremendously appealing to Bri.

First things first, she reminded herself as she pulled her hands free. It was time to give the devil his due.

Chapter Seventeen

B ri sawed through the rope that Powell had wrapped around her ankles. The process took a few minutes. Since she was buried in the bedspread, she couldn't tell how much attention Powell was paying to the wagon bed. Not much, she hoped.

Despite her throbbing headache, Bri mentally geared up to attempt escape. It would have to be quick and sudden, she reminded herself. Otherwise, Powell would have time to react.

Bri rolled over to her stomach and inched her way from the bedspread like a butterfly shedding its cocoon. When her head emerged, she could see that Sylvia and Powell were staring straight ahead as they drove the wagon down the north road in the cover of darkness.

This was her chance to attack.

Bri crouched down then sprang up to blindside Powell. He howled in surprise when she knocked him off balance then shoved him sideways. Powell squawked as he cartwheeled off the side of the wagon and landed facedown in the dirt.

Sylvia screamed bloody murder, spooking the two horses that thundered off into the night. Bri cursed mightily when the horses' momentum sent her sprawling in the wagon bed. She climbed onto hands and knees then pulled herself onto the vacant spot on the seat. The reins had slipped between the horses and whipped against their flanks, alarming them even more than Sylvia's high-pitched shriek.

"We're going to die!" Sylvia railed hysterically as the horses raced at breakneck speed.

"Stop being so melodramatic," Bri snapped as she jackknifed her body over the seat in attempt to reach the flapping reins.

"Stomp on the brake, Sylvia!" she yelled as she groped for the reins.

When Sylvia finally reacted she dived over Bri's legs to reach the brake. The horses reared up when the wagon wheels locked. Then they bolted sideways, causing Bri to tumble to the ground. Sylvia screeched again, setting off the frightened horses.

Bri didn't move a muscle until the horses and the wagon rolled forward and left her in the clear. Having had the wind knocked out of her, she lay there for a moment to catch her breath.

"For God's sake, woman, can't you take at least one day off from mayhem?"

Bri climbed to her knees then twisted around to see Hud mounted on Rambler. The marshal and her father were five horse-lengths behind him. He was glaring at her as he rode up to offer her a boost so she could climb on Rambler.

Sylvia was still screaming her head off as the horses headed north—and didn't show the slightest sign of stopping.

"Are you okay?" he asked as he half twisted in the saddle to brush a kiss over her cheek.

"No, I have a splitting headache. What is there about me that makes people want to pound on my skull?"

"Gee, I can't imagine. You being the calm, laidback, nonconfrontational person you are," he teased. "*I* want to club you over the head and I'm one of the people who *likes* you."

"You do?" She smiled as she snuggled closer.

"Yes, but I'm mad as hell because you've scared another ten years off my life. You just couldn't wait, could you? Had to go after Powell by yourself," he muttered.

"You know I like to nip problems in the bud instead of allowing them to fester."

"Yes well, sometimes those problems bite back. Like your ex-fiancé. I really hate that guy."

"I'm not fond of him, either… What are you doing here?"

"I changed my plans after Jarvis told me Powell paid him to abduct you from The Flat," he said in a gruff tone.

Even though she could tell he was annoyed with her, Bri looped her arms around his waist, leaned her head against his muscled back and breathed a gigantic sigh of relief.

"I must admit that the confrontation didn't go as I planned."

"Things rarely do." He nudged Rambler sideways when Marshal Long thundered past to overtake the runaway wagon.

"How did you find me?" Bri asked, enjoying the feel of Hud's swarthy body meshed against hers.

"We checked the hotel and found you gone," Hud replied. "Then we went looking in the alleys. Your three boys were visiting their old haunt and they saw Sylvia and her male companion toss something in the wagon behind the freight office. Naturally I thought *you* might be that *something,* given that you have plunged from one disastrous misadventure to the next since I met you."

Bri ignored the censure in his voice and gave him an affection hug. "When I found out that Sylvia was pretending to be me, so Powell could draw more attention to himself for his campaign, it infuriated me. I went after him immediately."

"It was a clever ruse," Hud remarked, "but no one can be you, Bri. You're one of a kind."

"Thank you."

"No, *thank God,*" he added sarcastically. "*One* of *you* is all the world can handle. Even your father is beating himself black and blue because he couldn't keep track of you, either. He's more understanding and forgiving of me since he fell into the same trap."

Hud slung his right leg over the pommel then hopped agilely to the ground. He handed the reins to Bri. "I'm going to chase down your ex-fiancé. When I catch him, you can have first crack at him like you wanted."

She peered into his amber-colored eyes and smiled gratefully. "Thank you. I appreciate that."

When Hud jogged off, her father reined up beside her. "Daughter, you are making me old before my time," he chastised her. "You were supposed to wait for me to provide reinforcement…just in case problems arose… which they did."

"I'm sorry, Papa. After I found out that Powell had pretended to rescue me and was taking all the glory to win votes I was too furious to wait. I certainly wanted to catch him unaware. I walked in on him and Sylvia, but he knocked me against the wall and I reinjured the knot on my head. When I woke up I was in the wagon bed, wrapped up like a mummy."

"Next time you tear off on a harrowing crusade, I'm giving Captain Stone a direct order to go with you," he huffed irritably.

When Hud saw Powell limping away from the road, favoring his left leg, he lowered his head and rammed the dirty, low-down politician in the back. Powell yelped in pain then his breath came out in a whoosh when Hud landed on top of him and slammed his face in the dirt—thrice for good measure.

"Oooff…ouch!" Powell grunted when Hud kneed him the back then grabbed him by the nape of his fashionable jacket and hoisted him none too gently to his feet.

Hud stared into Powell's smudged face and reminded himself that he'd promised to hand over this deceitful scoundrel to Bri. Nevertheless, before he could stop himself, he doubled his fist and punched Powell in the jaw.

The politician stumbled backward, lost his balance and sprawled spread-eagle in the dirt. Now, thought Hud, the man's expensive clothing is equally soiled on both sides.

"Bri!" Hud shouted. "If there's something you want to say to this worthless, conniving, murderer, do it now so I can kill him!"

Powell gaped apprehensively at Hud while Bri trotted up on Rambler. Glowering at Powell, she walked the horse over his prostrate body to hold him captive.

"I have known some sneaky, manipulative individuals in my time," Bri spat furiously at him. "But you are the most self-centered, maneuvering bastard ever to walk the earth." She glared pitchforks at him then snarled at him again. "Your family won't be able to *buy* you the election or *buy* your way out of jail because I will make the charges against you stick. Everyone in this state will know what kind of man you are because I'll be shouting it to high heaven. How *dare* you pay to have me abducted and then try to do it yourself when your scheme backfired!"

Hud grinned while he listened to Bri read Powell every line and paragraph of the riot act. Powell was afraid to move, for fear Rambler would stomp him in the ground. He had to lie there while Bri blasted away at him with both barrels blazing. She was magnificent in her fury and Hud thoroughly enjoyed watching Powell get what he had coming.

"Furthermore, you are not half the man Captain Hudson Stone is," she snapped at Powell. "He has impressive character, high morals and unwavering scruples. And for your information, I never had the slightest intention of marrying you, just because my mother made the arrangements. You are a hopeless bore and Hudson Stone has ten gallons more personality than you do," she ranted at Powell. "When word of your corruption and betrayal spreads across the state, even people who once associated with you will turn their backs on you. You are finished!"

Hud glanced sideways when Commander Price walked up beside him. "Has she taken a breath yet?" Winston asked, smiling at his daughter like a proud father.

"No, she's just getting warmed up."

"While she's giving Powell hell, I want to apologize for being so hard on you."

Hud shrugged nonchalantly. "I deserved it. I didn't

give your daughter full credit for being as capable, willful and courageous as she is, but I won't make that mistake ever again. I'm a lot happier now that I've accepted Bri for what she is, instead of measuring her against average women."

"You're a wise man, but even giving her credit isn't enough to keep in step with Bri," Winston remarked. "I found that out for myself tonight." He faced Hud directly. "I officially retract every insulting comment I made to you."

"Apology accepted. Even though she made me look bad repeatedly, this has been an interesting week. I was reluctant to take the assignment but I'm glad I didn't miss out on it."

Winston eyed him speculatively. "Correct me if I'm wrong, but I think you have taken a personal interest in my daughter, lively and high-spirited though she is. Am I right?"

"Yes, sir, I have," Hud admitted as he shifted awkwardly from one foot to the other. "If that offends you—"

"Glad to hear it," Winston interrupted, smiling. "It will take someone of your caliber and mettle to keep up with her, to watch over her…at a distance…because she has been smothered and restrained far too long already. Now that she's tested herself in difficult situations and discovered that she can handle herself effectively she won't back down."

Hud glanced at Bri, who was still chewing Powell up one side and down the other. Winston was right, he realized. Hovering over Bri only made her indignant, defensive and determined to fight her own battles and to make her own decisions. She wanted to enjoy the same privileges men took for granted. She was proud of her skills and abilities and she wanted the chance to use them. Restricting her made her rebellious.

"With your permission I'd like to take Bri back to the hotel to recuperate," Hud requested. "She told me she had a splitting headache after suffering another painful blow to the back of her head."

Winston nodded agreeably. "I'll help Marshal Long haul Powell and his lady friend to jail. Then I'll swing by one of the restaurants to bring food to our rooms since we missed out on supper."

No sooner had Winston stopped speaking than Sparrow arrived on the scene, driving the wagon. Sylvia was hunched over next to him on the seat, bawling her head off. While Winston mounted his horse, Hud borrowed Sparrow's pinto gelding. He walked the horse over to tap Bri on the shoulder.

"I'm not finished with him yet," she insisted hotly.

"You can march over to the jail in the morning and give Jarvis and Powell another tongue-lashing," Hud suggested helpfully. "Right now you need to rest and re-cuperate so don't try to talk me out of it. I'm putting my foot down in this instance, so don't argue with me because I'm the long arm of the law and I'll throw you in the calaboose if you cross me."

When he grinned teasingly at her, Bri drew in a steady-ing breath. She cast Powell one last mutinous glance while her father and the marshal put him in cuffs and tossed him—none too gently—in the back of the wagon.

"I'm sorry!" Sylvia wailed, startling the horses again.

Hud reached over to grab the reins before the horses tried to bolt and run away again.

Bri flapped her arms to gain the marshal's attention.

"Sylvia wasn't a willing participant in the murder scheme that Powell dreamed up," she announced.

Sylvia's jaw dropped open and she stared at Bri in stunned amazement.

"I overheard Sylvia trying to discourage Powell but he strong-armed her into accompanying him tonight. He even threatened her life if she didn't keep silent."

"Thank you," Sylvia mumbled brokenly.

"Just do me a favor and be more particular about the men you become involved with," Bri advised.

After the tearful actress and the men rode away, Hud leaned over to give Bri a quick peck on the lips.

"Does that mean you aren't mad at me anymore?" she asked.

"It means nothing of the kind," Hud replied as he walked his borrowed horse down the moonlit road. "But that was very sporting of you to let Sylvia off the hook. Also, I'm granting you a reprieve, even though I'd like to give you the kind of lecture you delivered to Powell, because you have a hellish headache."

"You are a most thoughtful and considerate man," she praised, and flashed him a bewitching smile.

"Not to mention my sterling character, upstanding morals and noble scruples," he teased, sitting up a little straighter in the saddle. "You made me sound like a saint."

"The veritable dark angel with one wing in the fire," she added, chuckling. "Best kind of angel there is."

"Just not the *guardian* angel who has been watching over you to make sure you emerge unscathed from your near brushes with disaster," Hud murmured as he reached into his pocket.

He dropped the misplaced watch in the palm of her hand. "I found this beside the buffalo wallow. I'm sure your friend Benji has been looking down from up above, exceptionally pleased at how well you've handled yourself in the face of adversity the past week."

He stared into her eyes, watching them well up with tears. Yet she was smiling as she rubbed her thumb over the watch. Hud wondered if he had purposely neglected to give her the watch this morning so he'd have an excuse to see her again. Letting go of her was turning out to be more difficult than he'd hoped. Hell, it bordered on impossible.

"You exposed a corrupt rancher and a crooked politician. You helped capture a ruthless murderer that I've been chasing and you have rescued three young boys from poverty and starvation." He reached over to wipe away the tears that dribbled down her cheeks and he grinned playfully. "I don't know how much more excitement and adventure you need to make your life complete, but there's always next week, I suppose."

"Hud, you probably don't want to hear this but I l—"

Bri caught herself the second before she blurted out her heartfelt feelings for him. She clamped her mouth shut and tucked the watch in her pocket.

"What were you saying?" Hud asked, refusing to break eye contact. "Finish the sentence, Bri."

When she compressed her lips, refusing to continue, Hud gave up and said, "I think I know why you have clung fiercely to Benji's memory. He taught you valuable survival skills and allowed you to see the world through his eyes. His impact on you is unmistakable and it influences you still today."

"You have made an impact on me, too." She reached over to give his hand a fond squeeze. More than he would ever know.

"Until now I've been envious of the orphan who be-friended you," Hud admitted as he brought her hand to his lips. "I don't resent him anymore. If not for him, you wouldn't see me for who I am and you wouldn't under-stand where I've come from. Also, Benji taught you to be a scrappy fighter who holds her own against difficult odds. I can't fault him for that."

Bri blinked back the tears that threatened to flood her eyes again. She wanted to launch herself from the saddle, throw herself into Hud's arms, and tell him that although Benji had been the infatuation of her youth, Hud had become the love of her life. Instead, she held her tongue and refused to burden him with a confession he probably didn't want to hear.

Not that she'd had the chance. The new Ranger recruit strode up to introduce himself. Bri made her own way to the hotel for a much-needed bath while Hud became acquainted with his new partner. She wondered if she'd see Hud again. She speculated how long it would take to get over loving him. Her best guess was about a hundred years.

An hour later Bri laid her head back against the stack of pillows on the bed in her hotel room and expelled a weary sigh. She had bathed and changed into her night-gown and her father had arrived with a supper tray. When he tried to spoon-feed her, as if she were a helpless invalid, she protested. Smiling good-naturedly, he handed over the silverware.

"So what's next for you?" her father inquired while she sipped the steamy soup.

"I'm not sure." Bri felt at loose ends since the boys had stopped by to check on her and announce that they had decided to remain with the troupe indefinitely. "I still want to see all the sights the western frontier has to offer. Maybe I should hire an escort to show me all the scenic places between here to California."

Winston snorted. "Probably wouldn't find any reputable takers. Besides, you like to live dangerously and anyone who is honorable enough to feel responsible for you would go crazy trying to protect you."

Bri blinked when her father's voice grew more agitated. Then she smiled cajolingly. "I have accepted the fact that being a conventional female doesn't suit me. I was hoping you could accept that, too."

Winston blew out his breath. "In my effort to make certain you were nothing like your mother, I think I might have overencouraged you to become a bit of a daredevil. Now there is no holding you back."

Bri shook her head ruefully. "I don't know what has gotten in to me lately. I seem to have developed a need that I can't fulfill, something that continues to elude me. The shallow life in high society's ballrooms and parlors isn't for me. Adventure and challenges inspire me."

Winston nodded in understanding. "High society didn't suit me, either. Which is why I made a better soldier and Ranger and left your mother to the world of socialites and soirées that she craves." He patted her arm then leaned over to press a kiss to her forehead. "I was pressured by my family and they made a poor match for me. I wish much more for you, sweetheart."

Bri watched her father walk away with the empty supper tray then she heaved a melancholy sigh. After all she'd endured the past week, she longed to savor every moment that she had cheated death. She didn't want to lie in bed alone. She wanted Hud, but he had met up with the new Ranger recruit and there was no telling where they were. In a saloon, perhaps, washing the trail dust from their throats.

She still didn't know if Hud intended to stop in to say goodbye before he rode back to the Rangers' camp. She couldn't sneak off to Hud's room, because she didn't know where it was.

An impish smile pursed her lips, wishing she could pop in on him as she had the first night they met.

Except this time she wouldn't dart off after one kiss.

"Damn it," she muttered, missing him like crazy. "Of all the men I've tolerated as suitors the past few years, I don't get to spend the rest of my life with the only man I truly want."

Bri pounded her pillows to relieve her frustration. It didn't help. "There should be a rule written down somewhere stating that the man who has your heart should love you back."

When someone knocked on her door unexpectedly, she glanced across the room. "Yes?"

"It's Hud. Can I bother you for a few minutes?"

You can bother me for the next fifty years and you won't hear me complain. "Come in."

Her gaze roamed appreciatively over his powerfully built frame when he stepped in and dominated her room with his presence. He smiled and breathed new life into her collapsed heart. Bri tried very hard not to blurt out her feelings for him, but it was difficult when the words ached to fly free.

"Feeling better?" Hud asked.

"Yes, thank you for asking," she said, then silently added, *By the way, I love you.* "How did your meeting with the Ranger recruit go?" *Stay the night. I want to be with you and the thought of losing you forever is killing me bit by excruciating bit!*

"He'll do," Hud said as he locked the door behind him.

Bri's eyebrows elevated two notches and her gaze leaped back and forth between him and the doorknob.

"Never can tell who might barge in unannounced. I was set upon by the kissing bandit in this very hotel."

"Really? How intriguing."

"Yes, it was. Very. Since then I've been chasing her all over creation." He came to stand at the foot of her bed. "There's something I need to talk to you about, Bri."

"Fire away," she invited with a casual flick of her wrist that belied the turmoil of emotions inside her.

Hud strode over to park himself on the edge of her bed. She caught a whiff of his fresh, clean scent and noticed his raven hair was still damp from a recent bath. He was also clean-shaven and she thought he was the most ruggedly handsome man she had ever laid eyes on.

What a shame that all the Price and Roland money combined couldn't buy his love. What good was all that money now? In Hud's eyes, she was just the assignment gone bad, the troublemaker who delayed him and frustrated him.

When he skimmed his forefinger over the bruises on her chin and cheek, she nearly melted into a sentimental puddle. "What did you want to talk to me about?" she managed to say without her voice cracking completely.

"Remember that night when I moved my pallet to the far side of the cavern?" he murmured as his thumb brushed over her lips.

Bri couldn't speak. Her tongue was stuck to the roof of her mouth so she just nodded mutely.

"You got the wrong idea."

"I did?" she chirped.

"Yes, you did," Hud confirmed. "I didn't move to get away from you because I was tired of you. I knew I couldn't keep my hands off you when you were only an arm's length away. After the ordeal with the flash flood, I wanted you to have the chance to rest."

Her lashes swept up to stare into his mesmerizing golden eyes. "I tossed money at you the next morning because my pride was smarting," she admitted. "So…you aren't opposed to being with me?"

A wide smile spread across his sensuous lips. "No, I was sort of hoping that you weren't opposed to being with me. I've been wondering all evening what it would be like to make love with you on a bed instead of the rock floor in that cave."

Bri beamed in anticipation as she scooted over to make room for him beside her. "I'd love to find out myself."

"How's your tender head?" he asked as he trailed moist kisses down the column of her throat.

"It just got better." She peeled off his leather vest and sent it flying. "One of us is overdressed." She helped him out of his shirt so she could splay her hand over his broad chest and sketch the washboarded muscles of his belly.

"Mmm…" Hud groaned in pleasure. "Your father tells me that you're looking to hire an escort for your tour of the West."

"I can afford to pay well," she whispered as she leaned sideways to skim her lips over his male nipples. "Know anyone who might be interested?"

"Me, but I'm here to negotiate." He tugged the nightgown over her head and tossed it on top of his vest and shirt. "I'm in the market for a wife who will help me build my ranch on the land grant I'll receive when I retire from Ranger service very soon."

She reared back and gaped at him. *"Wife?"*

He nodded and grinned. "I asked your father for permission to propose and he said you were blind and foolish if you didn't snatch up a fine catch like me immediately."

"I wouldn't want to be called blind and foolish," she said, feeling her heart swell with so much happiness and contentment that she was afraid it might burst wide open.

"Is that a yes?" he asked as his hand glided up her ribcage to caress the peaks of her breasts.

"Yes..." she breathed raggedly as hot sensations scalded her from inside out.

"I'm in love with you, Bri," Hud confided as he stared intently into her indigo eyes. "When I'm with you, I'm at peace with my life. I can't lay the world at your feet, but I promise I will love you all the rest of my days. If you want adventure then I'll be by your side to make sure you have it."

"You are my world, Hud," she whispered as she cupped his face in her hands and stared deeply into his eyes. "All I'll ever need is you because I love you, too. I almost blurted it out earlier this evening."

He smiled crookedly. "I was hoping that was what you intended to say but I couldn't pry it out of you."

"I was afraid you didn't want to hear that from a troublemaker like me," she replied as she trailed the pad of her thumb over his sensuous lower lip.

He chuckled lightly as he lowered his head, his lips a scant few inches from her lush mouth. "You're my kind of trouble, sweetheart," he assured her. "I tried to do the honorable thing and walk away but I couldn't tolerate the thought of life without you. Plus, I've recently discovered that sometimes you don't have to let go of your most precious treasure." He stared intently at her so she would understand that he meant every word he said. "That's what you are to me, Bri. A treasure. You're all I need to make me happy."

She smiled impishly at him, her indigo eyes sparkling as she draped her arms around his shoulders and snuggled suggestively against him. "Really? Prove it."

"Gladly," he whispered before he kissed her as if he were starved for the taste of her—which he always had been and always would be. Bri reciprocated with the kind of fiery passion that never ceased to amaze and arouse him. Then he offered all that he was to the only woman his heart desired.

And he loved her devotedly…from that day forward until the end of forever…

* * * * *

*Celebrate 60 years of pure reading pleasure
with Harlequin® Books!*

*Harlequin Romance® is celebrating by
showering you with DIAMOND BRIDES
in February 2009.
Six stories that promise to bring a touch of
sparkle to your life, with diamond proposals
and dazzling weddings, sparkling brides
and gorgeous grooms!*

*Enjoy a sneak peek at Caroline Anderson's
TWO LITTLE MIRACLES,
available February 2009
from Harlequin Romance®.*

'I've found her.'

Max froze.

It was what he'd been waiting for since June, but now—now he was almost afraid to voice the question. His heart stalling, he leaned slowly back in his chair and scoured the investigator's face for clues. 'Where?' he asked, and his voice sounded rough and unused, like a rusty hinge.

'In Suffolk. She's living in a cottage.'

Living. His heart crashed back to life, and he sucked in a long, slow breath. All these months he'd feared—

'Is she well?'

'Yes, she's well.'

He had to force himself to ask the next question. 'Alone?'

The man paused. 'No. The cottage belongs to a man called John Blake. He's working away at the moment, but he comes and goes.'

God. He felt sick. So sick he hardly registered the next few words, but then gradually they sank in. 'She's got *what?*'

'Babies. Twin girls. They're eight months old.'

'Eight—?' he echoed under his breath. 'They must be his.'

He was thinking out loud, but the P.I. heard and corrected him.

'Apparently not. I gather they're hers. She's been there since mid-January last year, and they were born during the summer—June, the woman in the post office thought. She was more than helpful. I think there's been a certain amount of speculation about their relationship.'

He'd just bet there had. God, he was going to kill her. Or Blake. Maybe both of them.

'Of course, looking at the dates, she was presumably pregnant when she left you, so they could be yours, or she could have been having an affair with this Blake character before…'

He glared at the unfortunate P.I. 'Just stick to your job. I can do the math,' he snapped, swallowing the unpalatable possibility that she'd been unfaithful to him before she'd left. 'Where is she? I want the address.'

'It's all in here,' the man said, sliding a large envelope across the desk to him. 'With my invoice.'

'I'll get it seen to. Thank you.'

'If there's anything else you need, Mr Gallagher, any further information—'

'I'll be in touch.'

'The woman in the post office told me Blake was away at the moment, if that helps,' he added quietly, and opened the door.

Max stared down at the envelope, hardly daring to open it, but when the door clicked softly shut behind the P.I., he eased up the flap, tipped it and felt his breath jam in his throat as the photos spilled out over the desk.

Oh, lord, she looked gorgeous. Different, though. It took him a moment to recognise her, because she'd grown her hair, and it was tied back in a ponytail, making her look younger and somehow freer. The blond highlights were gone, and it was back to its natural soft golden-brown, with a little curl in the end of the ponytail that he wanted to thread his finger through and tug, just gently, to draw her back to him.

Crazy. She'd put on a little weight, but it suited her. She looked well and happy and beautiful, but oddly, considering how desperate he'd been for news of her for the past year—one year, three weeks and two days, to be exact—it wasn't only Julia who held his attention after the initial shock. It was the babies sitting side by side in a supermarket trolley. Two identical and absolutely beautiful little girls.

* * * * *

When Max Gallagher hires a P.I. to find his estranged wife, Julia, he discovers she's not alone— she has twin baby girls, and they might be his. Now workaholic Max has just two weeks to prove that he can be a wonderful husband and father to the family he wants to treasure.

Look for TWO LITTLE MIRACLES
by Caroline Anderson,
available February 2009
from Harlequin Romance®.

HARLEQUIN® Romance®

This February the Harlequin® Romance series
will feature six Diamond Brides stories featuring
diamond proposals and gorgeous grooms.

Share your dream wedding proposal and you could WIN!

The most romantic entry will win a diamond
necklace and will inspire a proposal in one of
our upcoming Diamond Grooms books in 2010.

In 100 words or less, tell us the most romantic
way that you dream of being proposed to.

For more information, and to enter
the Diamond Brides Proposal contest, please visit
www.DiamondBridesProposal.com

Or mail your entry to us at:

IN THE U.S.: 3010 Walden Ave., P.O. Box 9069, Buffalo, NY 14269-9069
IN CANADA: 225 Duncan Mill Road, Don Mills, ON M3B 3K9

REQUEST YOUR FREE BOOKS!

Harlequin® Historical
Historical Romantic Adventure!

2 FREE NOVELS PLUS 2 FREE GIFTS!

YES! Please send me 2 FREE Harlequin® Historical novels and my 2 FREE gifts (gifts are worth about $10). After receiving them, if I don't wish to receive any more books, I can return the shipping statement marked "cancel". If I don't cancel, I will receive 6 brand-new novels every month and be billed just $4.94 per book in the U.S. or $5.49 per book in Canada, plus 25¢ shipping and handling per book and applicable taxes, if any*. That's a savings of 20% off the cover price! I understand that accepting the 2 free books and gifts places me under no obligation to buy anything. I can always return a shipment and cancel at any time. Even if I never buy another book, the two free books and gifts are mine to keep forever.

246 HDN ERUM 349 HDN ERUA

Name _____ (PLEASE PRINT) _____

Address _____ Apt. # _____

City _____ State/Prov. _____ Zip/Postal Code _____

Signature (if under 18, a parent or guardian must sign)

Mail to the **Harlequin Reader Service:**
IN U.S.A.: P.O. Box 1867, Buffalo, NY 14240-1867
IN CANADA: P.O. Box 609, Fort Erie, Ontario L2A 5X3

Not valid to current subscribers of Harlequin Historical books.

Want to try two free books from another line?
Call 1-800-873-8635 or visit www.morefreebooks.com.

HH

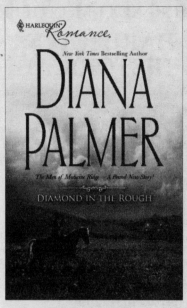

Diamond in the Rough

John Callister is a millionaire rancher, yet when he meets
lovely Sassy Peale and she thinks he's a cowboy, he goes along
with her misconception. He's had enough of gold diggers,
and this is a chance to be valued for himself, not his money.
But when Sassy finds out the truth, she feels John was merely
playing with her. John will have to convince her that he's truly
the man she fell in love with—a diamond in the rough.

The Men of Medicine Ridge—a brand-new miniseries
set in the wilds of Montana!

Available April 2009 wherever you buy books.

COMING NEXT MONTH FROM

HARLEQUIN®
HISTORICAL

- **WANTED IN ALASKA**
by **Kate Bridges**
(Western)
Outlaw Quinn Rowlan kidnaps a nurse—only to discover he's got
the wrong woman! Desperate to feel proud about his life once
again, he needs Autumn MacNeil's help to clear his name in town.
But Quinn had never expected a curvy, blond, ambitious singer to make
him feel so whole again....

- **THE RAKE'S UNCONVENTIONAL MISTRESS**
by **Juliet Landon**
(Regency)
Miss Letitia Boyce didn't begrudge her sisters the pick of London's
available bachelors. She'd chosen her own path, and book learning and
marriage rarely mixed. Notorious rakehell Lord Seton Rayne had every
heiress hurling herself at him. So his sudden kissing of unconventional
Letitia took them both by surprise....

- **THE EARL'S UNTOUCHED BRIDE**
by **Annie Burrows**
(Regency)
Charles Fawley, Earl of Walton, never thought he'd fall for plain
Heloise Bergeron in Paris, the city of romance! But Heloise needed
to escape a vile betrothal, so they married quickly. And then Charles
discovered just how untouched his French bride really was....

- **THE VIKING'S DEFIANT BRIDE**
by **Joanna Fulford**
(Viking)
Since her father's death, Elgiva needs protection more than ever.
When a brooding dark-haired Viking warrior rescues her young nephew
he looks at her and her fate is sealed.... Earl Wulfrum
has come to conquer, and he takes the beautiful, spirited woman
as his bride—but now he must break down the walls of his defiant
bride's heart!